SPIDER-MAN

MONSTERS ON THE PROWL

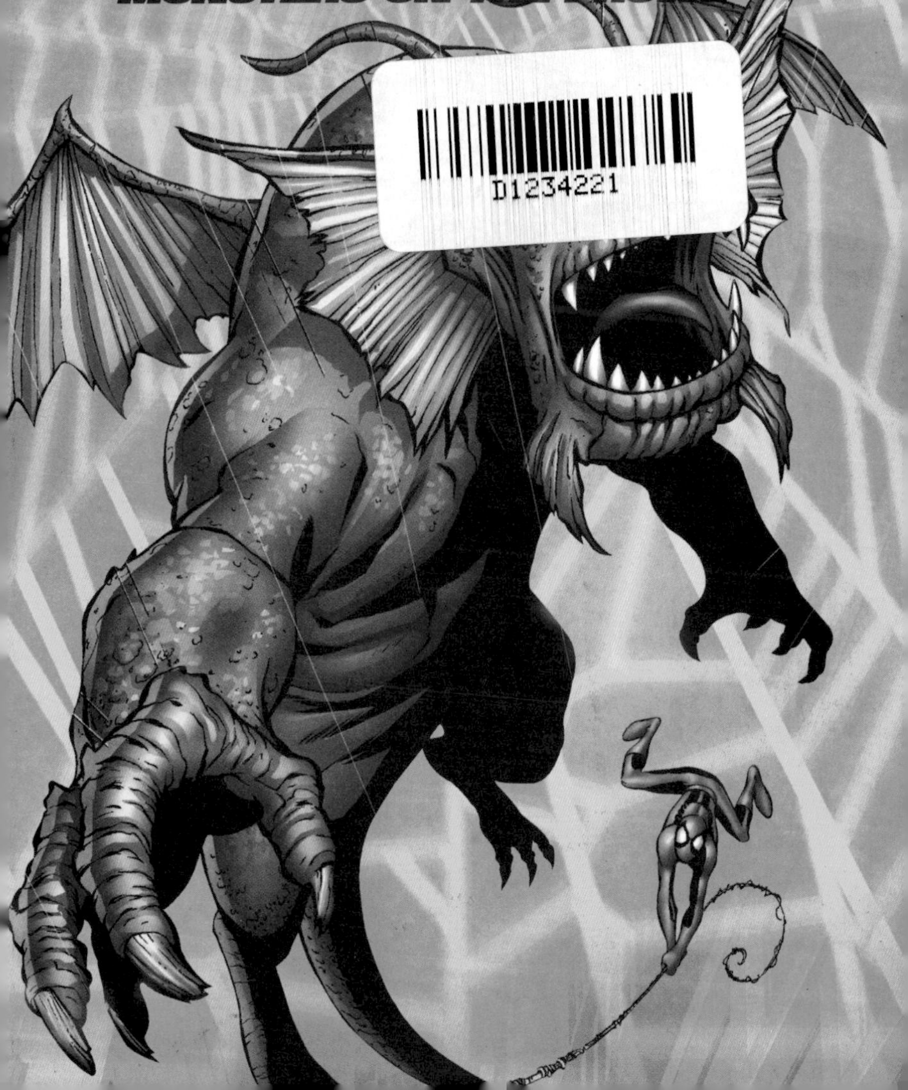

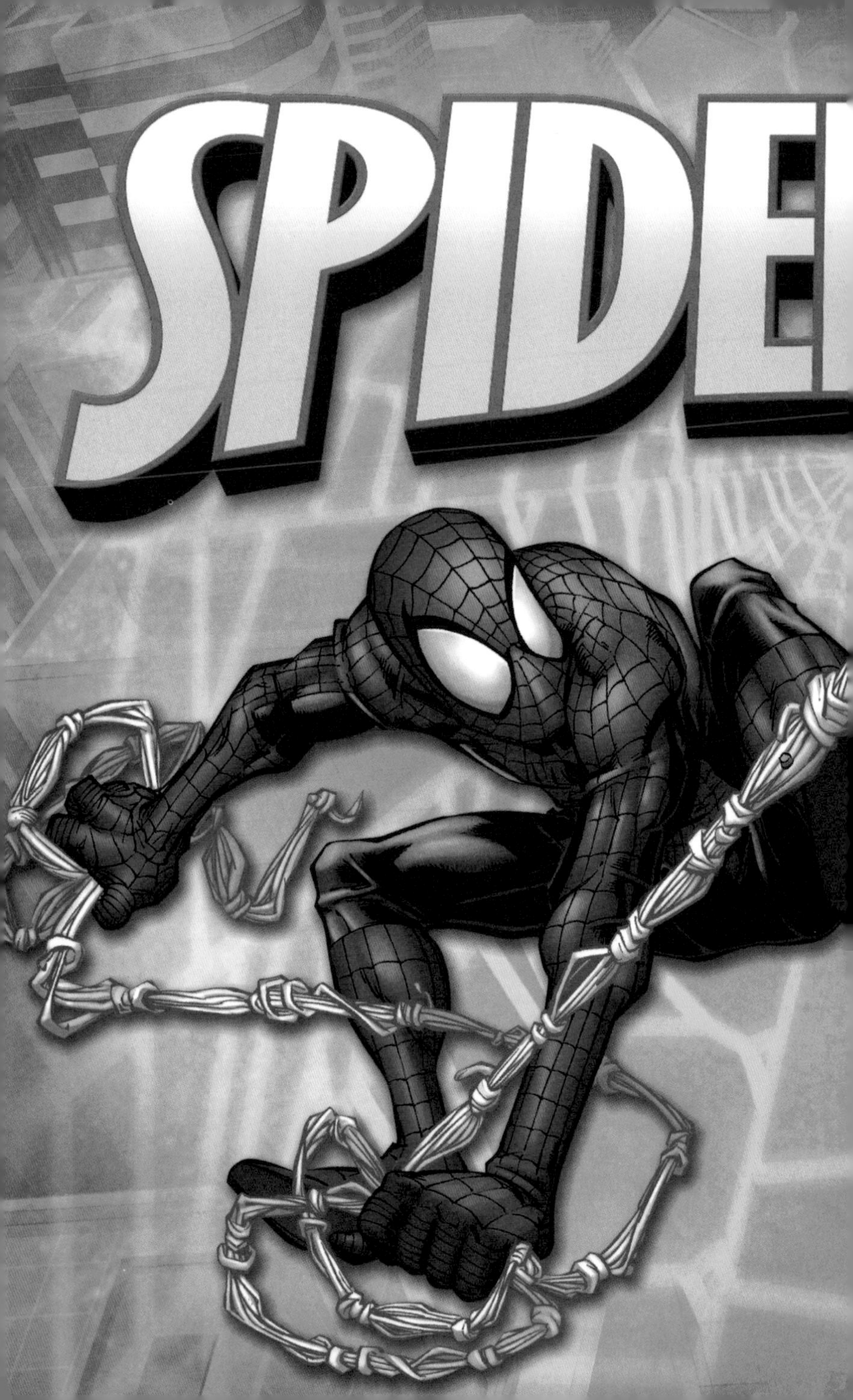
SPIDE

?-MAN

MONSTERS ON THE PROWL

Writer
Peter David
Pencils
Mike Norton

Inks: **Norman Lee**
Colors: **Guru eFX**
Letters: **Dave Sharpe**
Cover Art: **Cameron Stewart & Christina Strain**
Assistant Editor: **Nathan Cosby**
Editor: **Mark Paniccia**

Collection Editor: **Jennifer Grünwald**
Assistant Editor: **Michael Short**
Associate Editor: **Mark D. Beazley**
Senior Editor, Special Projects: **Jeff Youngquist**
Vice President of Sales: **David Gabriel**
Production: **Jerron Quality Color**
Vice President of Creative: **Tom Marvelli**

Editor in Chief: **Joe Quesada**
Publisher: **Dan Buckley**

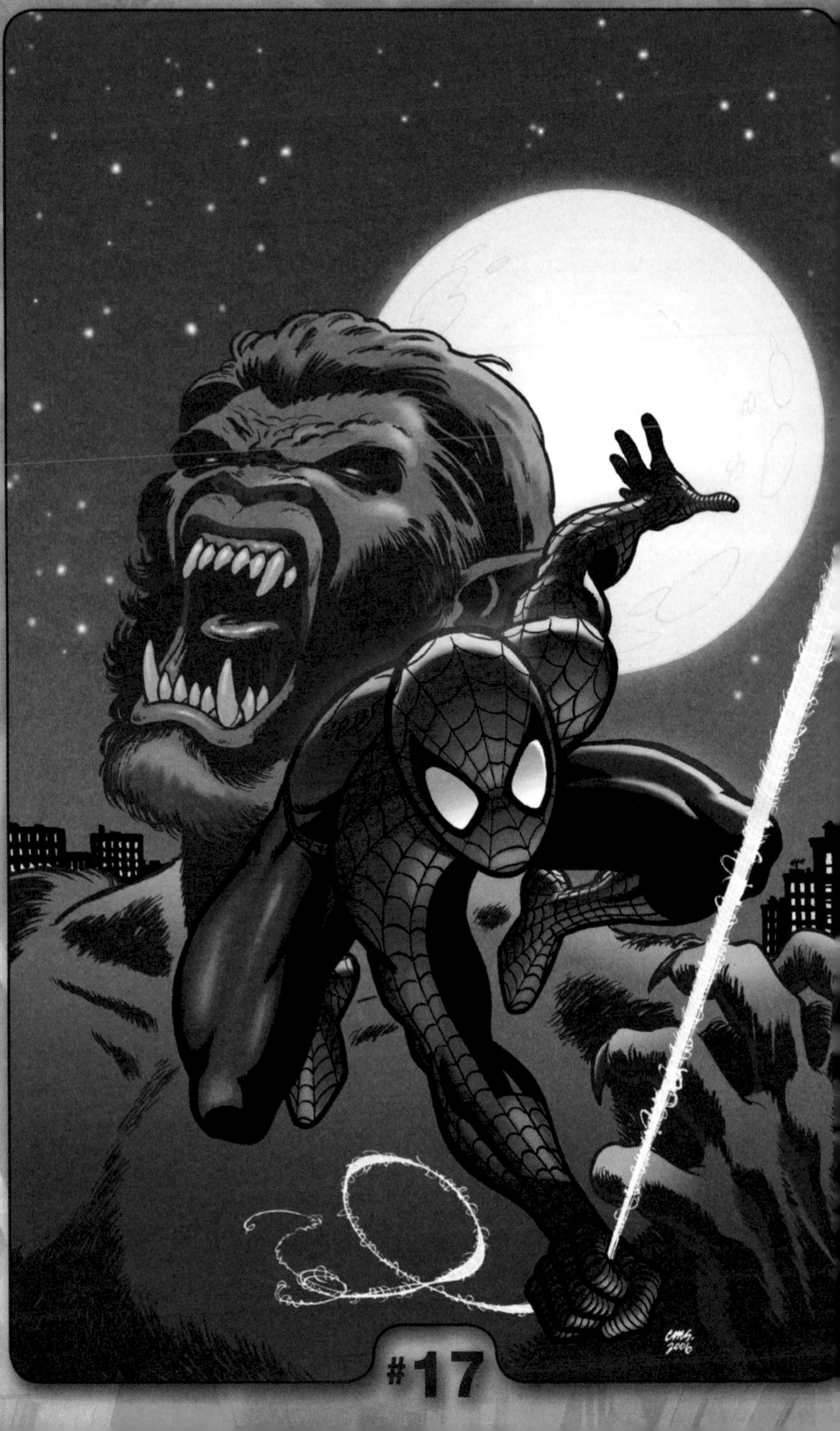
#17

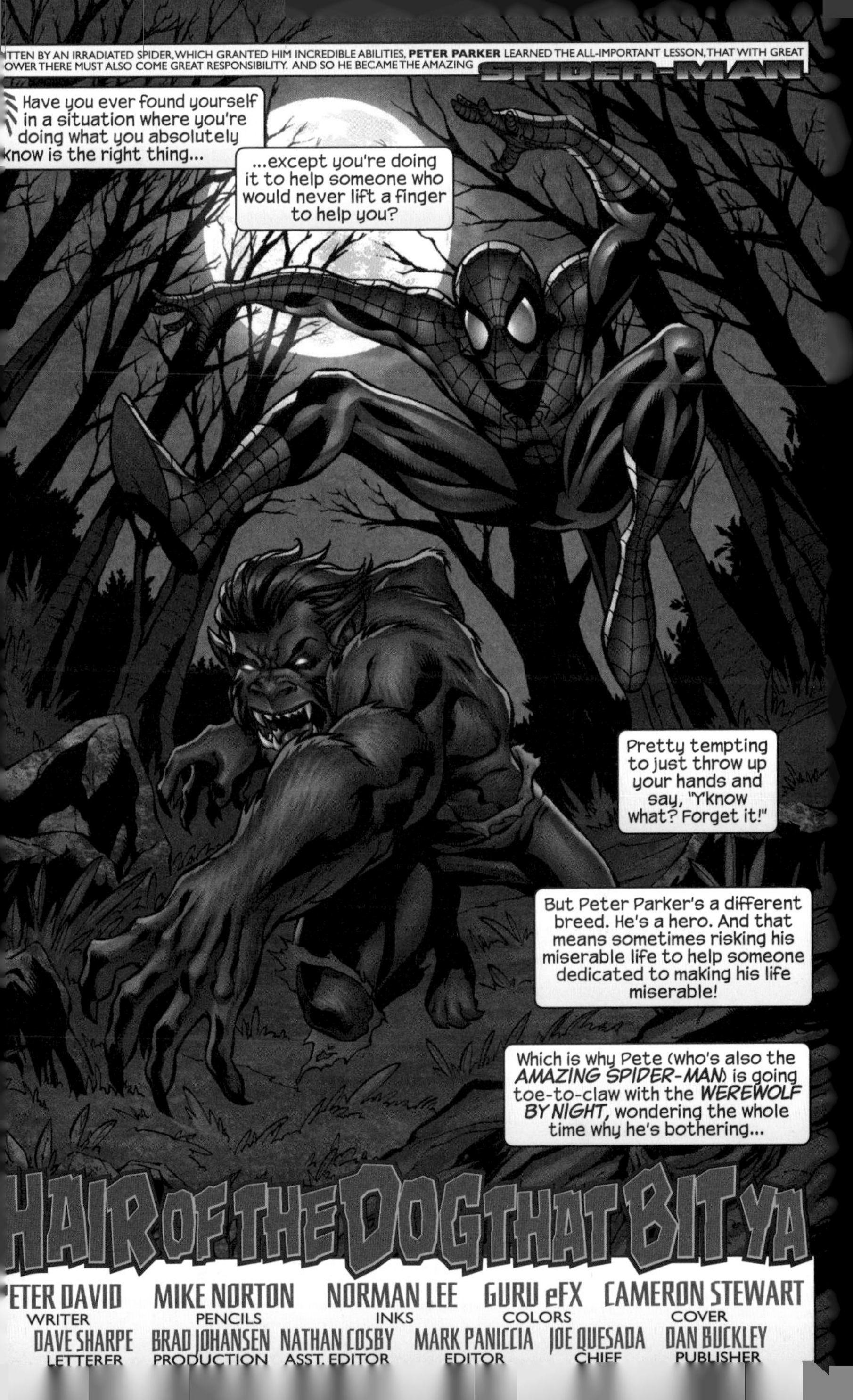
TTEN BY AN IRRADIATED SPIDER, WHICH GRANTED HIM INCREDIBLE ABILITIES, PETER PARKER LEARNED THE ALL-IMPORTANT LESSON, THAT WITH GREAT
OWER THERE MUST ALSO COME GREAT RESPONSIBILITY. AND SO HE BECAME THE AMAZING
SPIDER-MAN
Have you ever found yourself in a situation where you're doing what you absolutely know is the right thing...
...except you're doing it to help someone who would never lift a finger to help you?
Pretty tempting to just throw up your hands and say, "Y'know what? Forget it!"
But Peter Parker's a different breed. He's a hero. And that means sometimes risking his miserable life to help someone dedicated to making his life miserable!
Which is why Pete (who's also the AMAZING SPIDER-MAN) is going toe-to-claw with the WEREWOLF BY NIGHT, wondering the whole time why he's bothering...
HAIR OF THE DOG THAT BIT YA
ETER DAVID WRITER
MIKE NORTON PENCILS
NORMAN LEE INKS
GURU eFX COLORS
CAMERON STEWART COVER
DAVE SHARPE LETTERER
BRAD JOHANSEN PRODUCTION
NATHAN COSBY ASST. EDITOR
MARK PANICCIA EDITOR
JOE QUESADA CHIEF
DAN BUCKLEY PUBLISHER

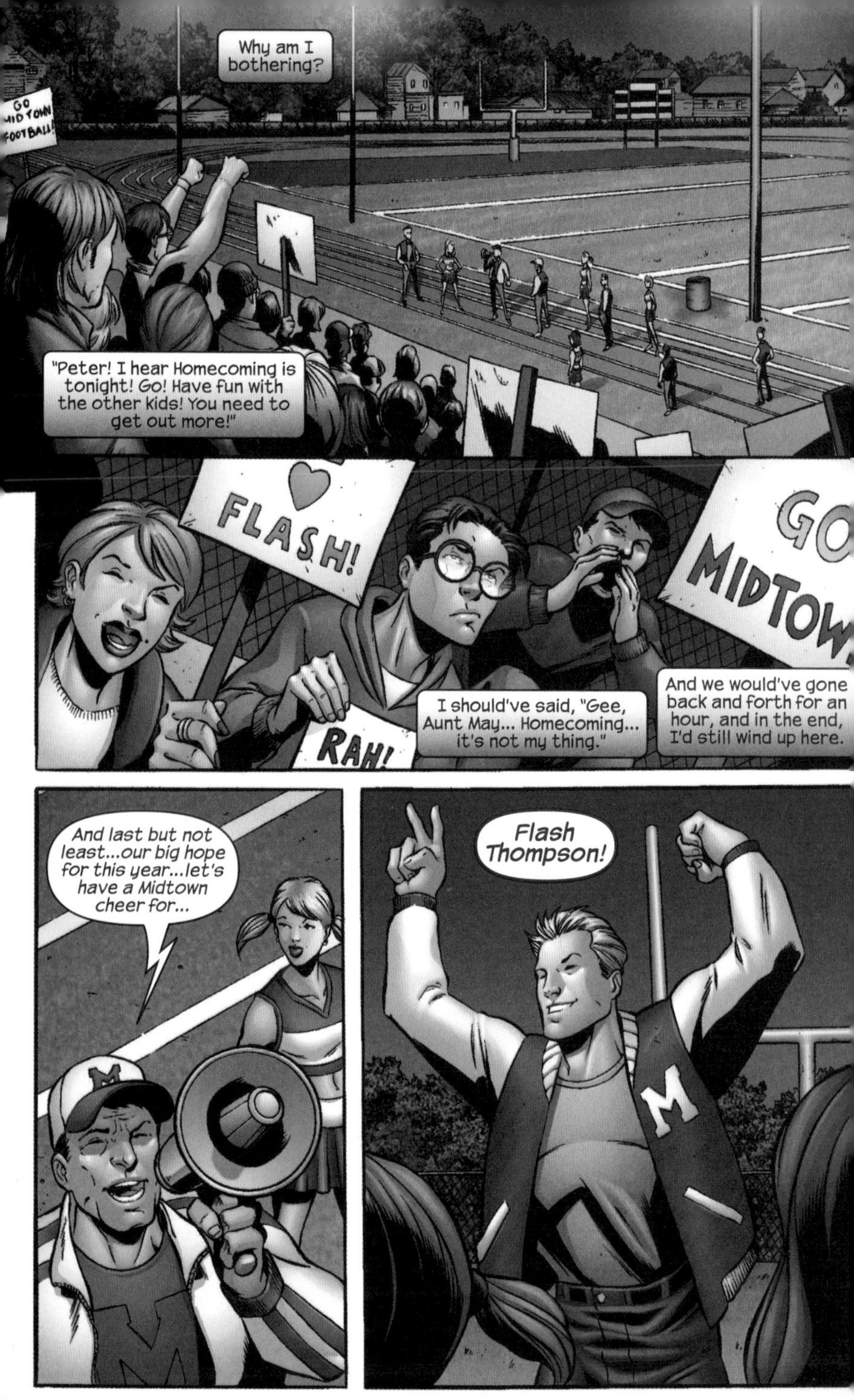

Why am I bothering?
GO MID TOWN FOOTBALL!
"Peter! I hear Homecoming is tonight! Go! Have fun with the other kids! You need to get out more!"
FLASH!
GO MIDTOW
RAH!
I should've said, "Gee, Aunt May... Homecoming... it's not my thing."
And we would've gone back and forth for an hour, and in the end, I'd still wind up here.
And last but not least...our big hope for this year...let's have a Midtown cheer for...
Flash Thompson!

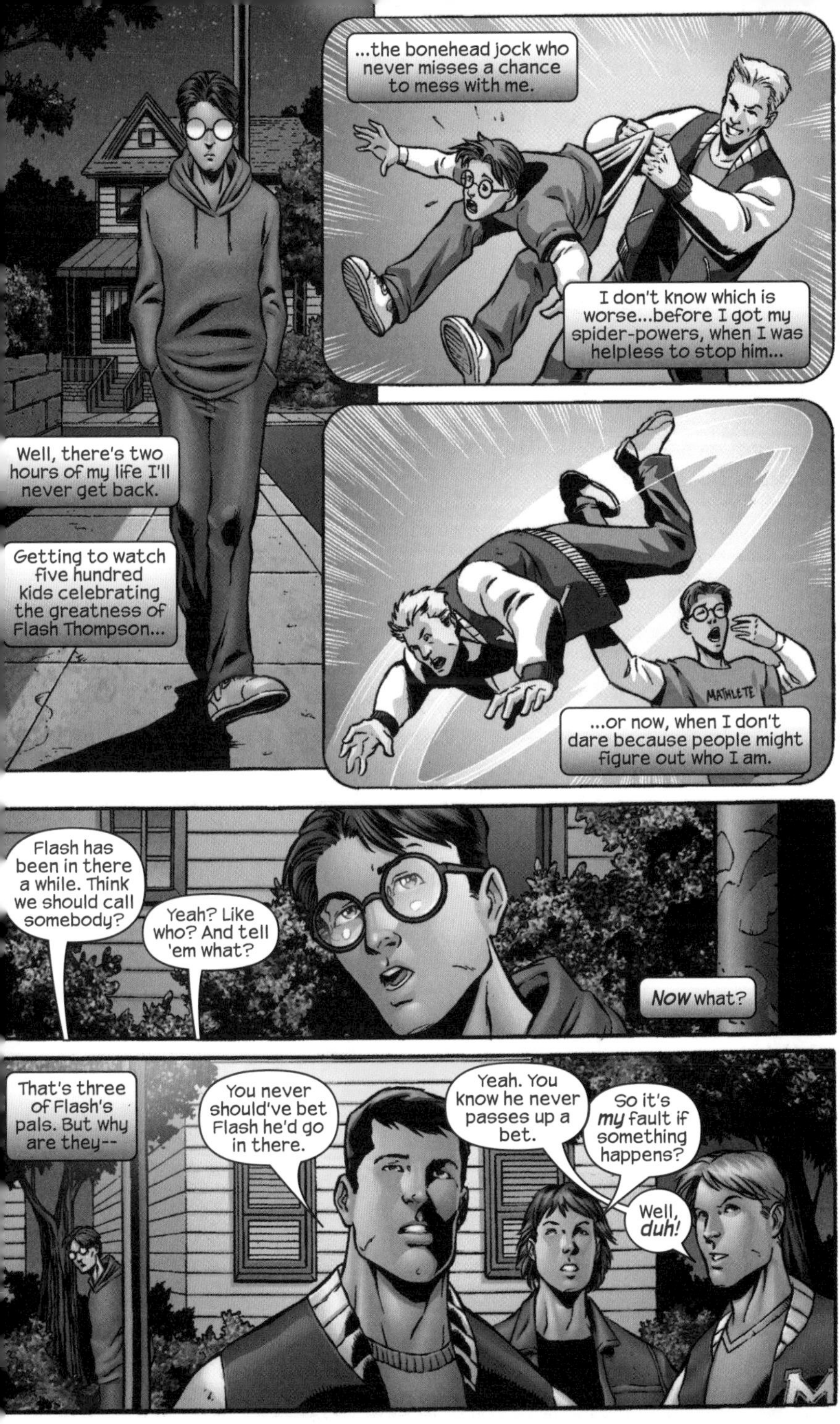
Well, there's two hours of my life I'll never get back.
Getting to watch five hundred kids celebrating the greatness of Flash Thompson...
...the bonehead jock who never misses a chance to mess with me.
I don't know which is worse...before I got my spider-powers, when I was helpless to stop him...
MATHLETE
...or now, when I don't dare because people might figure out who I am.
Flash has been in there a while. Think we should call somebody?
Yeah? Like who? And tell 'em what?
NOW what?
That's three of Flash's pals. But why are they--
You never should've bet Flash he'd go in there.
Yeah. You know he never passes up a bet.
So it's my fault if something happens?
Well, duh!

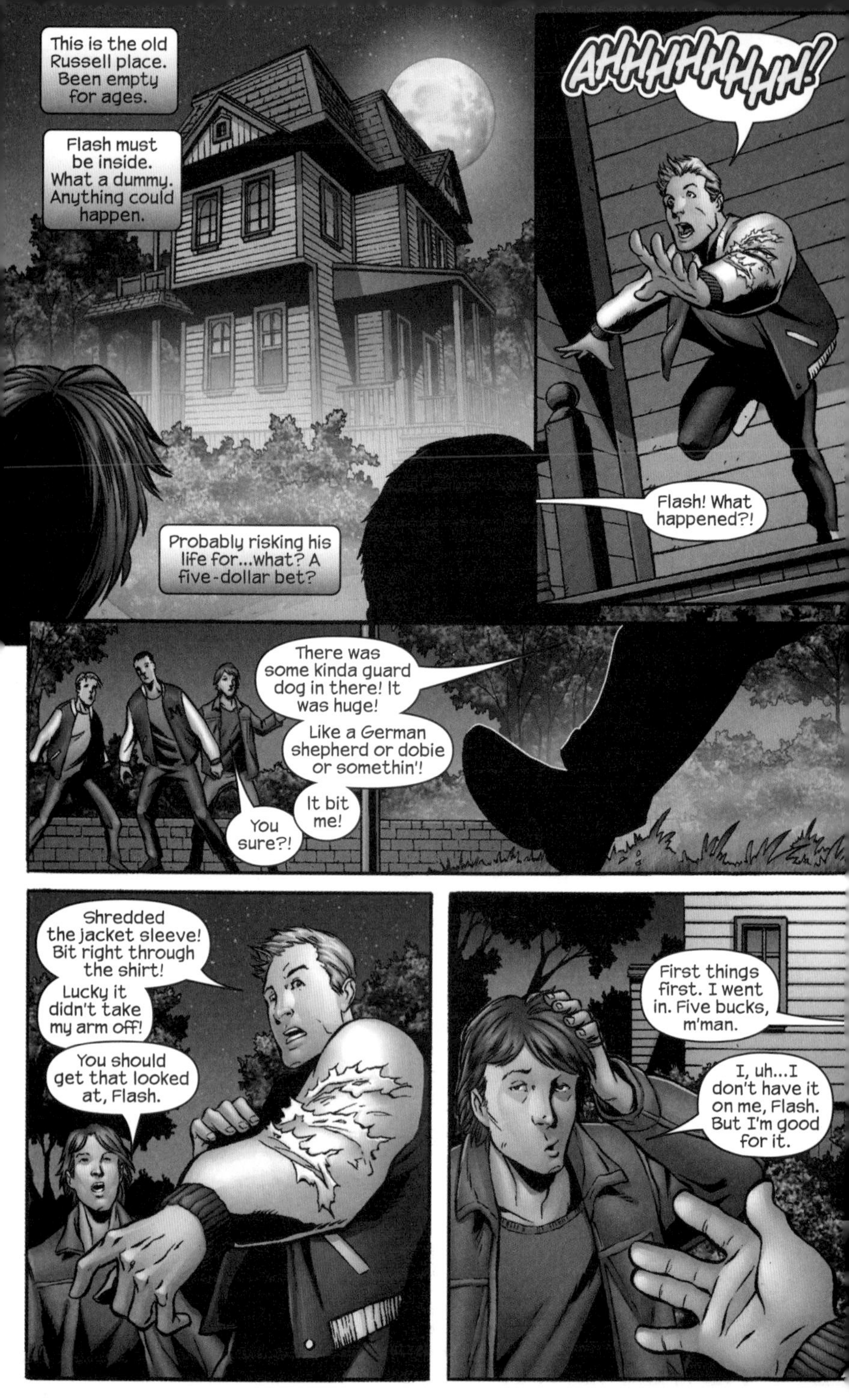
This is the old Russell place. Been empty for ages.
Flash must be inside. What a dummy. Anything could happen.
Probably risking his life for...what? A five-dollar bet?
AHHHHHHHHH!
Flash! What happened?!
There was some kinda guard dog in there! It was huge!
Like a German shepherd or dobie or somethin'!
It bit me!
You sure?!
Shredded the jacket sleeve! Bit right through the shirt!
Lucky it didn't take my arm off!
You should get that looked at, Flash.
First things first. I went in. Five bucks, m'man.
I, uh...I don't have it on me, Flash. But I'm good for it.

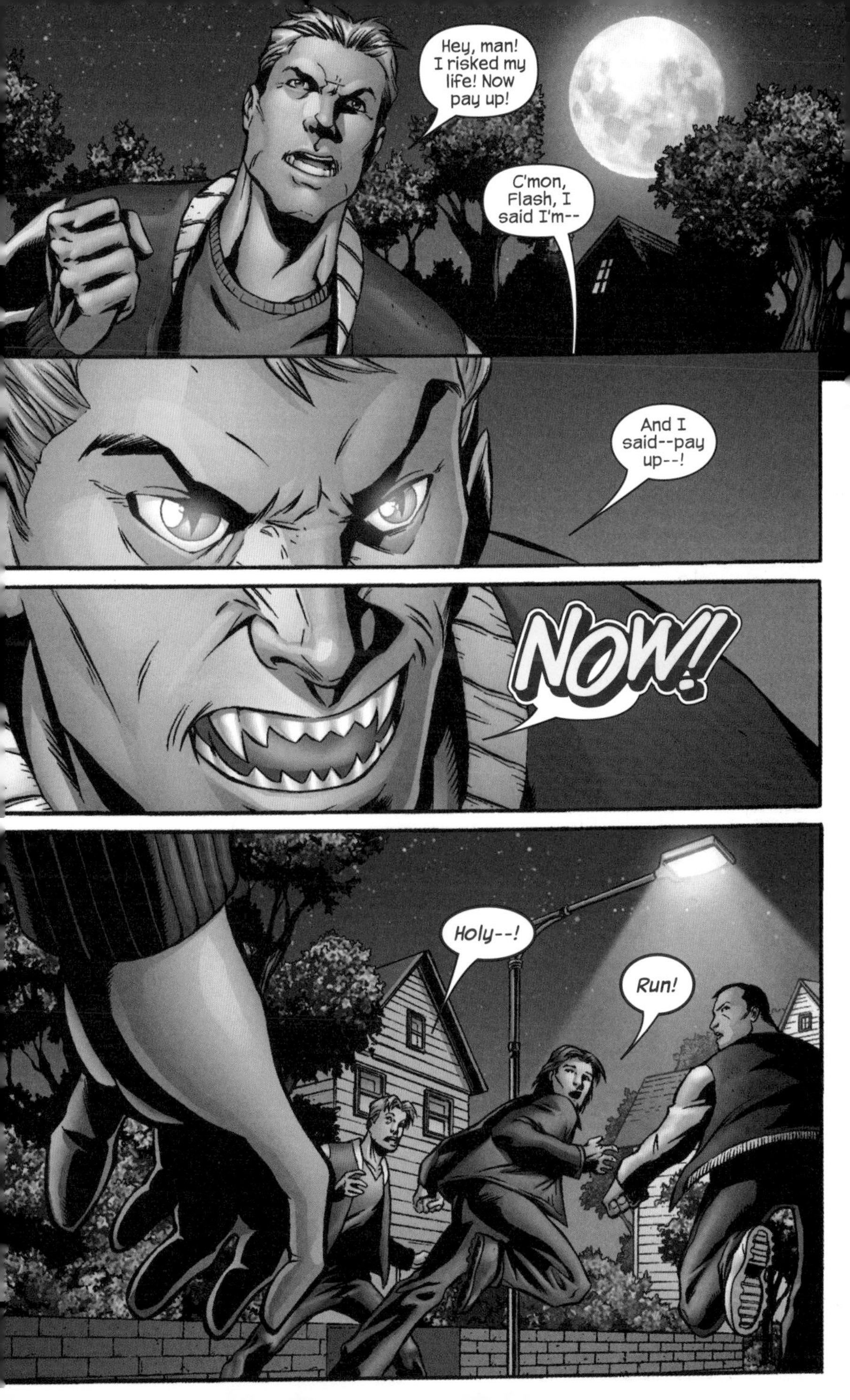
Hey, man! I risked my life! Now pay up!
C'mon, Flash, I said I'm--
And I said--pay up--!
NOW!
Holy--!
Run!

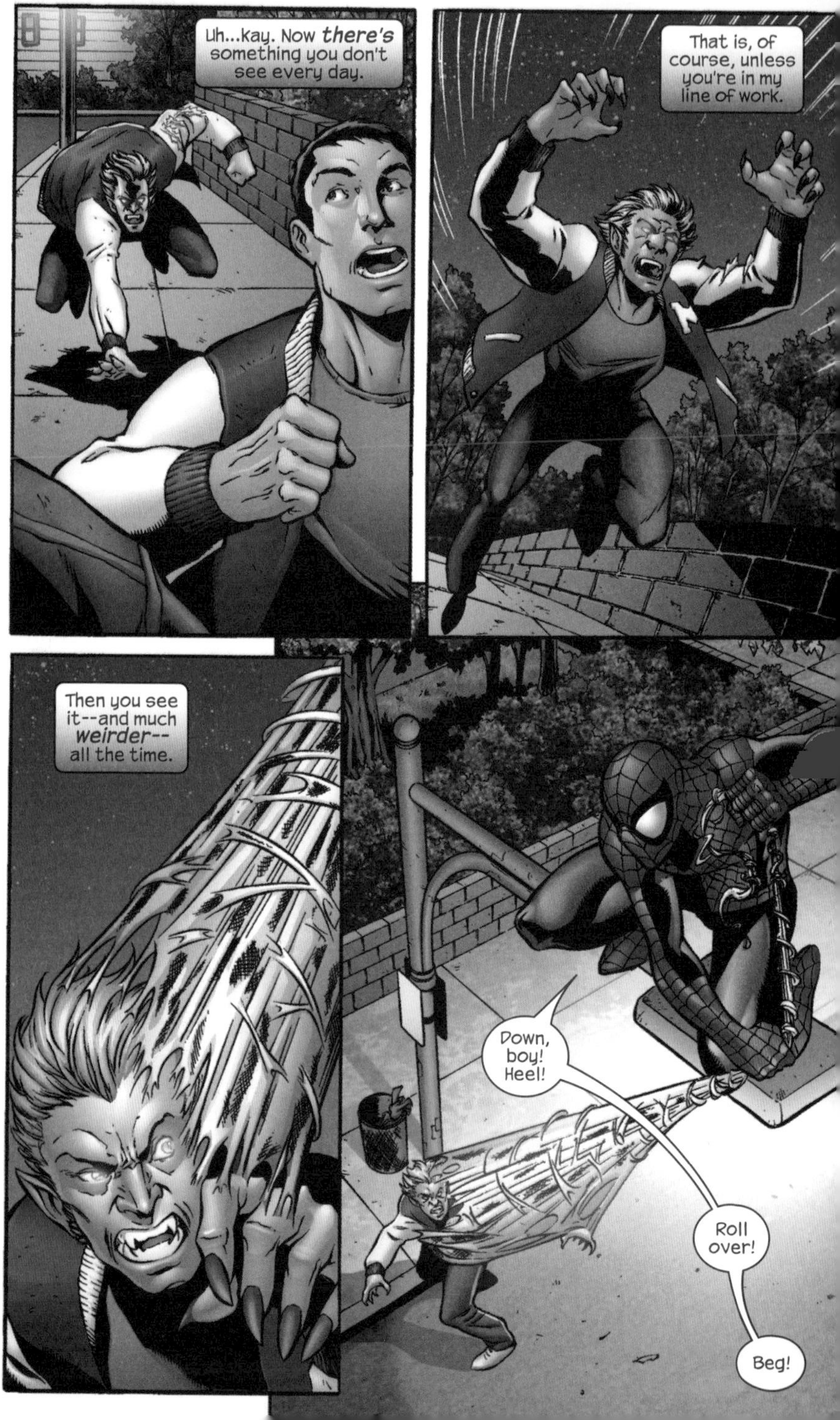

Uh...kay. Now there's something you don't see every day.
That is, of course, unless you're in my line of work.
Then you see it--and much weirder--all the time.
Down, boy! Heel!
Roll over!
Beg!

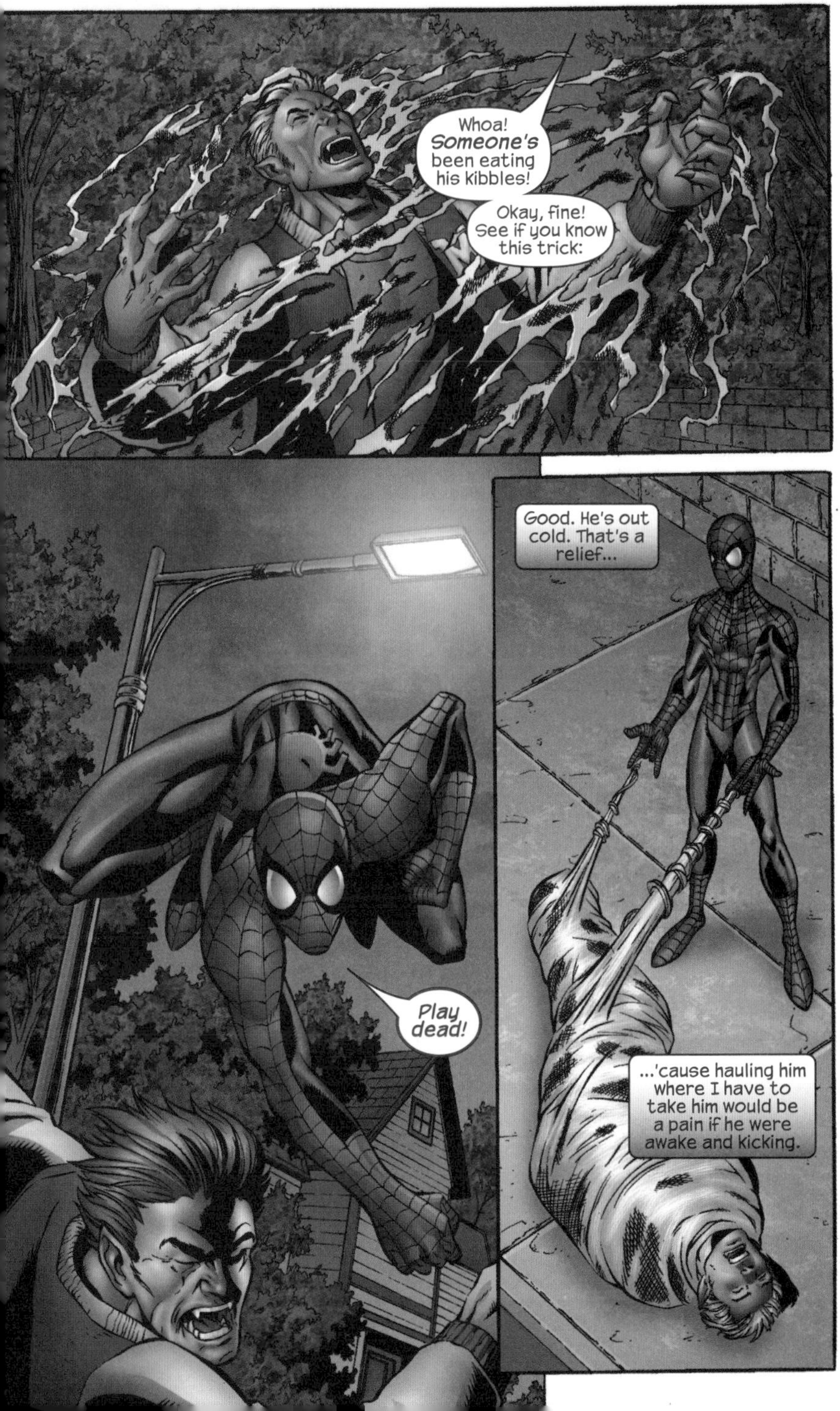
Whoa! Someone's been eating his kibbles!
Okay, fine! See if you know this trick:
Play dead!
Good. He's out cold. That's a relief...
...'cause hauling him where I have to take him would be a pain if he were awake and kicking.

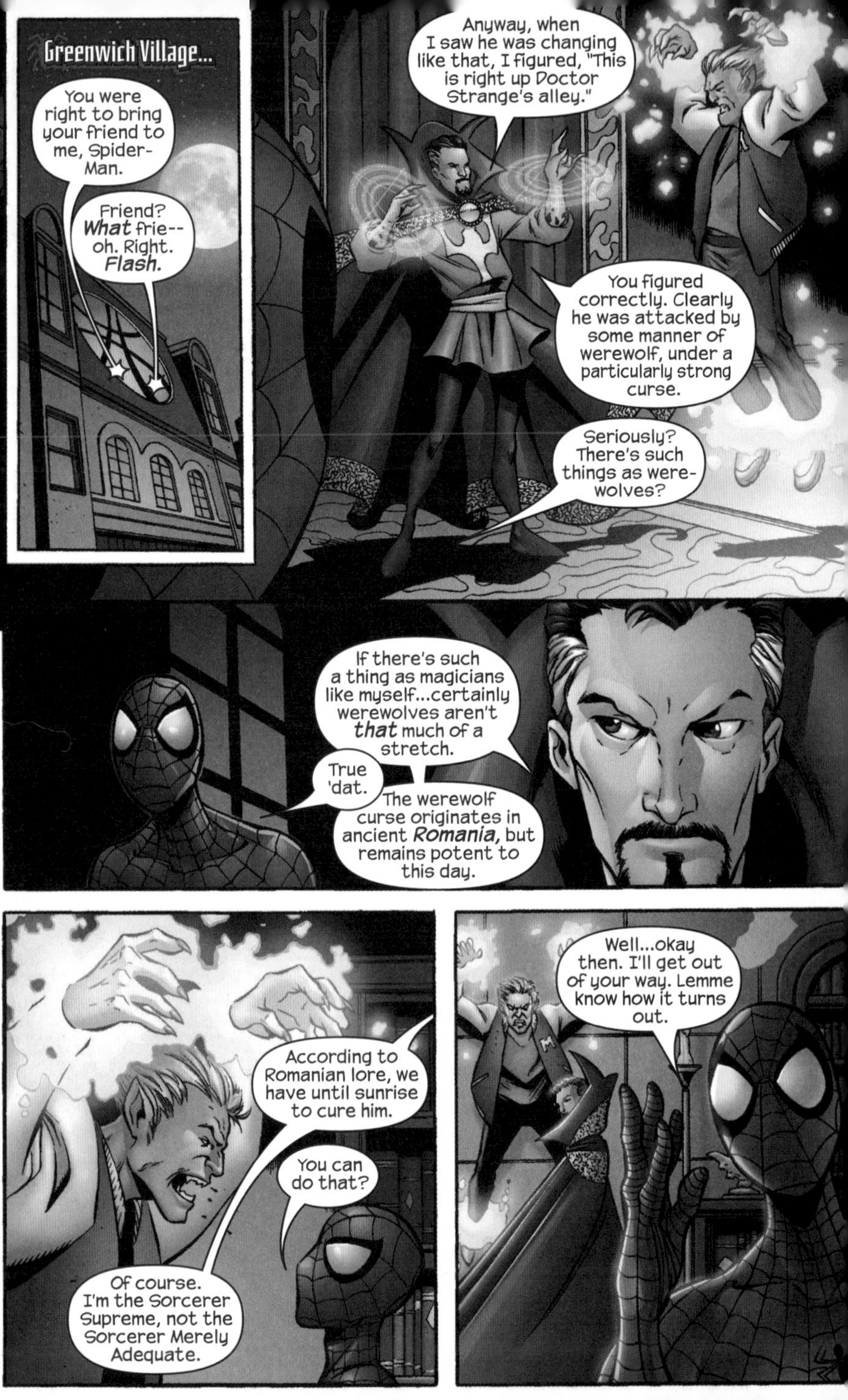
Greenwich Village...
You were right to bring your friend to me, Spider-Man.
Friend? What frie-- oh. Right. Flash.
Anyway, when I saw he was changing like that, I figured, "This is right up Doctor Strange's alley."
You figured correctly. Clearly he was attacked by some manner of werewolf, under a particularly strong curse.
Seriously? There's such things as were-wolves?
If there's such a thing as magicians like myself...certainly werewolves aren't that much of a stretch.
True 'dat.
The werewolf curse originates in ancient Romania, but remains potent to this day.
According to Romanian lore, we have until sunrise to cure him.
You can do that?
Of course. I'm the Sorcerer Supreme, not the Sorcerer Merely Adequate.
Well...okay then. I'll get out of your way. Lemme know how it turns out.

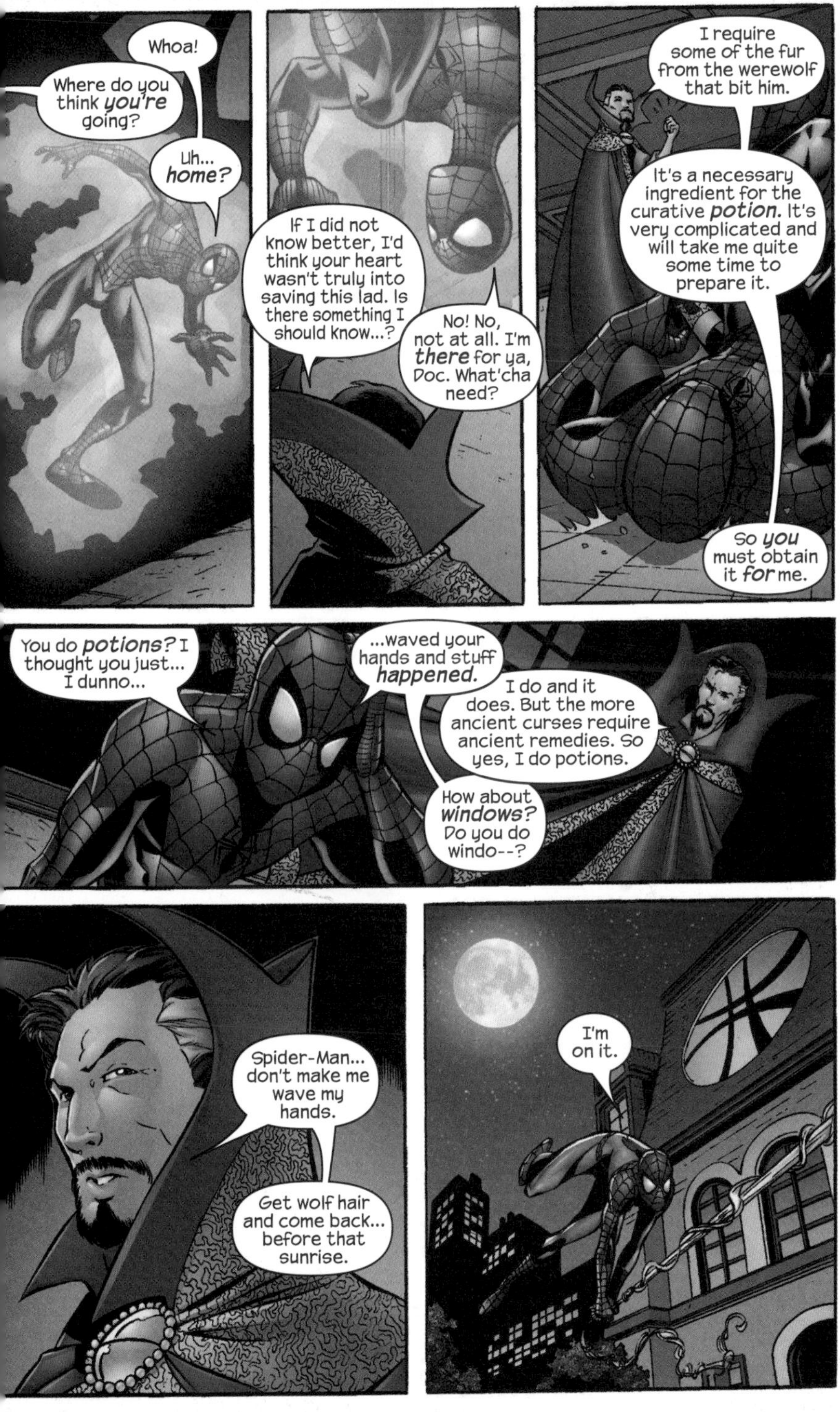
Whoa!
Where do you think *you're* going?
Uh... *home?*
If I did not know better, I'd think your heart wasn't truly into saving this lad. Is there something I should know...?
No! No, not at all. I'm *there* for ya, Doc. What'cha need?
I require some of the fur from the werewolf that bit him.
It's a necessary ingredient for the curative *potion.* It's very complicated and will take me quite some time to prepare it.
So *you* must obtain it *for* me.
You do *potions?* I thought you just... I dunno...
...waved your hands and stuff *happened.*
I do and it does. But the more ancient curses require ancient remedies. So yes, I do potions.
How about *windows?* Do you do windo--?
Spider-Man... don't make me wave my hands.
Get wolf hair and come back... before that sunrise.
I'm on it.

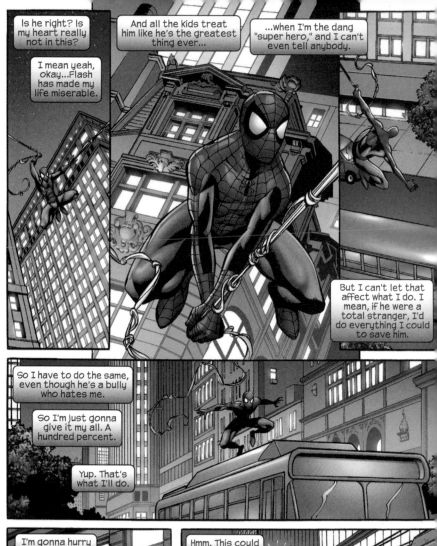

Is he right? Is my heart really not in this?

I mean yeah, okay...Flash has made my life miserable.

And all the kids treat him like he's the greatest thing ever...

...when I'm the dang "super hero," and I can't even tell anybody.

But I can't let that affect what I do. I mean, if he were a total stranger, I'd do everything I could to save him.

So I have to do the same, even though he's a bully who hates me.

So I'm just gonna give it my all. A hundred percent.

Yup. That's what I'll do.

I'm gonna hurry as fast as I c--

Uh-oh.

Hmm. This could take a while.

Should've brought a book. Or maybe I could just take a nap.

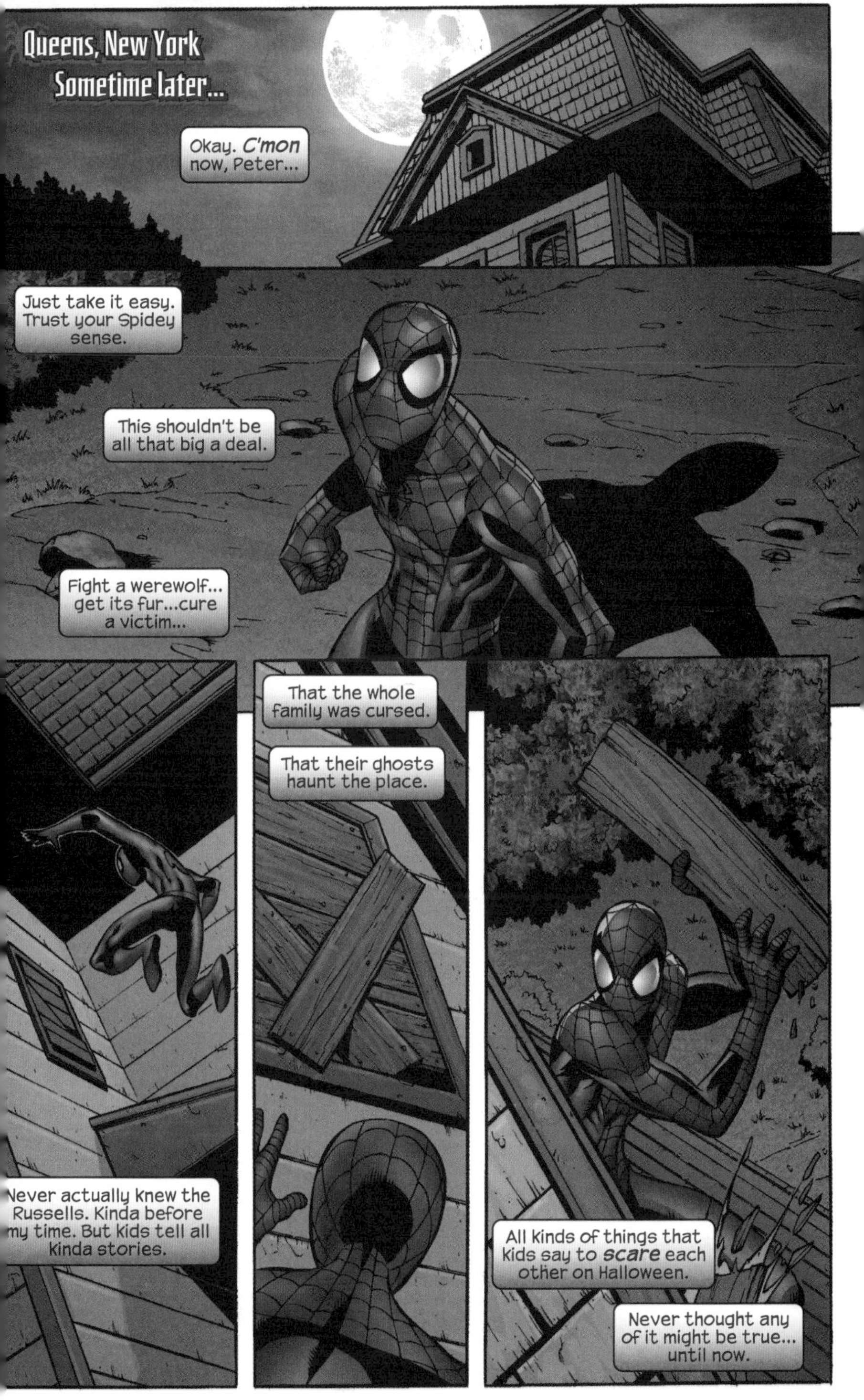
Queens, New York
Sometime later...
Okay. C'mon now, Peter...
Just take it easy. Trust your Spidey sense.
This shouldn't be all that big a deal.
Fight a werewolf... get its fur...cure a victim...
Never actually knew the Russells. Kinda before my time. But kids tell all kinda stories.
That the whole family was cursed.
That their ghosts haunt the place.
All kinds of things that kids say to scare each other on Halloween.
Never thought any of it might be true... until now.

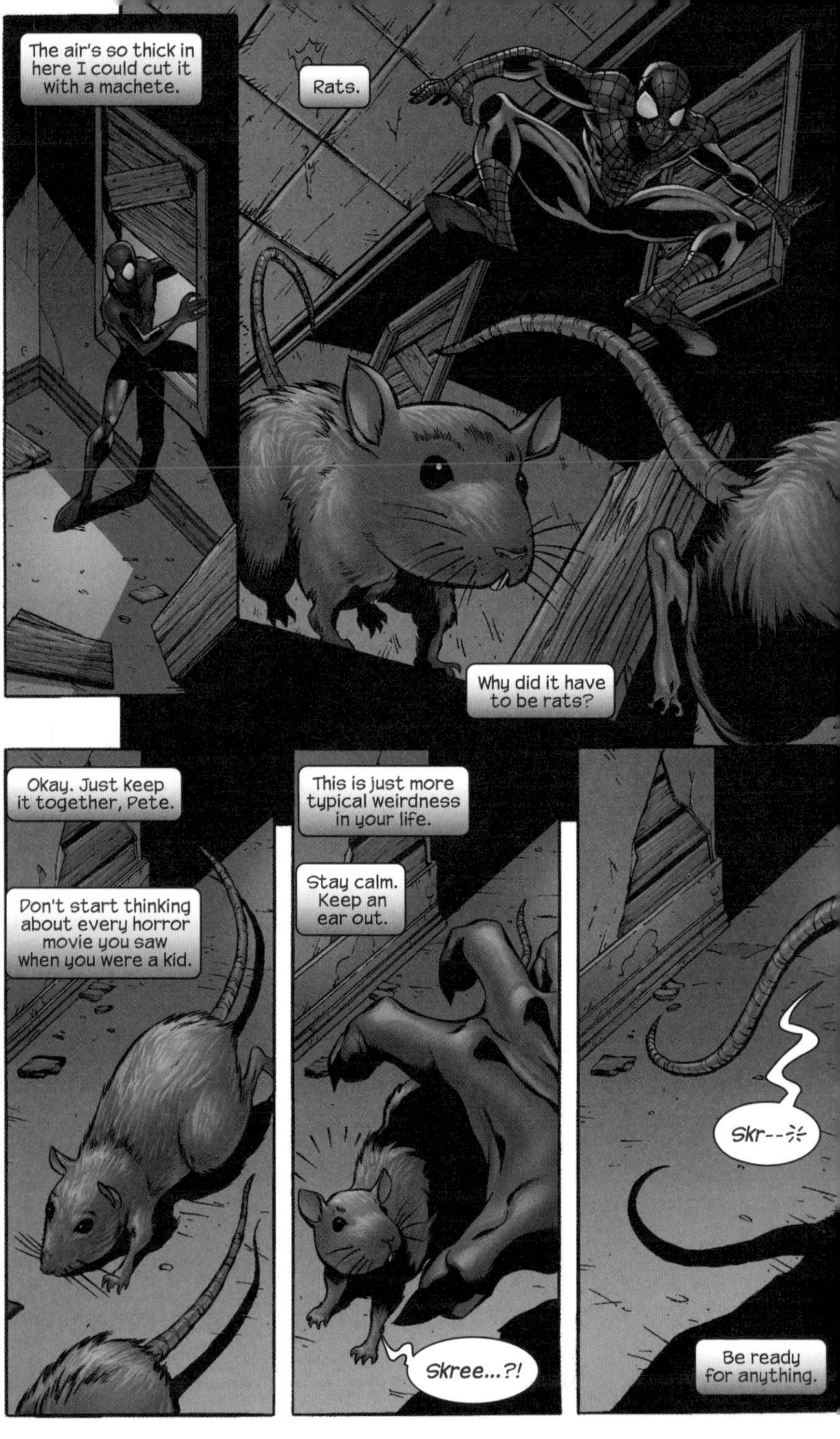

The air's so thick in here I could cut it with a machete.
Rats.
Why did it have to be rats?
Okay. Just keep it together, Pete.
Don't start thinking about every horror movie you saw when you were a kid.
This is just more typical weirdness in your life.
Stay calm. Keep an ear out.
Skree...?!
Skr--
Be ready for anything.

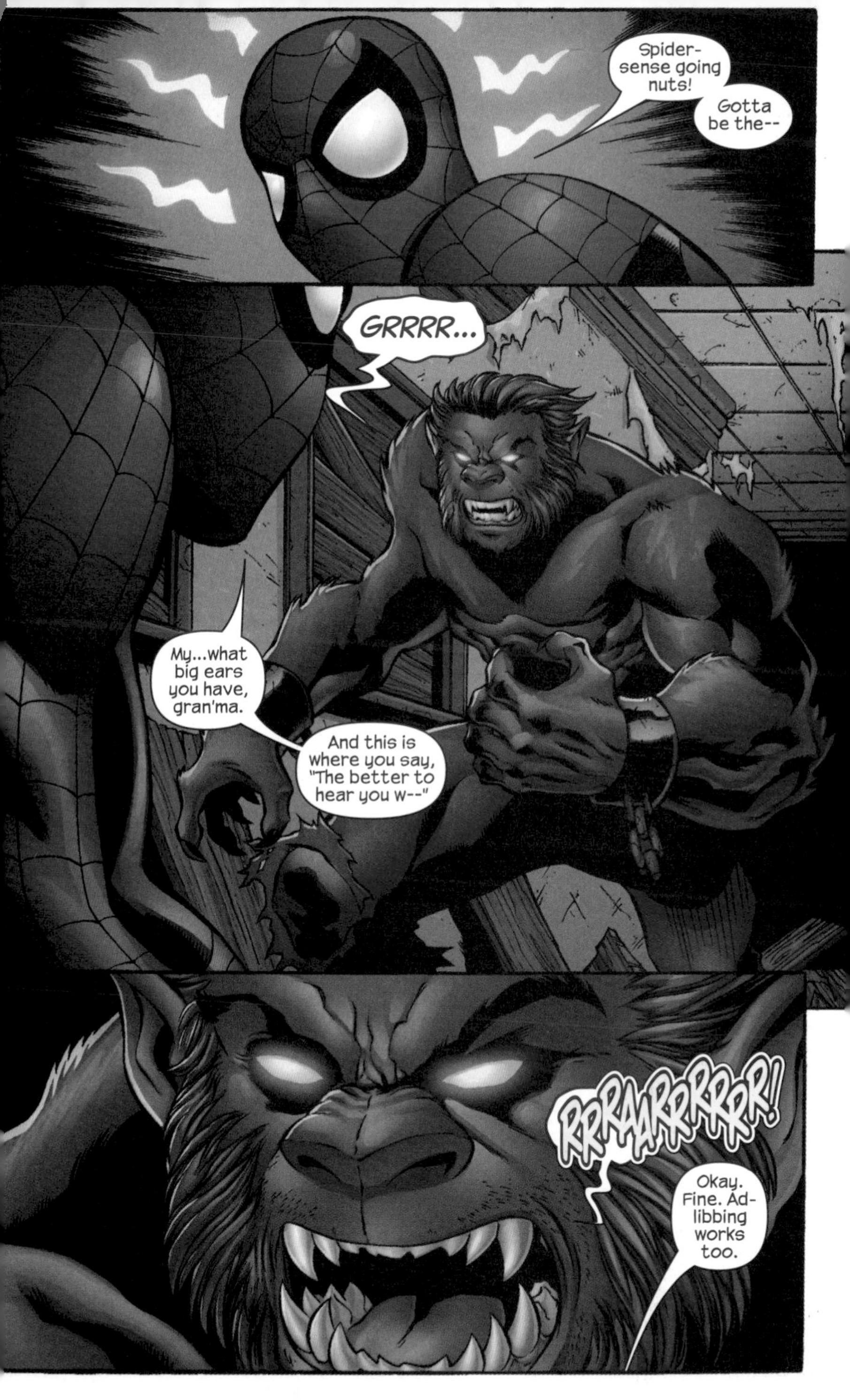
Spider-sense going nuts!
Gotta be the--
GRRRR...
My...what big ears you have, gran'ma.
And this is where you say, "The better to hear you w--"
RRRAARRRRRR!
Okay. Fine. Ad-libbing works too.

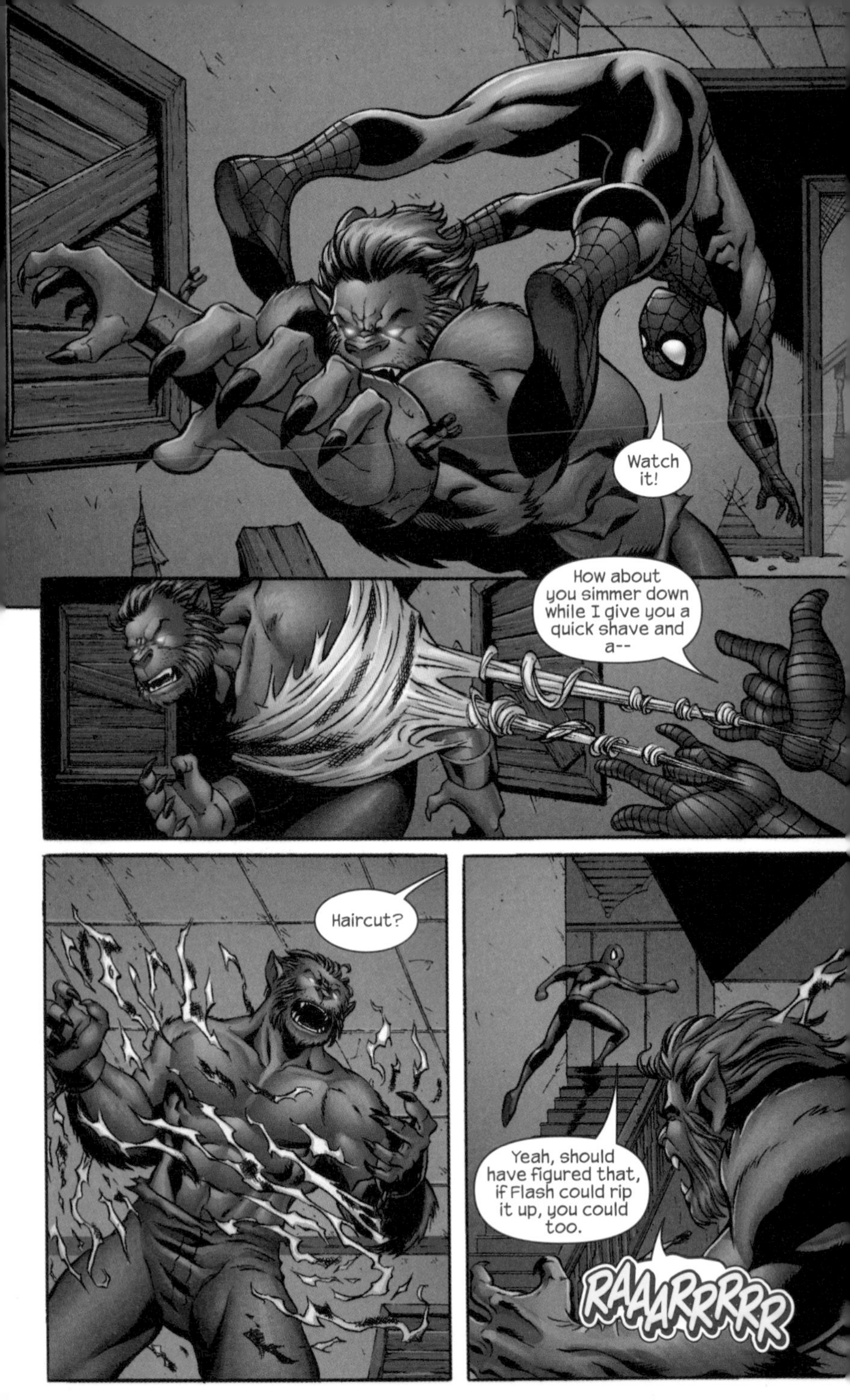
Watch it!
How about you simmer down while I give you a quick shave and a--
Haircut?
Yeah, should have figured that, if Flash could rip it up, you could too.
RAAARRRRR

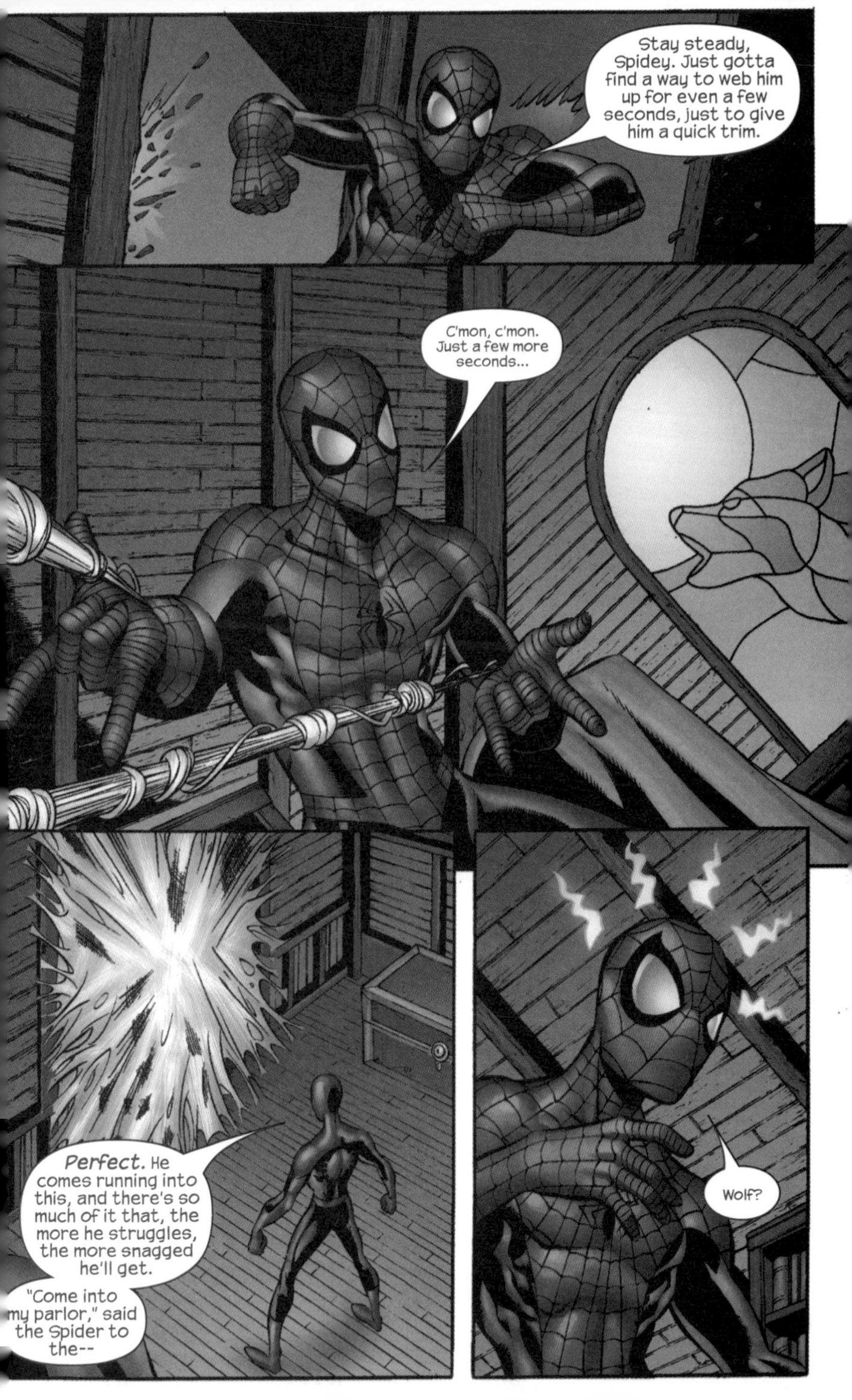
Stay steady, Spidey. Just gotta find a way to web him up for even a few seconds, just to give him a quick trim.
C'mon, c'mon. Just a few more seconds...
Perfect. He comes running into this, and there's so much of it that, the more he struggles, the more snagged he'll get.
"Come into my parlor," said the Spider to the--
Wolf?

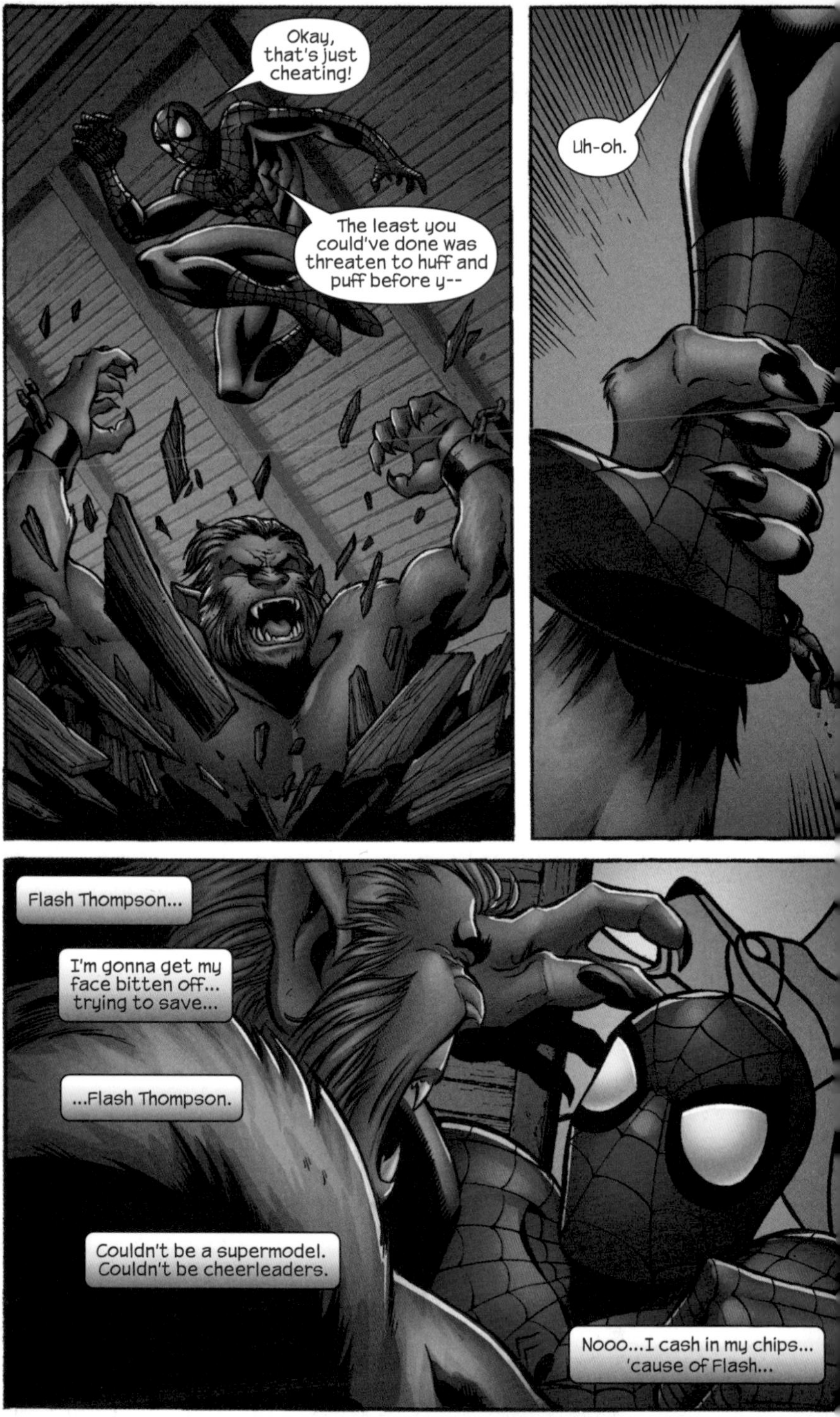
Okay, that's just cheating!
The least you could've done was threaten to huff and puff before y--
Uh-oh.
Flash Thompson...
I'm gonna get my face bitten off... trying to save...
...Flash Thompson.
Couldn't be a supermodel. Couldn't be cheerleaders.
Nooo...I cash in my chips... 'cause of Flash...

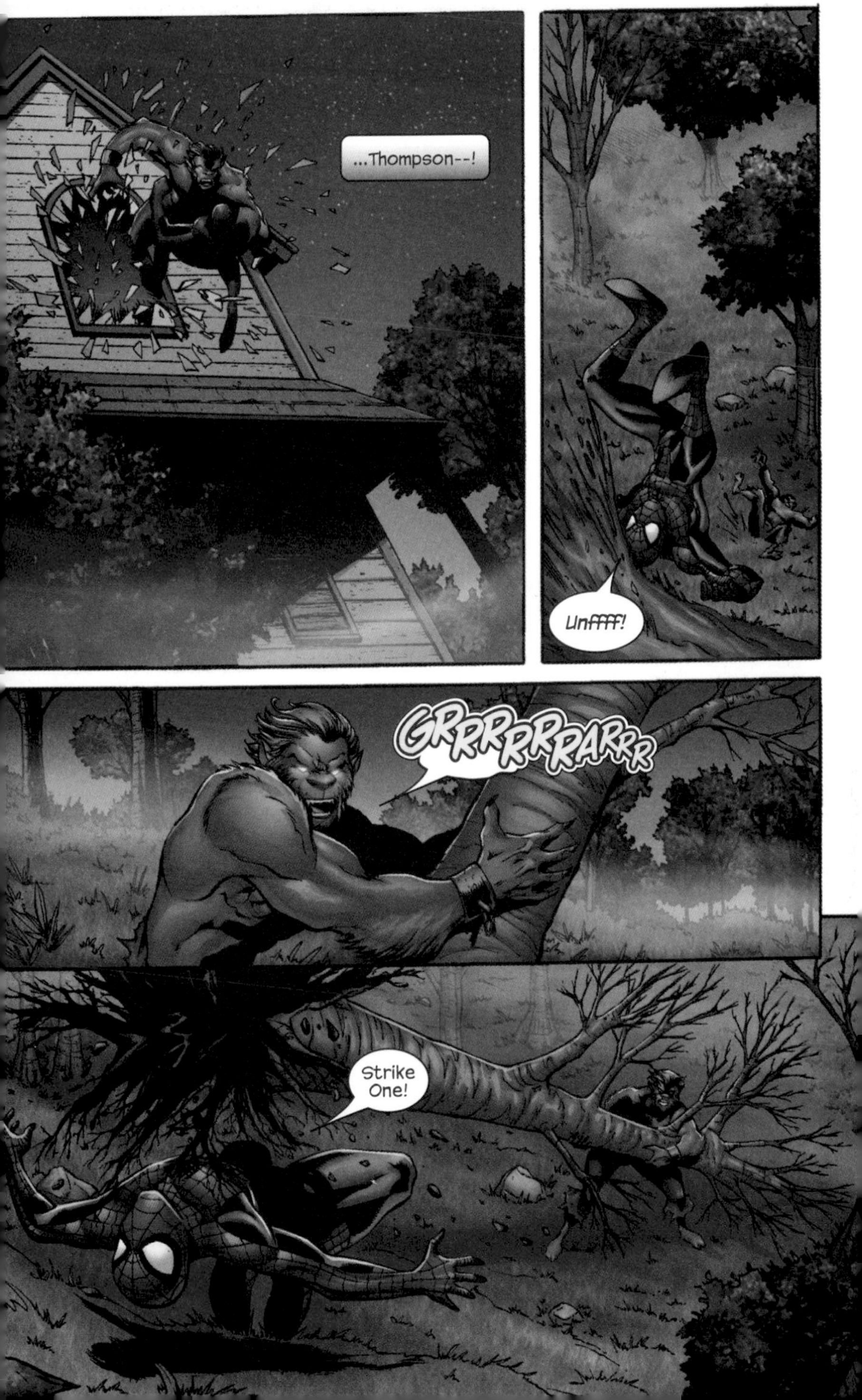
...Thompson--!
Unffff!
GRRRRRRARRR
Strike One!

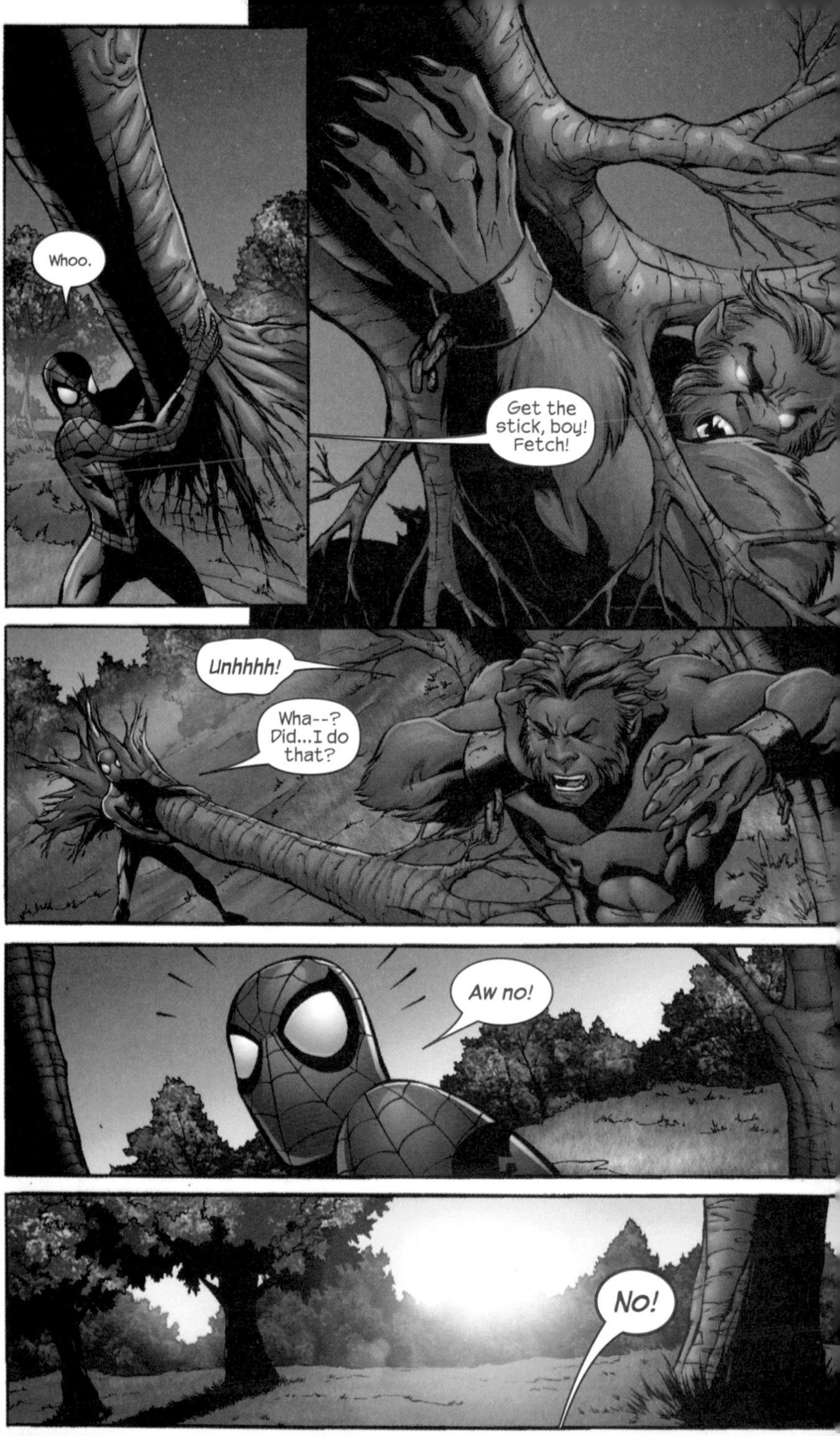

Whoo.
Get the stick, boy! Fetch!
Unhhhh!
Wha--? Did...I do that?
Aw no!
No!

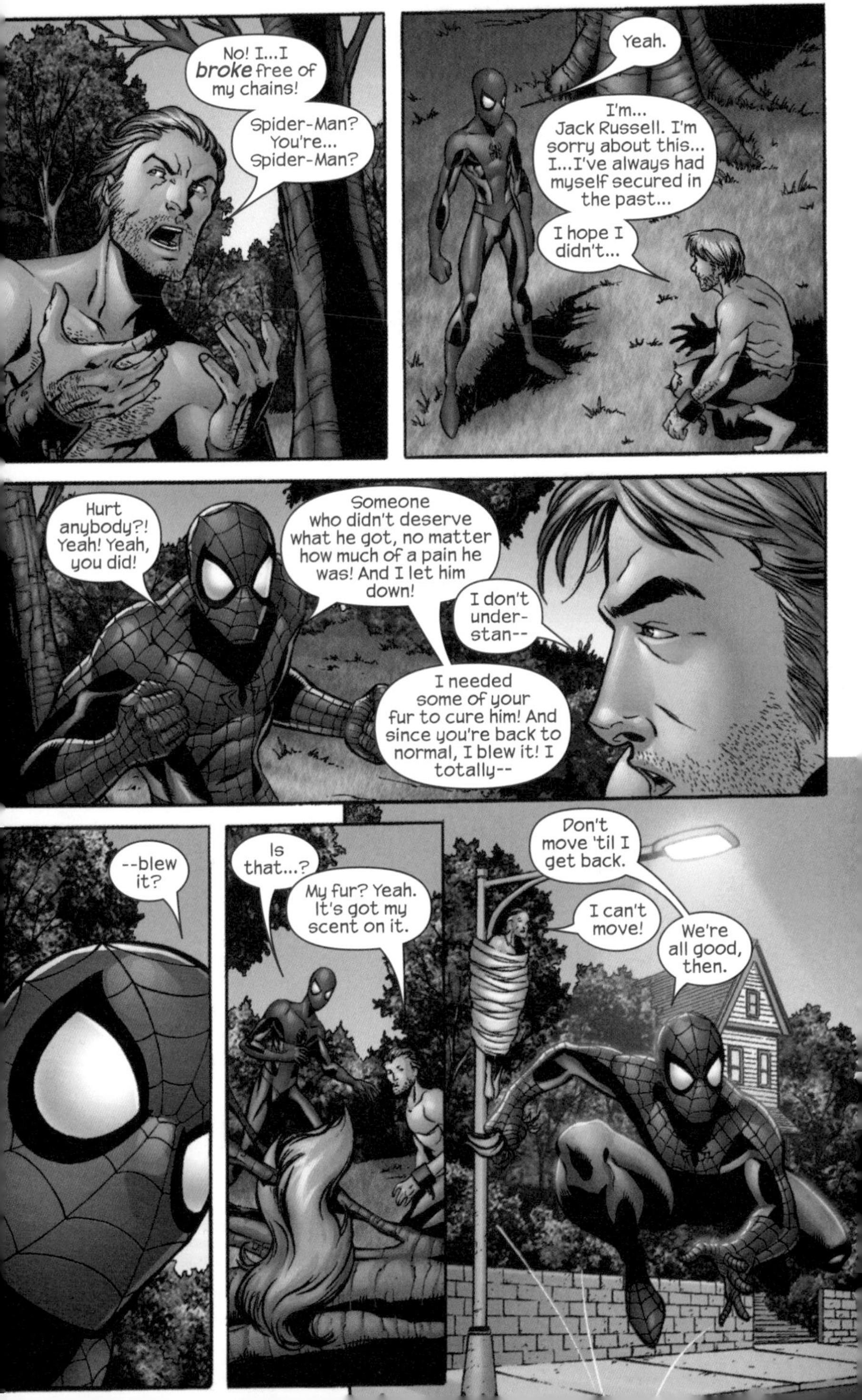
No! I...I *broke* free of my chains!
Spider-Man? You're... Spider-Man?
Yeah.
I'm... Jack Russell. I'm sorry about this... I...I've always had myself secured in the past...
I hope I didn't...
Hurt anybody?! Yeah! Yeah, you did!
Someone who didn't deserve what he got, no matter how much of a pain he was! And I let him down!
I don't under-stan--
I needed some of your fur to cure him! And since you're back to normal, I blew it! I totally--
--blew it?
Is that...?
My fur? Yeah. It's got my scent on it.
Don't move 'til I get back.
I can't move!
We're all good, then.

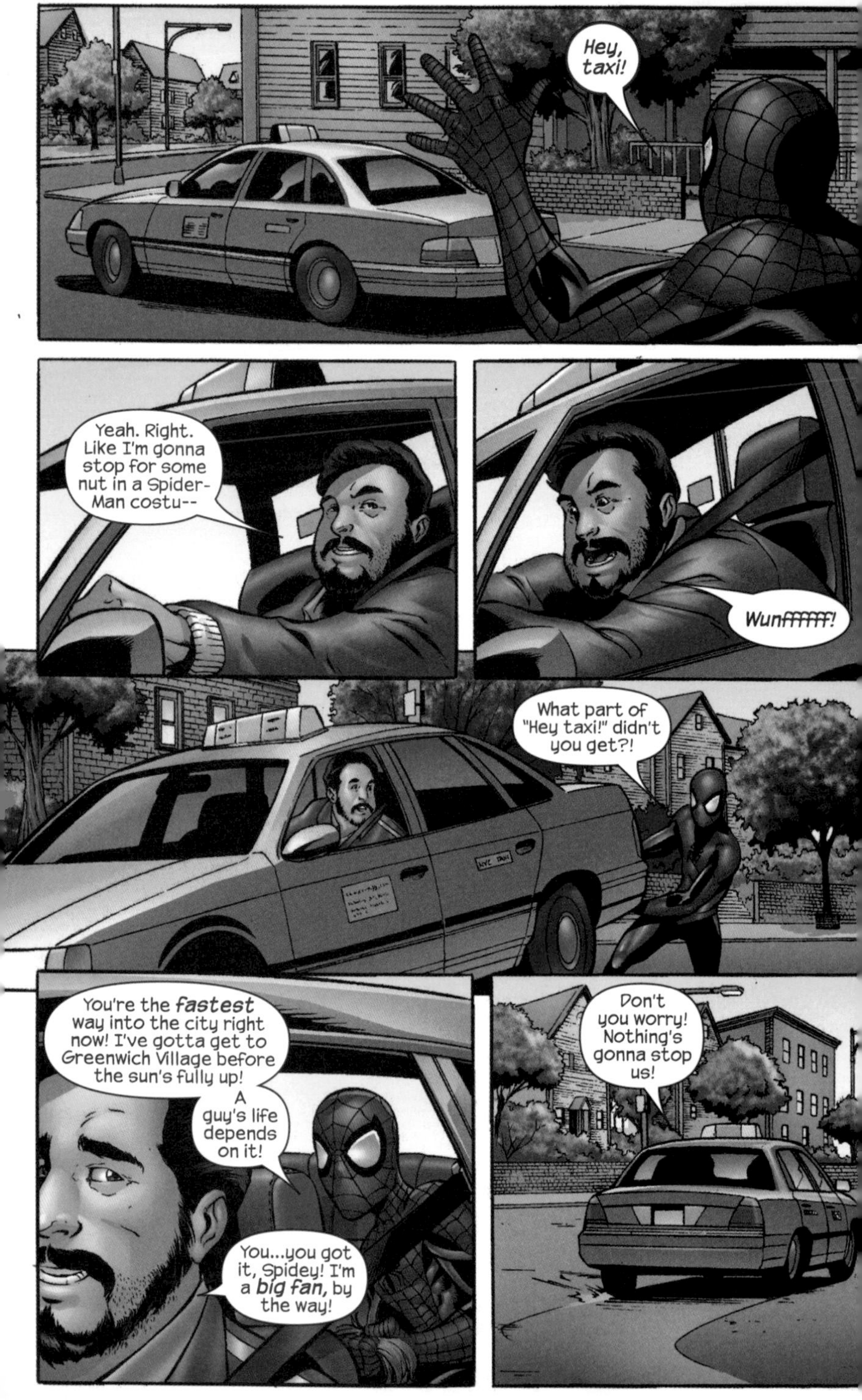
Hey, taxi!
Yeah. Right. Like I'm gonna stop for some nut in a Spider-Man costu--
Wunffffff!
What part of "Hey taxi!" didn't you get?!
You're the *fastest* way into the city right now! I've gotta get to Greenwich Village before the sun's fully up!
A guy's life depends on it!
You...you got it, Spidey! I'm a *big fan,* by the way!
Don't you worry! Nothing's gonna stop us!

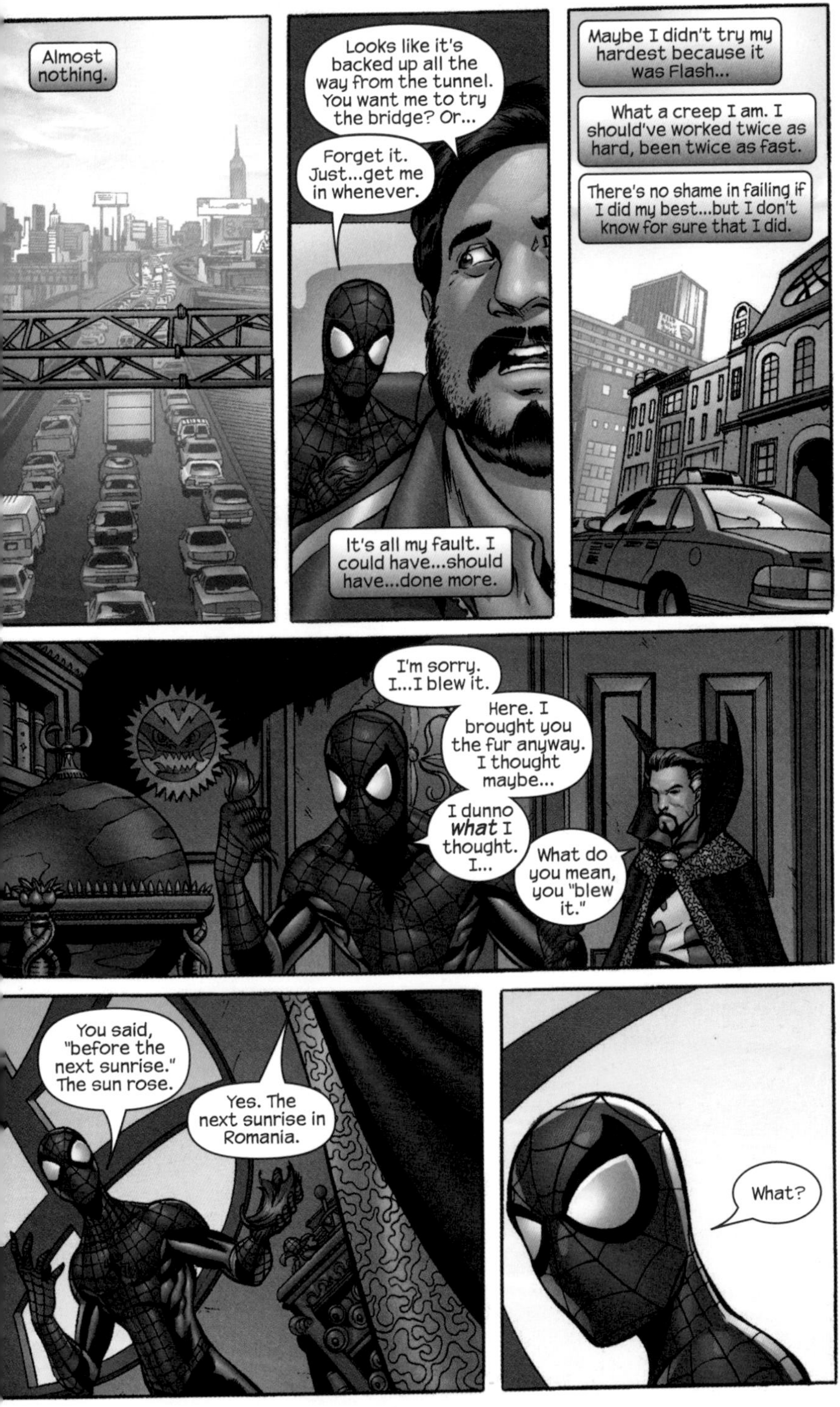
Almost nothing.
Looks like it's backed up all the way from the tunnel. You want me to try the bridge? Or...
Forget it. Just...get me in whenever.
It's all my fault. I could have...should have...done more.
Maybe I didn't try my hardest because it was Flash...
What a creep I am. I should've worked twice as hard, been twice as fast.
There's no shame in failing if I did my best...but I don't know for sure that I did.
I'm sorry. I...I blew it.
Here. I brought you the fur anyway. I thought maybe...
I dunno *what* I thought. I...
What do you mean, you "blew it."
You said, "before the next sunrise." The sun rose.
Yes. The next sunrise in Romania.
What?

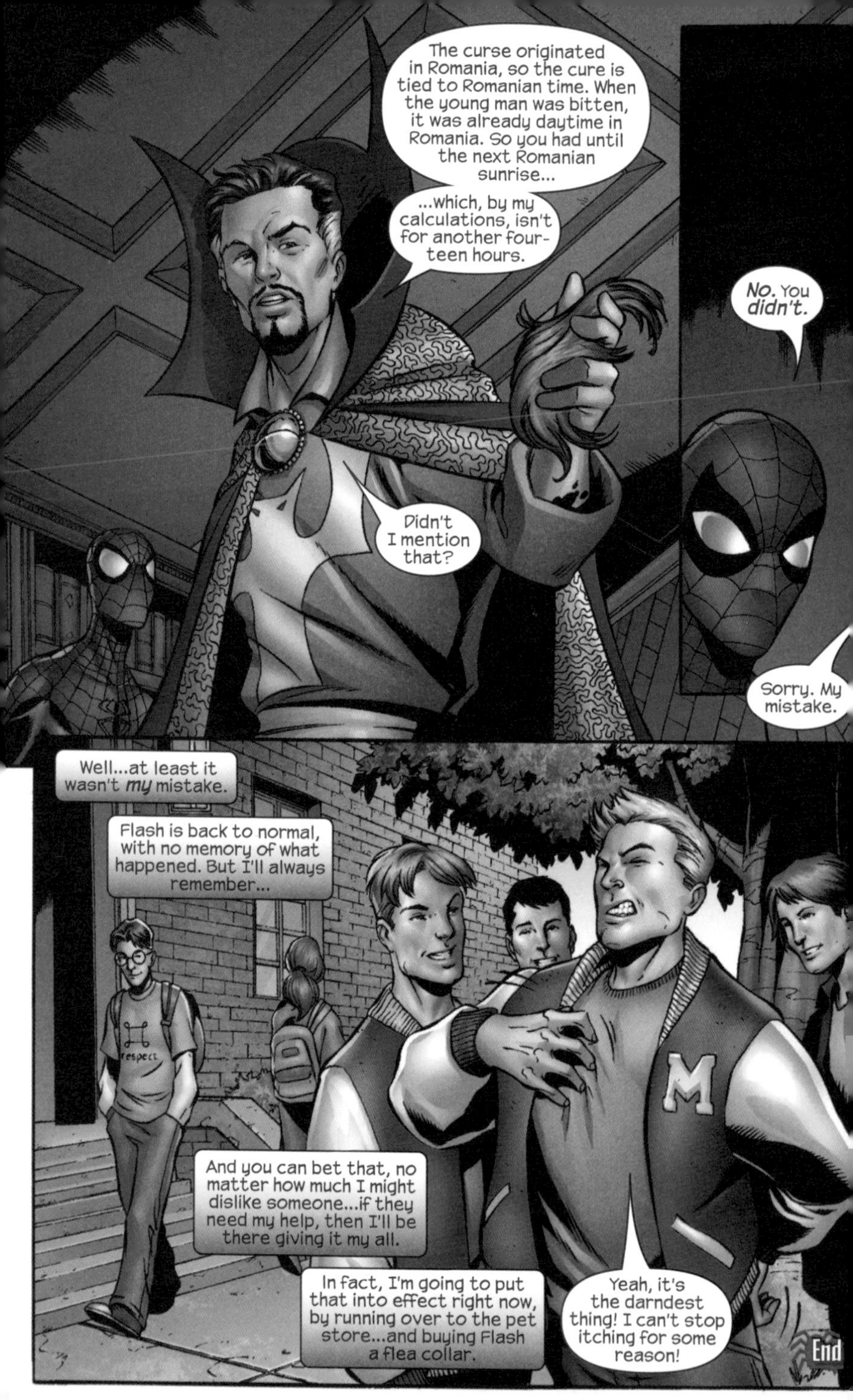
The curse originated in Romania, so the cure is tied to Romanian time. When the young man was bitten, it was already daytime in Romania. So you had until the next Romanian sunrise...
...which, by my calculations, isn't for another four-teen hours.
No. You didn't.
Didn't I mention that?
Sorry. My mistake.
Well...at least it wasn't my mistake.
Flash is back to normal, with no memory of what happened. But I'll always remember...
respect
M
And you can bet that, no matter how much I might dislike someone...if they need my help, then I'll be there giving it my all.
In fact, I'm going to put that into effect right now, by running over to the pet store...and buying Flash a flea collar.
Yeah, it's the darndest thing! I can't stop itching for some reason!
End

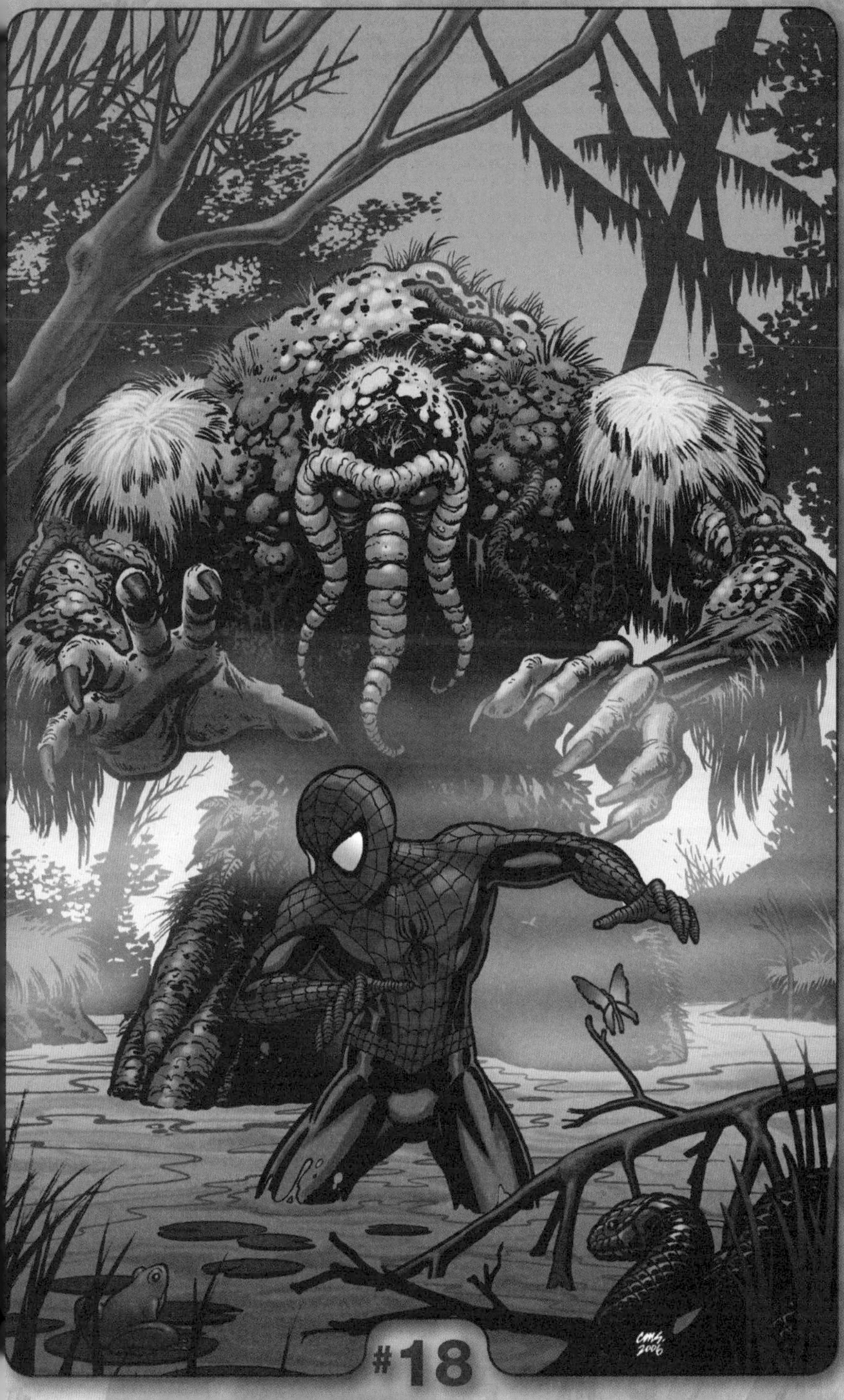
#18

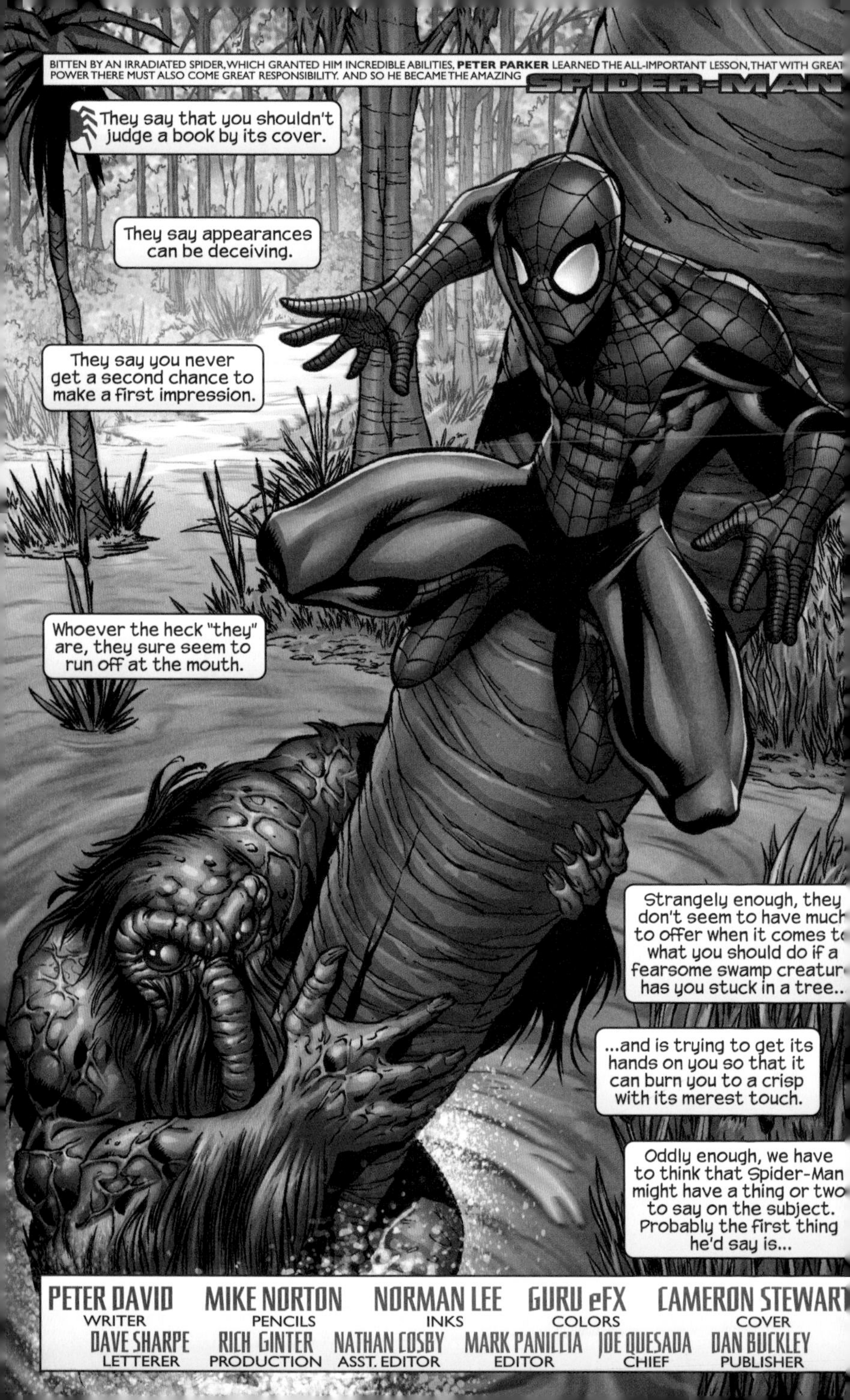

BITTEN BY AN IRRADIATED SPIDER, WHICH GRANTED HIM INCREDIBLE ABILITIES, PETER PARKER LEARNED THE ALL-IMPORTANT LESSON, THAT WITH GREAT POWER THERE MUST ALSO COME GREAT RESPONSIBILITY. AND SO HE BECAME THE AMAZING
SPIDER-MAN
They say that you shouldn't judge a book by its cover.
They say appearances can be deceiving.
They say you never get a second chance to make a first impression.
Whoever the heck "they" are, they sure seem to run off at the mouth.
Strangely enough, they don't seem to have muc to offer when it comes t what you should do if a fearsome swamp creatur has you stuck in a tree..
...and is trying to get its hands on you so that it can burn you to a crisp with its merest touch.
Oddly enough, we have to think that Spider-Man might have a thing or two to say on the subject. Probably the first thing he'd say is...
PETER DAVID WRITER
MIKE NORTON PENCILS
NORMAN LEE INKS
GURU eFX COLORS
CAMERON STEWART COVER
DAVE SHARPE LETTERER
RICH GINTER PRODUCTION
NATHAN COSBY ASST. EDITOR
MARK PANICCIA EDITOR
JOE QUESADA CHIEF
DAN BUCKLEY PUBLISHER

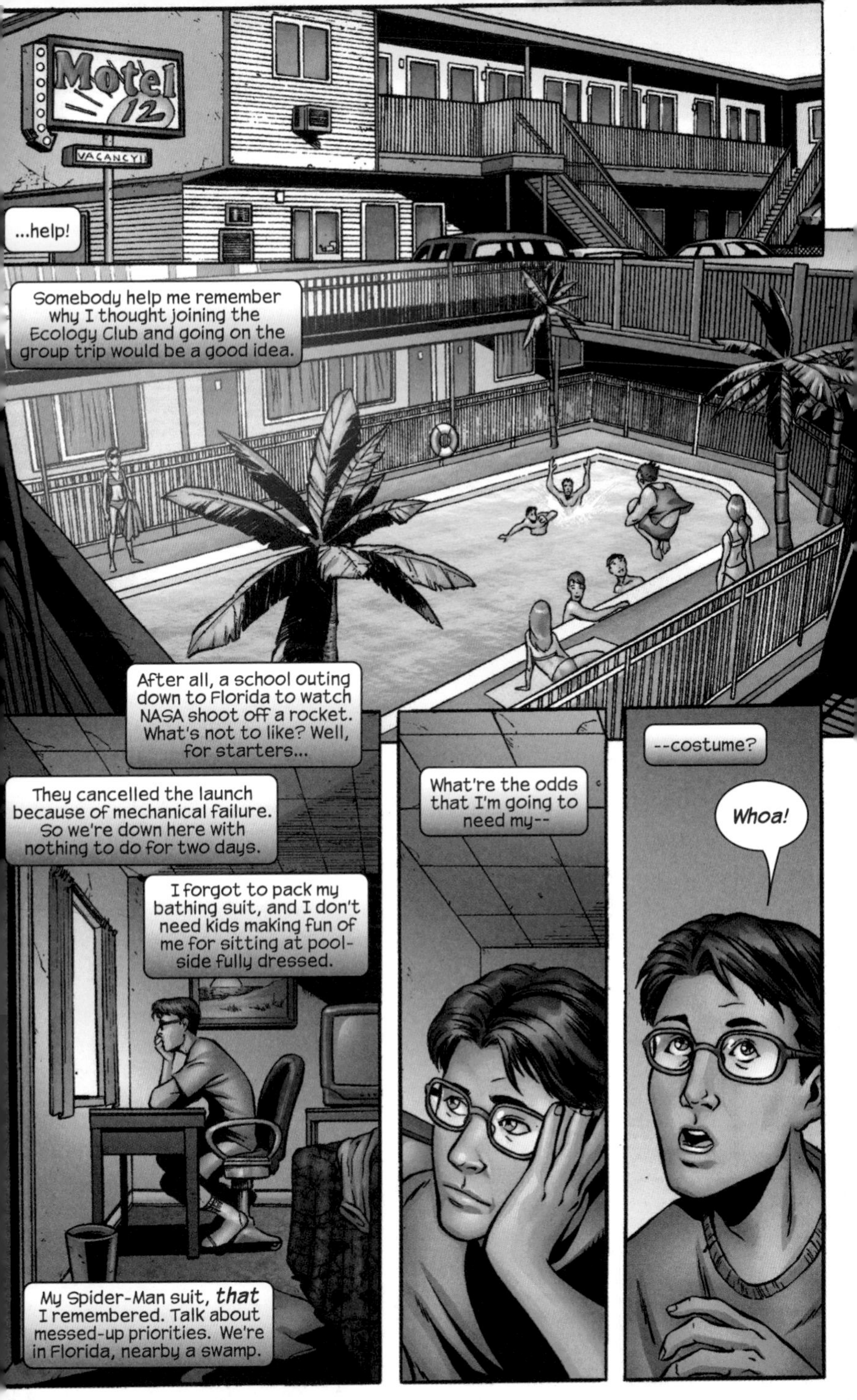

Motel 12
VACANCY!
...help!
Somebody help me remember why I thought joining the Ecology Club and going on the group trip would be a good idea.
After all, a school outing down to Florida to watch NASA shoot off a rocket. What's not to like? Well, for starters...
They cancelled the launch because of mechanical failure. So we're down here with nothing to do for two days.
I forgot to pack my bathing suit, and I don't need kids making fun of me for sitting at pool-side fully dressed.
My Spider-Man suit, *that* I remembered. Talk about messed-up priorities. We're in Florida, nearby a swamp.
What're the odds that I'm going to need my--
--costume?
Whoa!

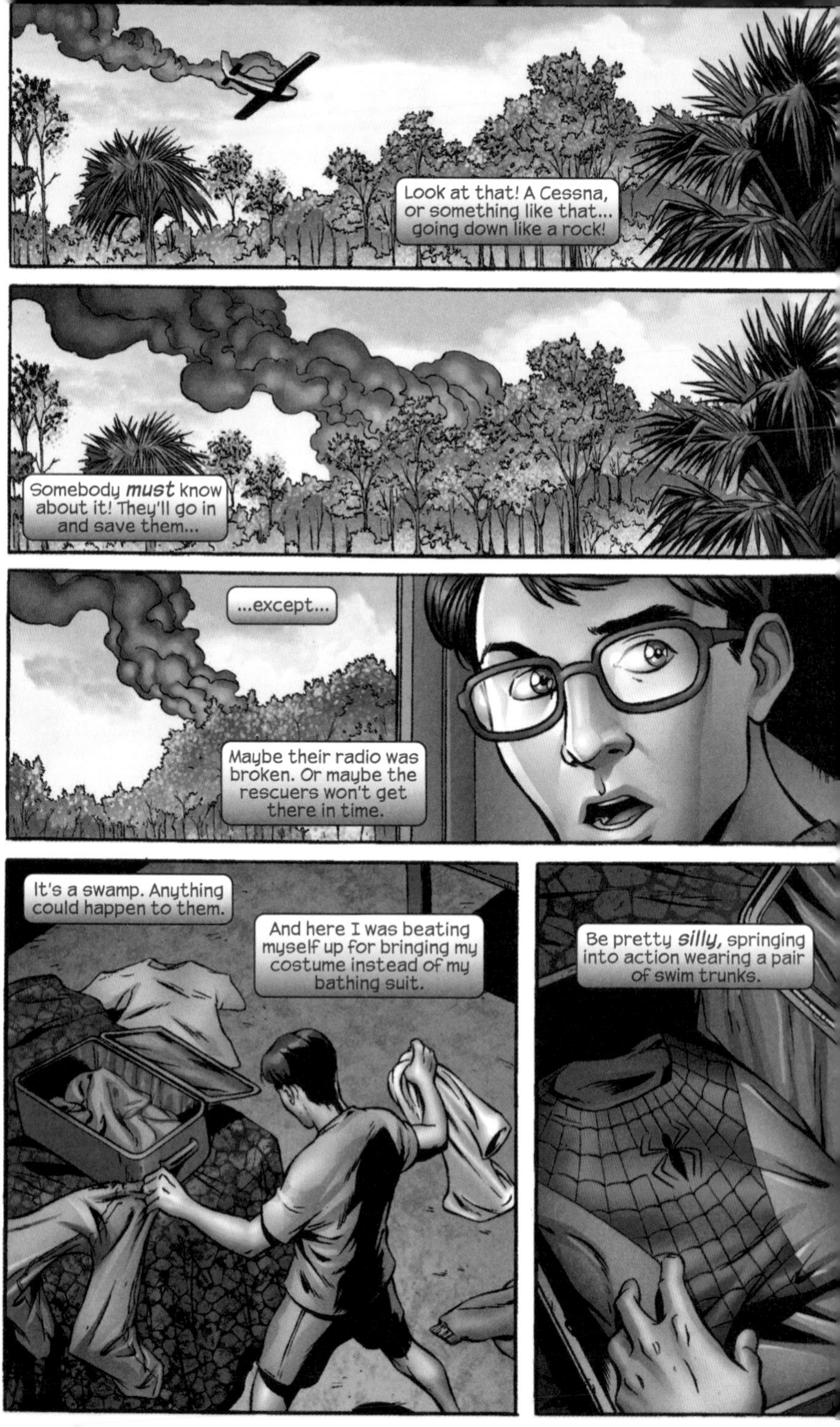

Look at that! A Cessna, or something like that... going down like a rock!
Somebody *must* know about it! They'll go in and save them...
...except...
Maybe their radio was broken. Or maybe the rescuers won't get there in time.
It's a swamp. Anything could happen to them.
And here I was beating myself up for bringing my costume instead of my bathing suit.
Be pretty *silly*, springing into action wearing a pair of swim trunks.

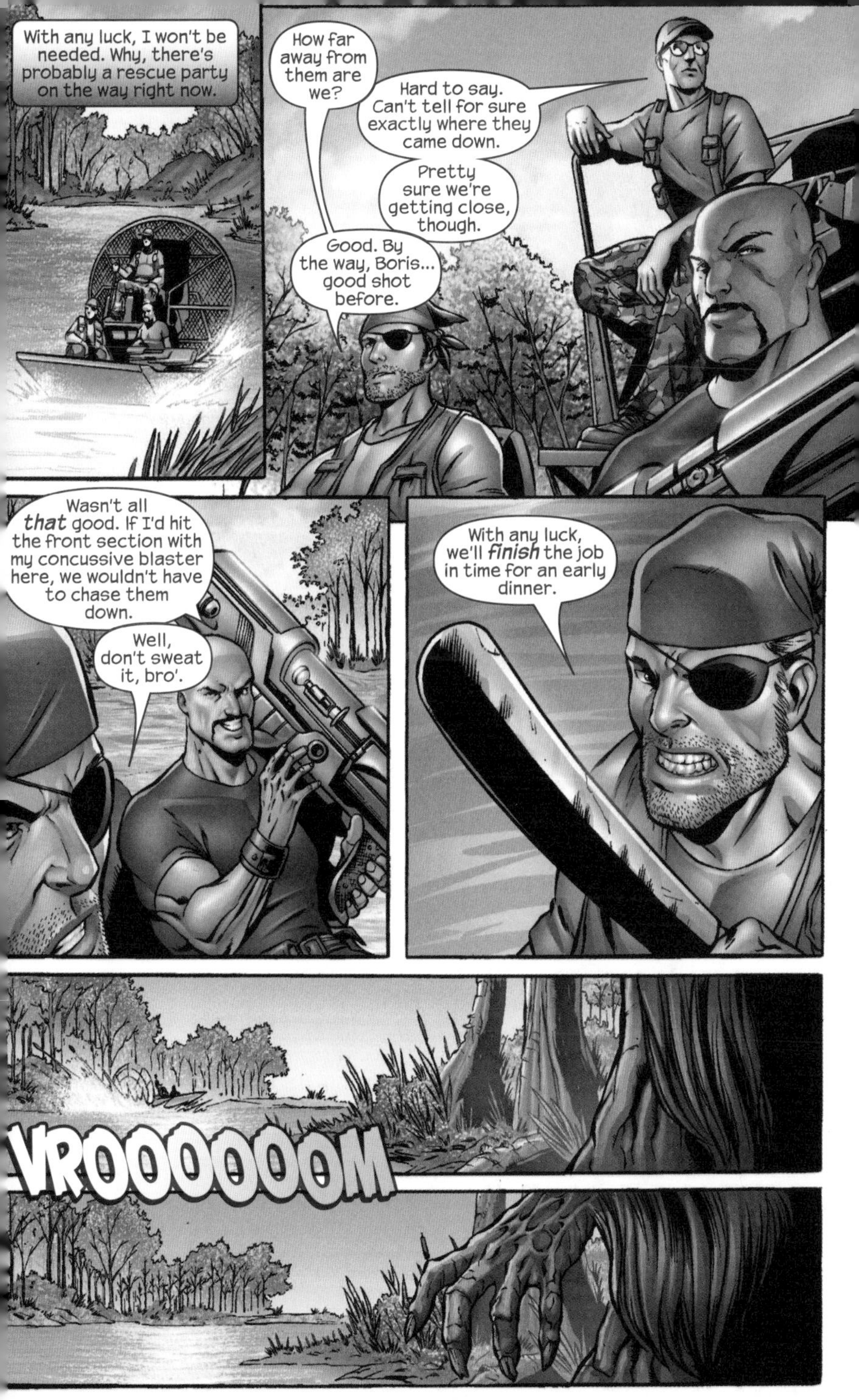

With any luck, I won't be needed. Why, there's probably a rescue party on the way right now.
How far away from them are we?
Hard to say. Can't tell for sure exactly where they came down.
Pretty sure we're getting close, though.
Good. By the way, Boris... good shot before.
Wasn't all *that* good. If I'd hit the front section with my concussive blaster here, we wouldn't have to chase them down.
Well, don't sweat it, bro'.
With any luck, we'll *finish* the job in time for an early dinner.
VROOOOOOM

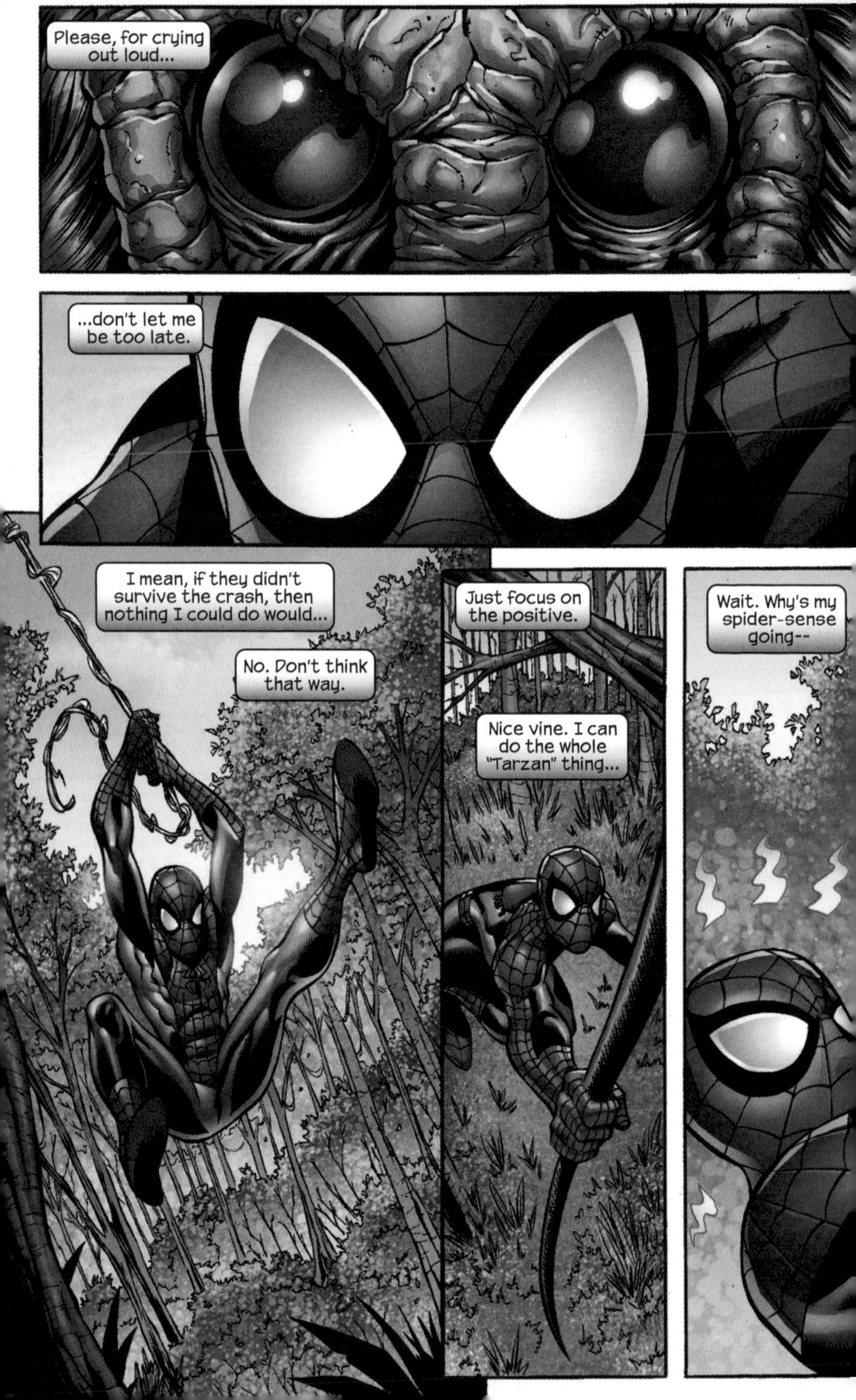
Please, for crying out loud...
...don't let me be too late.
I mean, if they didn't survive the crash, then nothing I could do would...
No. Don't think that way.
Just focus on the positive.
Nice vine. I can do the whole "Tarzan" thing...
Wait. Why's my spider-sense going--

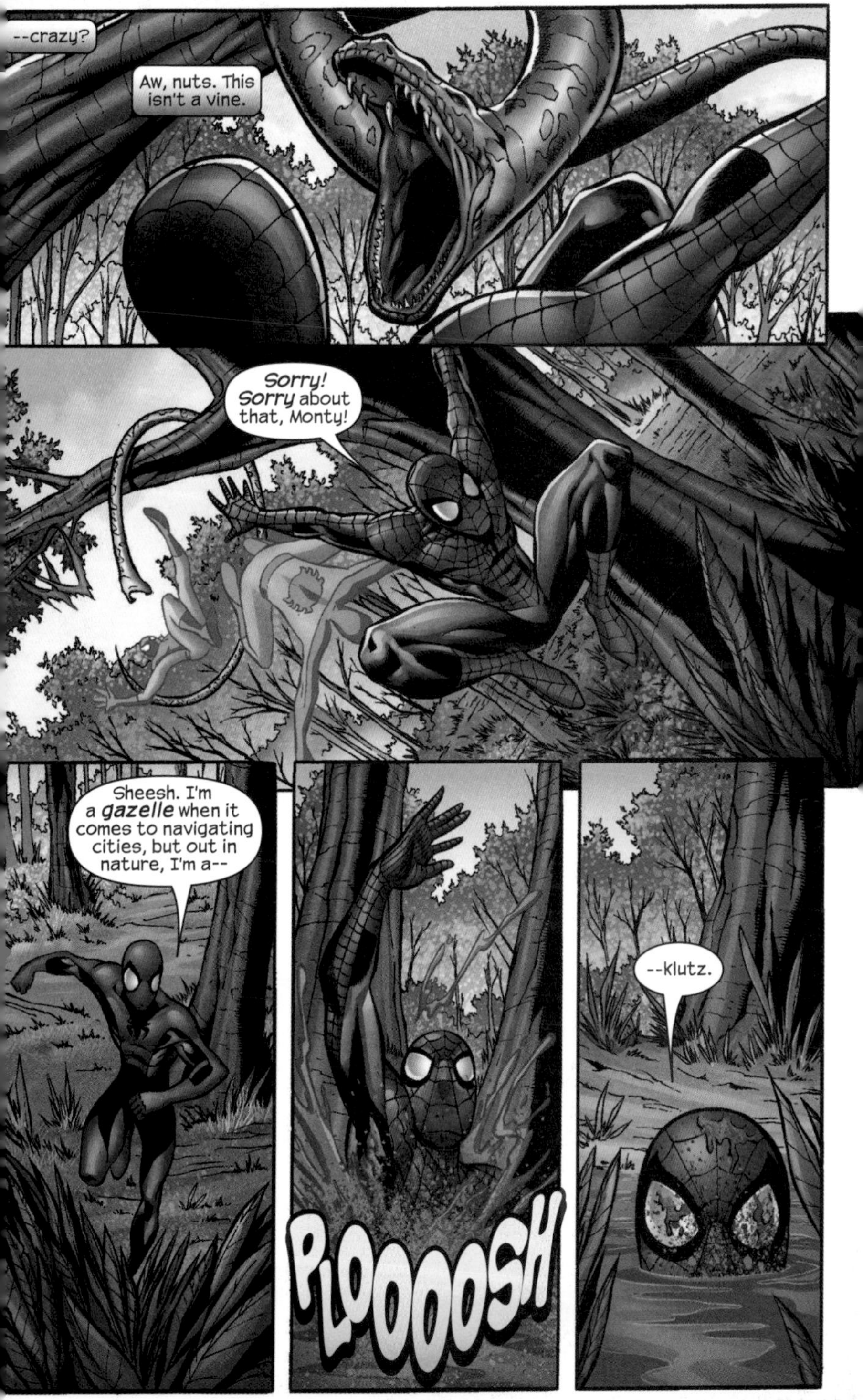
--crazy?
Aw, nuts. This isn't a vine.
Sorry! Sorry about that, Monty!
Sheesh. I'm a gazelle when it comes to navigating cities, but out in nature, I'm a--
PLOOOOSH
--klutz.

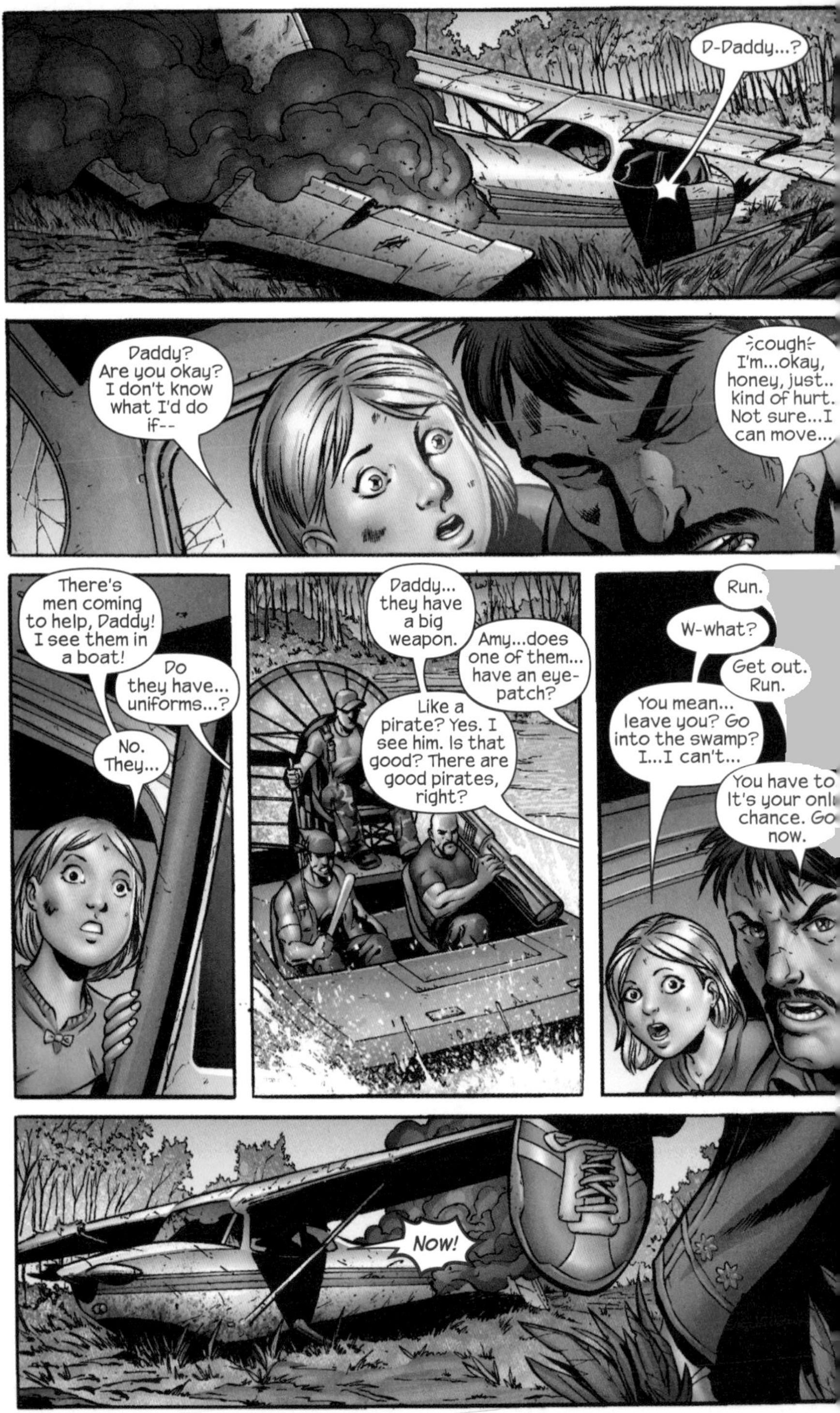
D-Daddy...?
Daddy? Are you okay? I don't know what I'd do if--
cough I'm...okay, honey, just.. kind of hurt. Not sure...I can move...
There's men coming to help, Daddy! I see them in a boat!
Do they have... uniforms...?
No. They...
Daddy... they have a big weapon.
Amy...does one of them... have an eye-patch?
Like a pirate? Yes. I see him. Is that good? There are good pirates, right?
Run.
W-what?
Get out. Run.
You mean... leave you? Go into the swamp? I...I can't...
You have to It's your onl chance. Go now.
NOW!

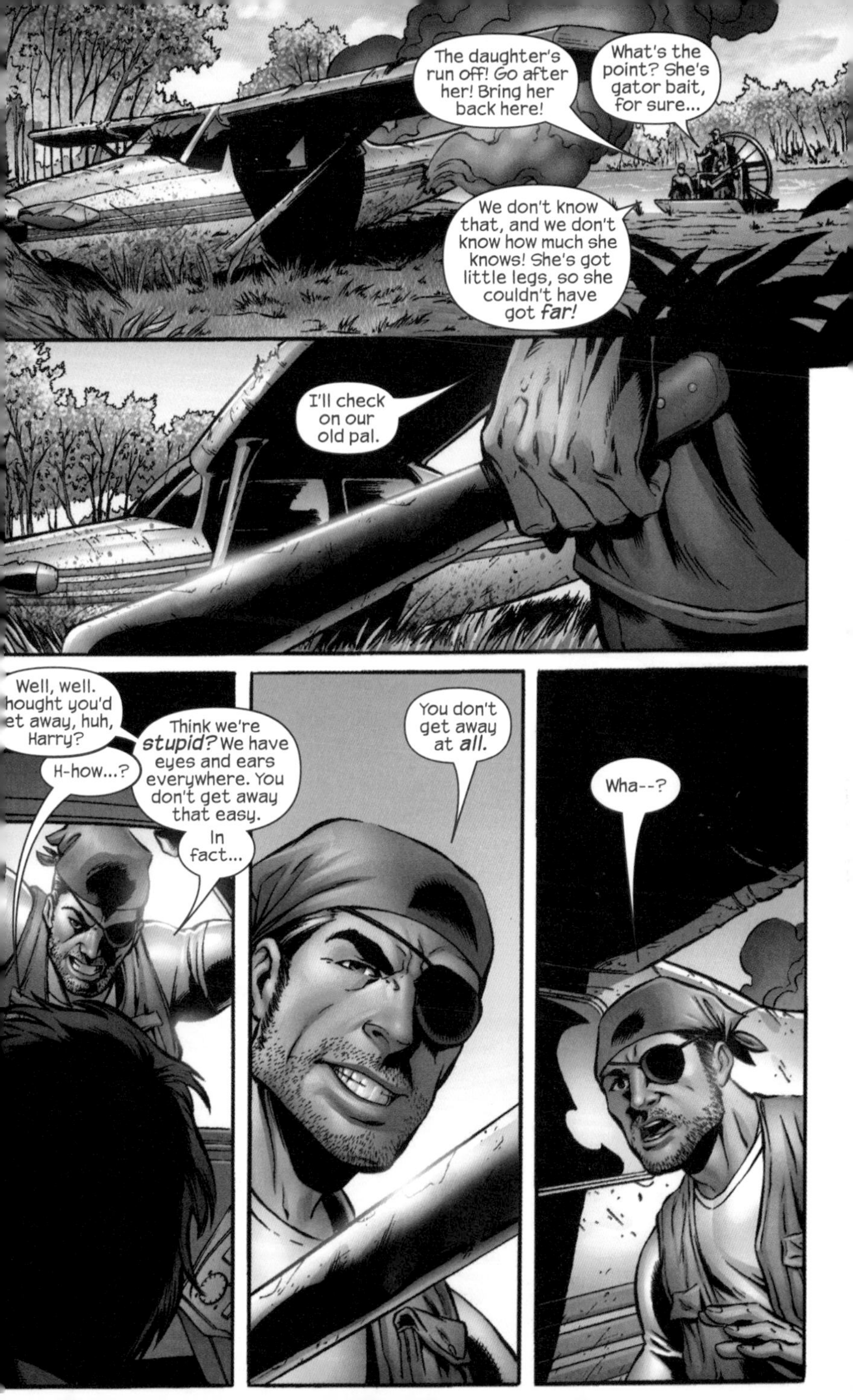

The daughter's run off! Go after her! Bring her back here!
What's the point? She's gator bait, for sure...
We don't know that, and we don't know how much she knows! She's got little legs, so she couldn't have got *far!*
I'll check on our old pal.
Well, well. hought you'd et away, huh, Harry?
H-how...?
Think we're *stupid?* We have eyes and ears everywhere. You don't get away that easy.
In fact...
You don't get away at *all.*
Wha--?

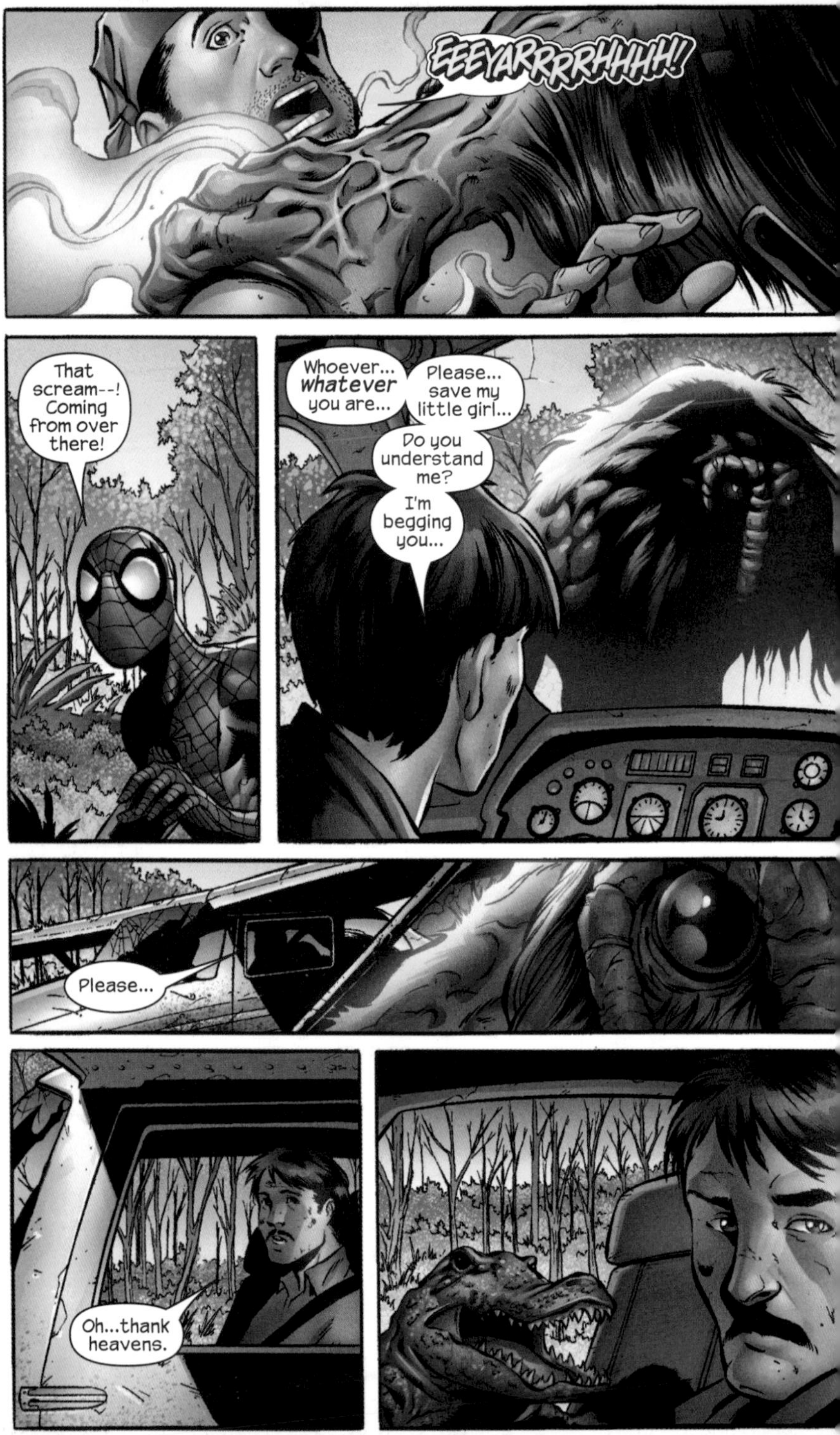
EEEYARRRRHHHH!
That scream--! Coming from over there!
Whoever... *whatever* you are...
Please... save my little girl...
Do you understand me?
I'm begging you...
Please...
Oh...thank heavens.

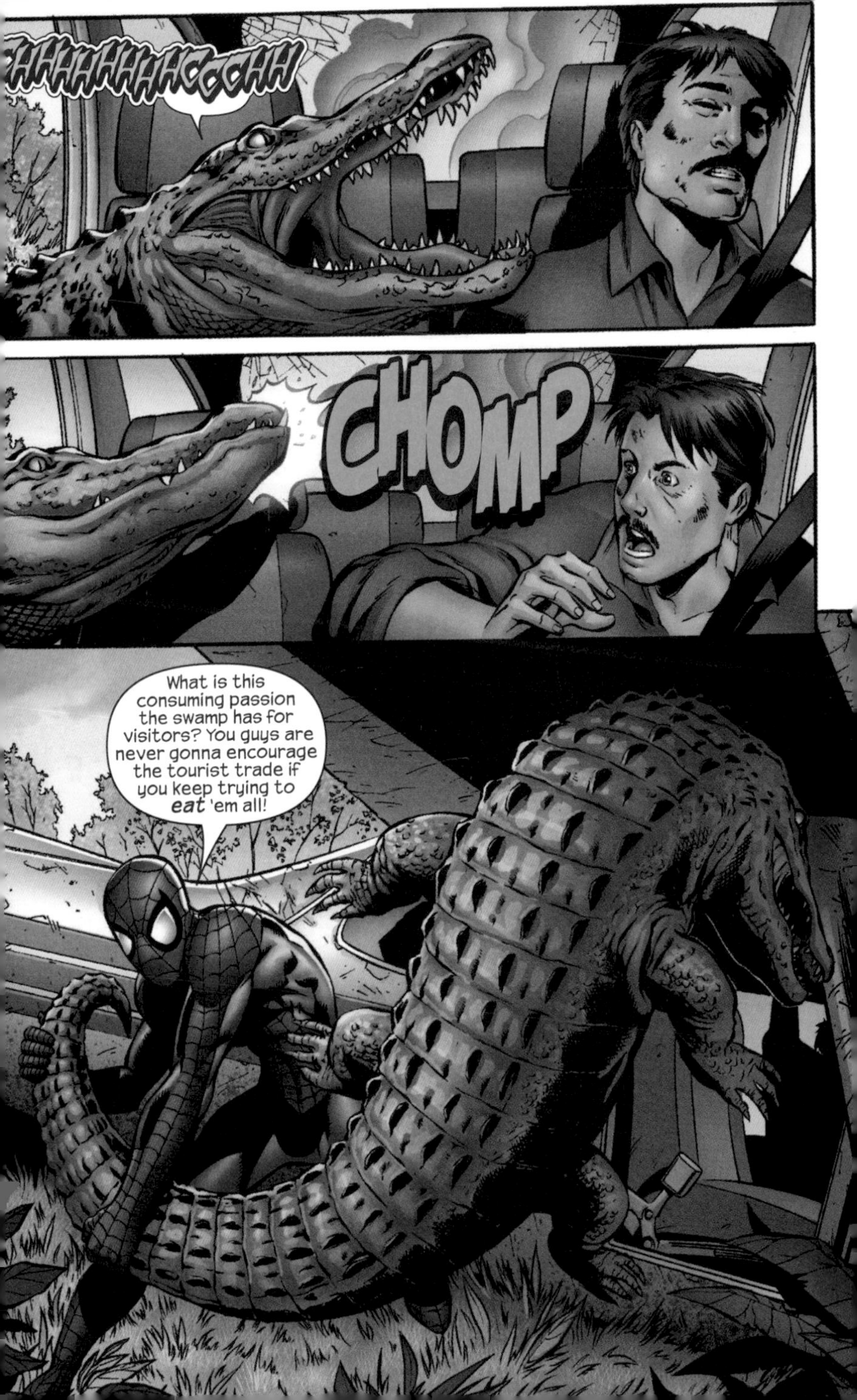
HHHHHHHHACCCAHH
CHOMP
What is this consuming passion the swamp has for visitors? You guys are never gonna encourage the tourist trade if you keep trying to *eat* 'em all!

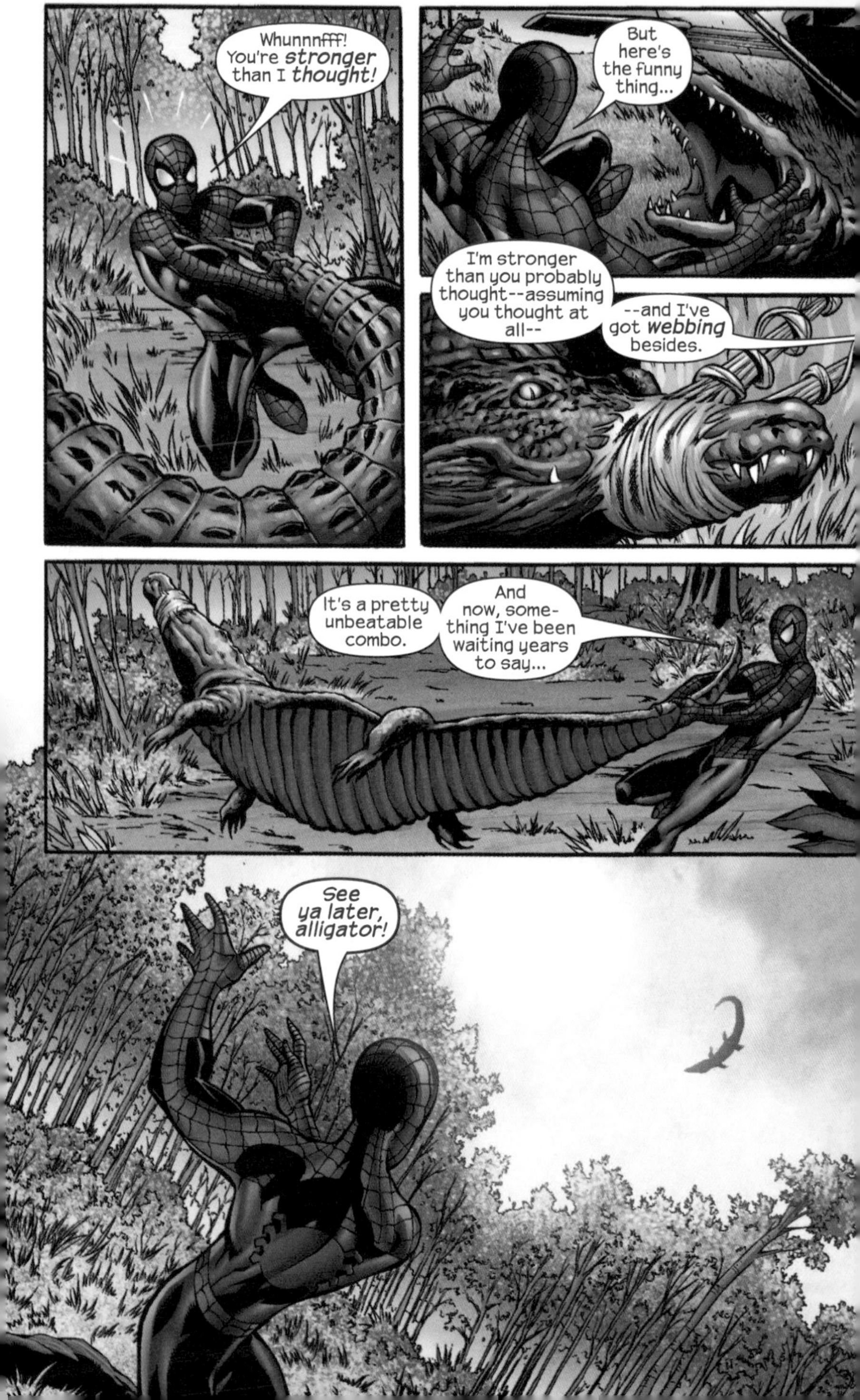
Whunnnfff! You're *stronger* than I *thought*!
But here's the funny thing...
I'm stronger than you probably thought--assuming you thought at all--
--and I've got *webbing* besides.
It's a pretty unbeatable combo.
And now, something I've been waiting years to say...
See ya later, alligator!

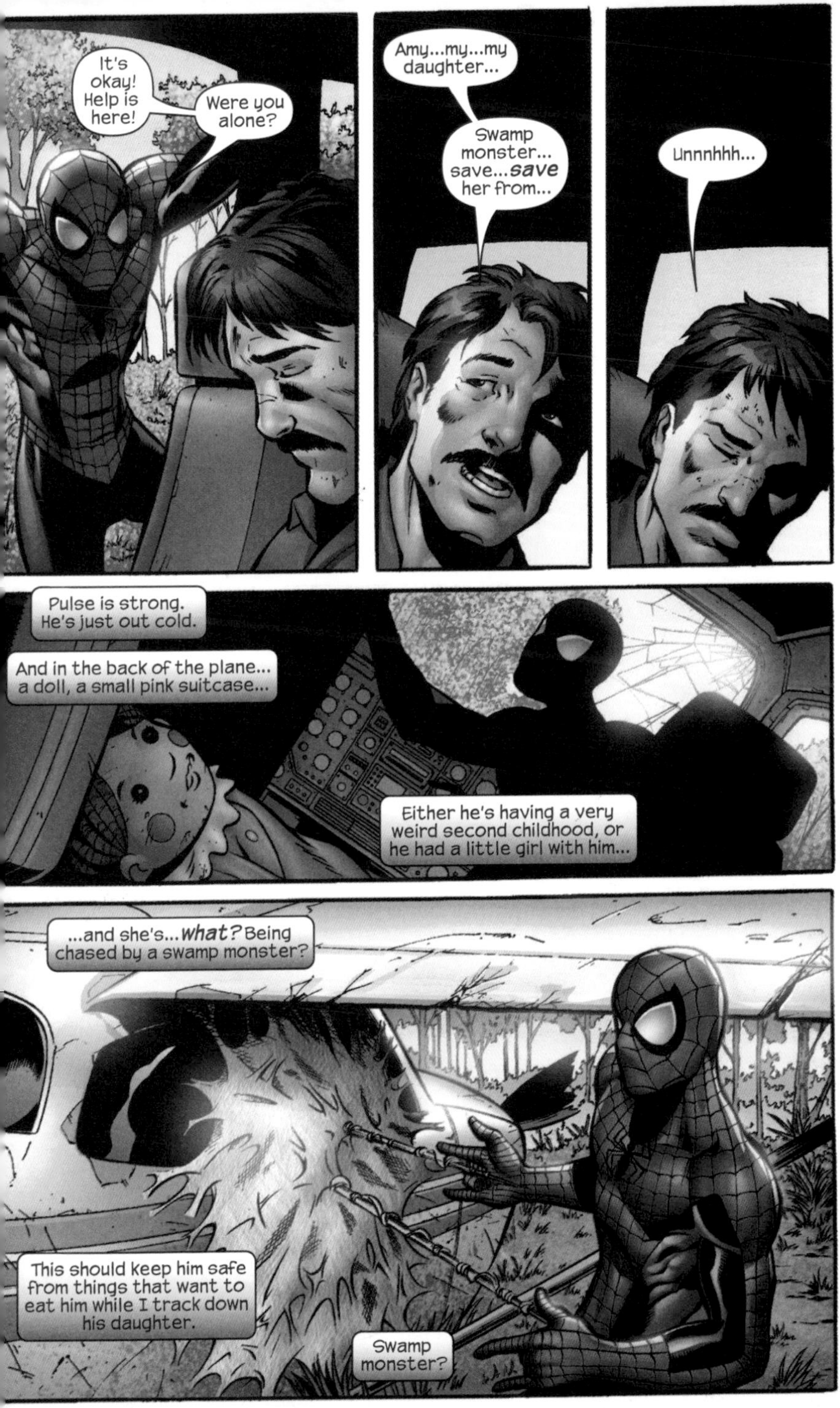

It's okay! Help is here!
Were you alone?
Amy...my...my daughter...
Swamp monster... save...*save* her from...
Unnnhhh...
Pulse is strong. He's just out cold.
And in the back of the plane... a doll, a small pink suitcase...
Either he's having a very weird second childhood, or he had a little girl with him...
...and she's...*what?* Being chased by a swamp monster?
This should keep him safe from things that want to eat him while I track down his daughter.
Swamp monster?

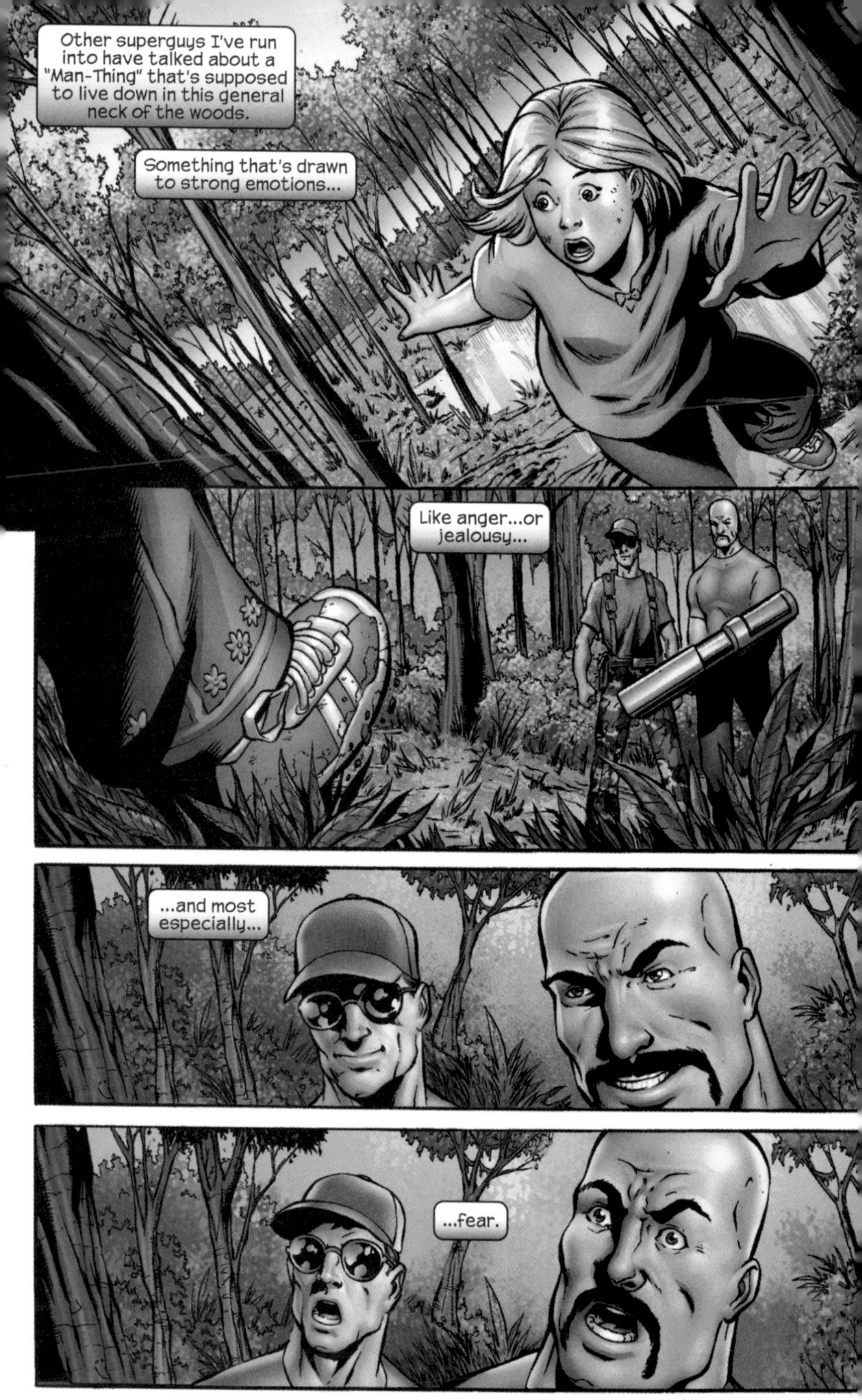
Other superguys I've run into have talked about a "Man-Thing" that's supposed to live down in this general neck of the woods.
Something that's drawn to strong emotions...
Like anger...or jealousy...
...and most especially...
...fear.

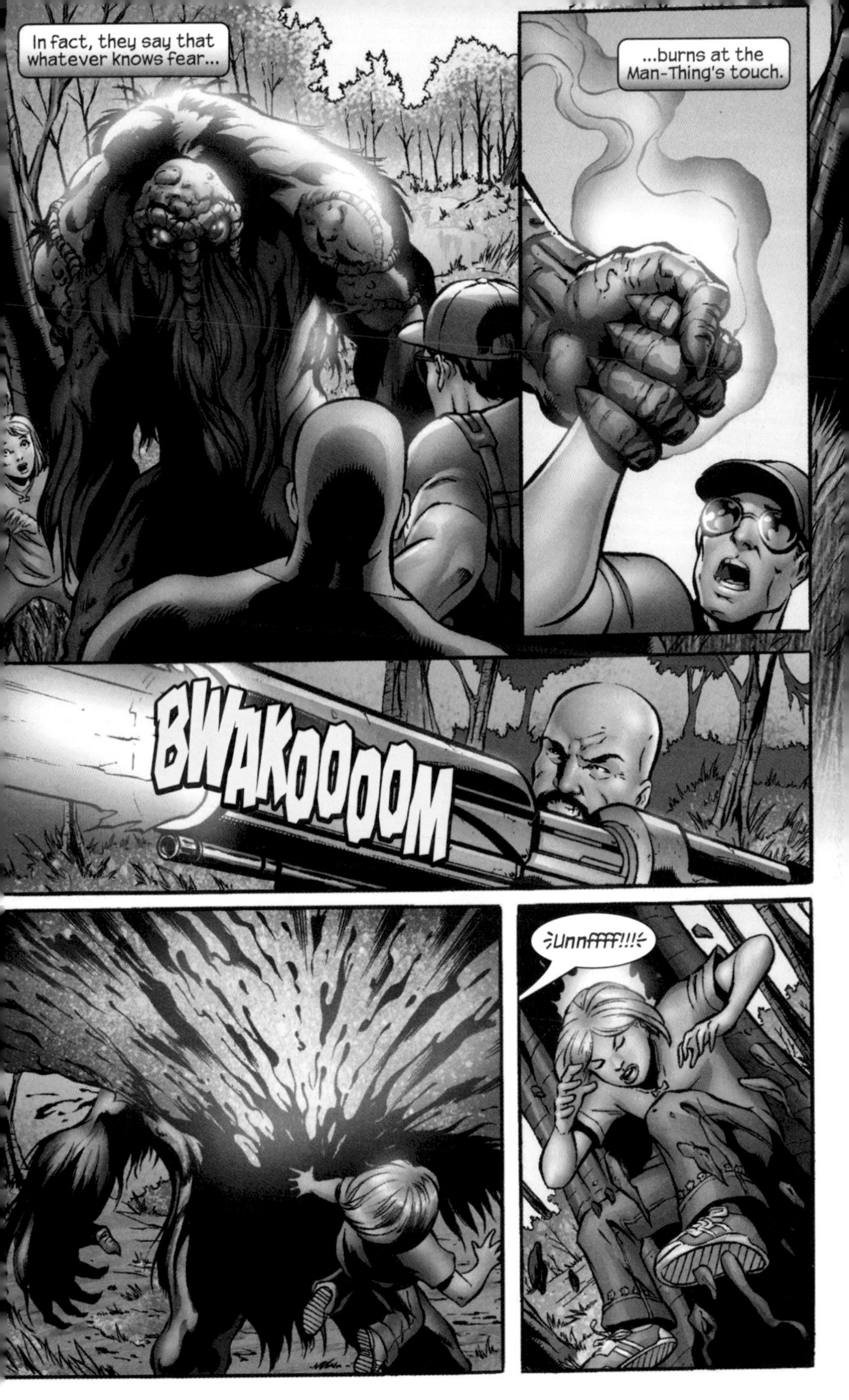
In fact, they say that whatever knows fear...
...burns at the Man-Thing's touch.
BWAKOOOOM
Unnffff!!!

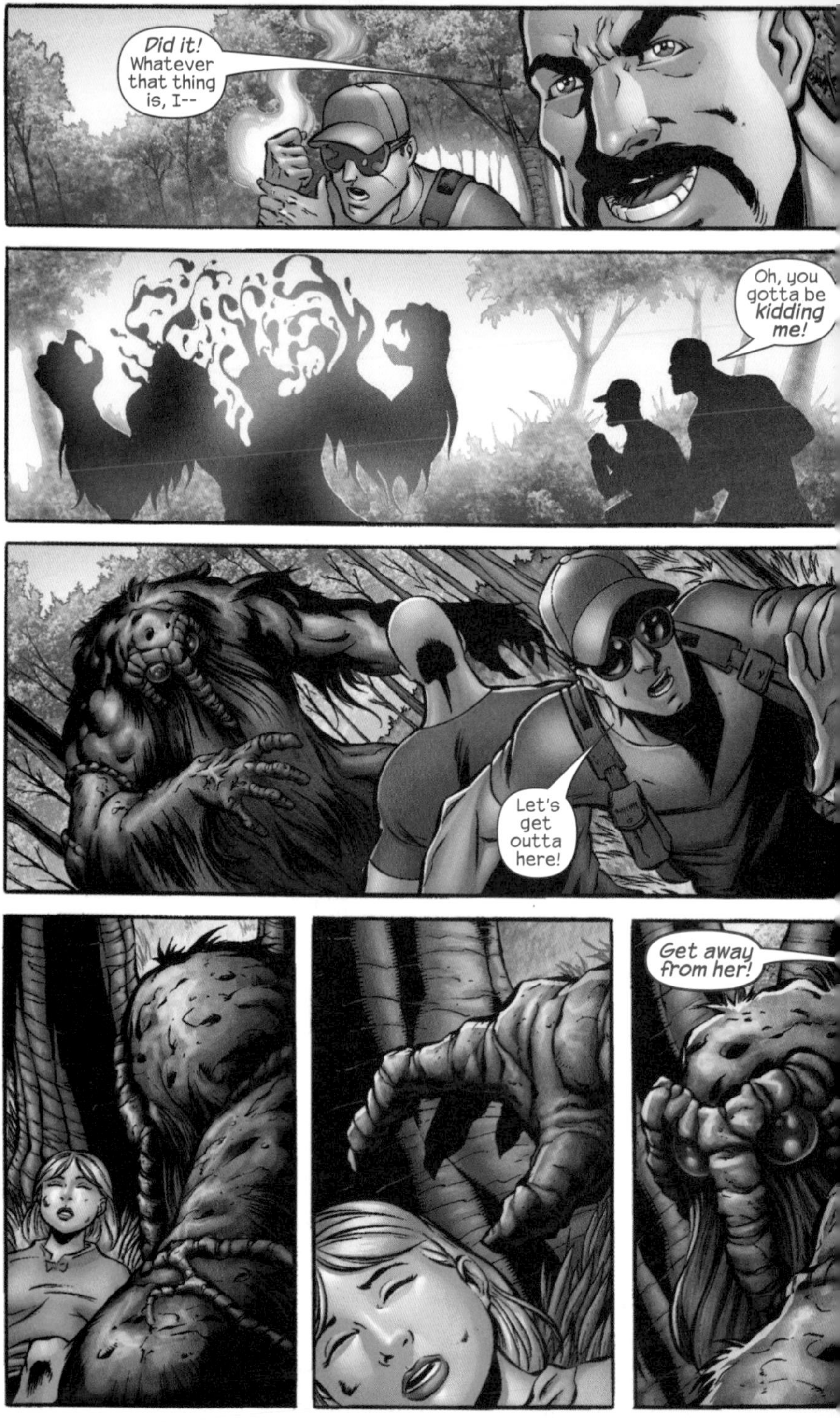
Did it! Whatever that thing is, I--
Oh, you gotta be kidding me!
Let's get outta here!
Get away from her!

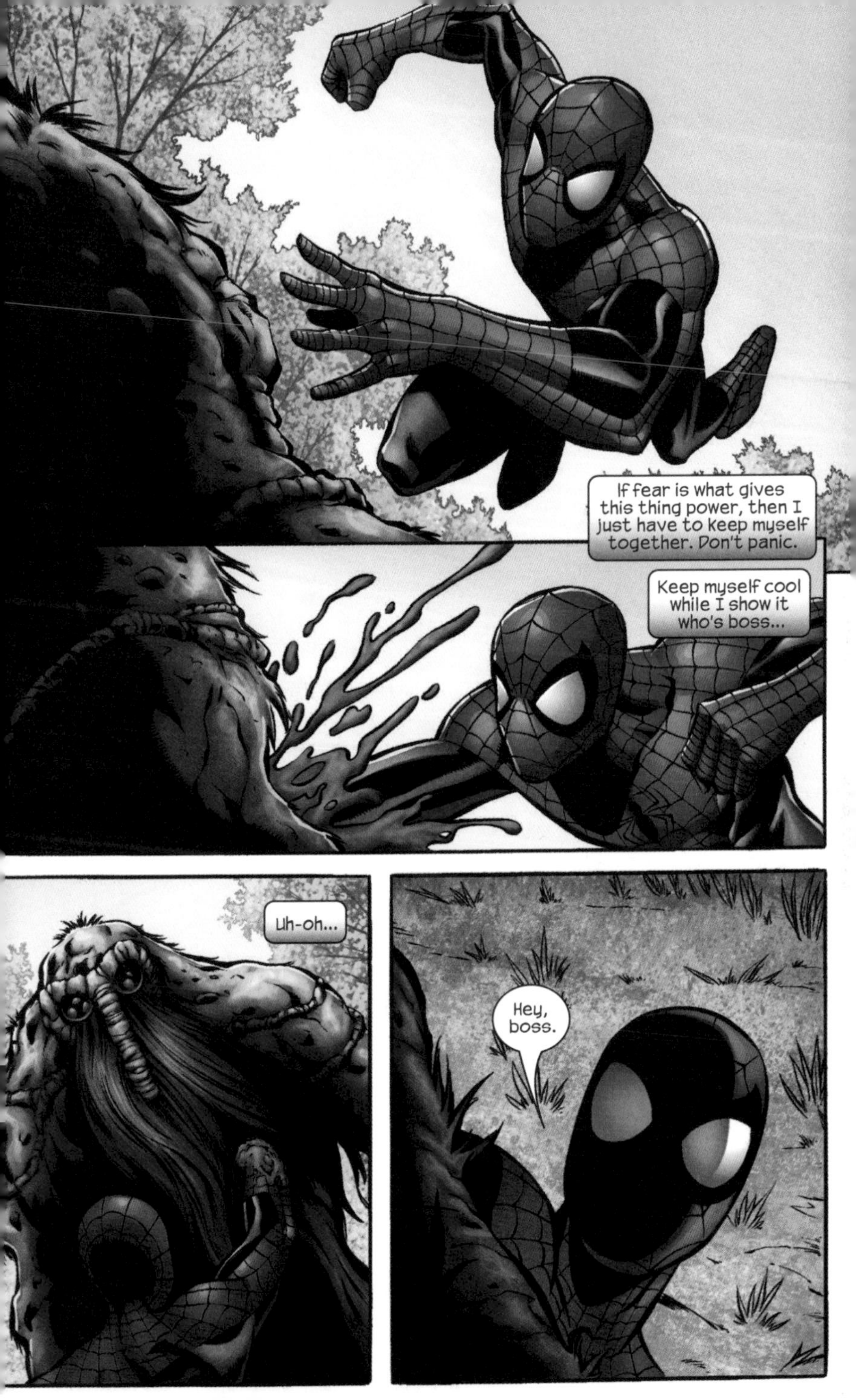
If fear is what gives this thing power, then I just have to keep myself together. Don't panic.
Keep myself cool while I show it who's boss...
Uh-oh...
Hey, boss.

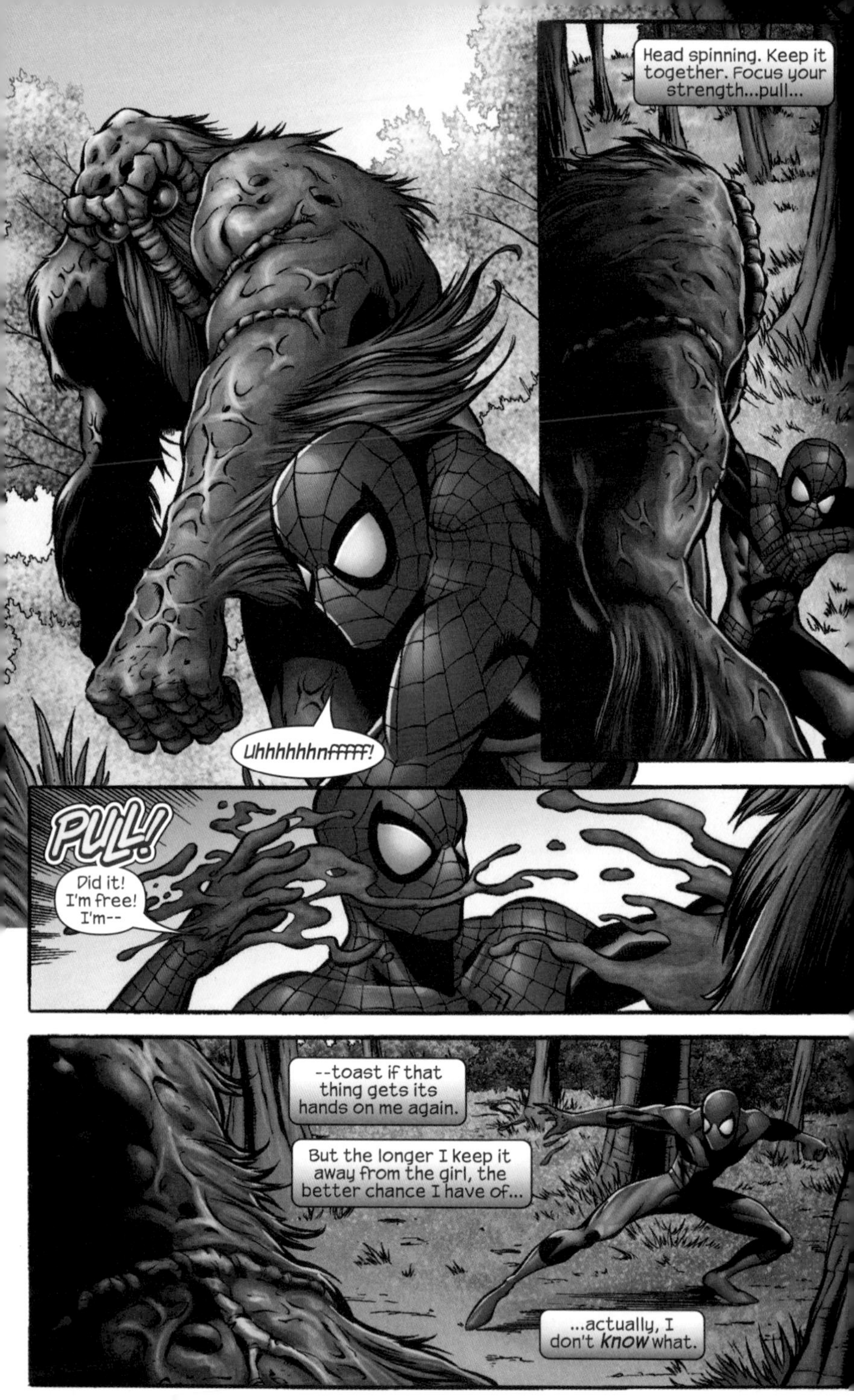
Head spinning. Keep it together. Focus your strength...pull...
Uhhhhhhnffff!
PULL!
Did it! I'm free! I'm--
--toast if that thing gets its hands on me again.
But the longer I keep it away from the girl, the better chance I have of...
...actually, I don't *know* what.

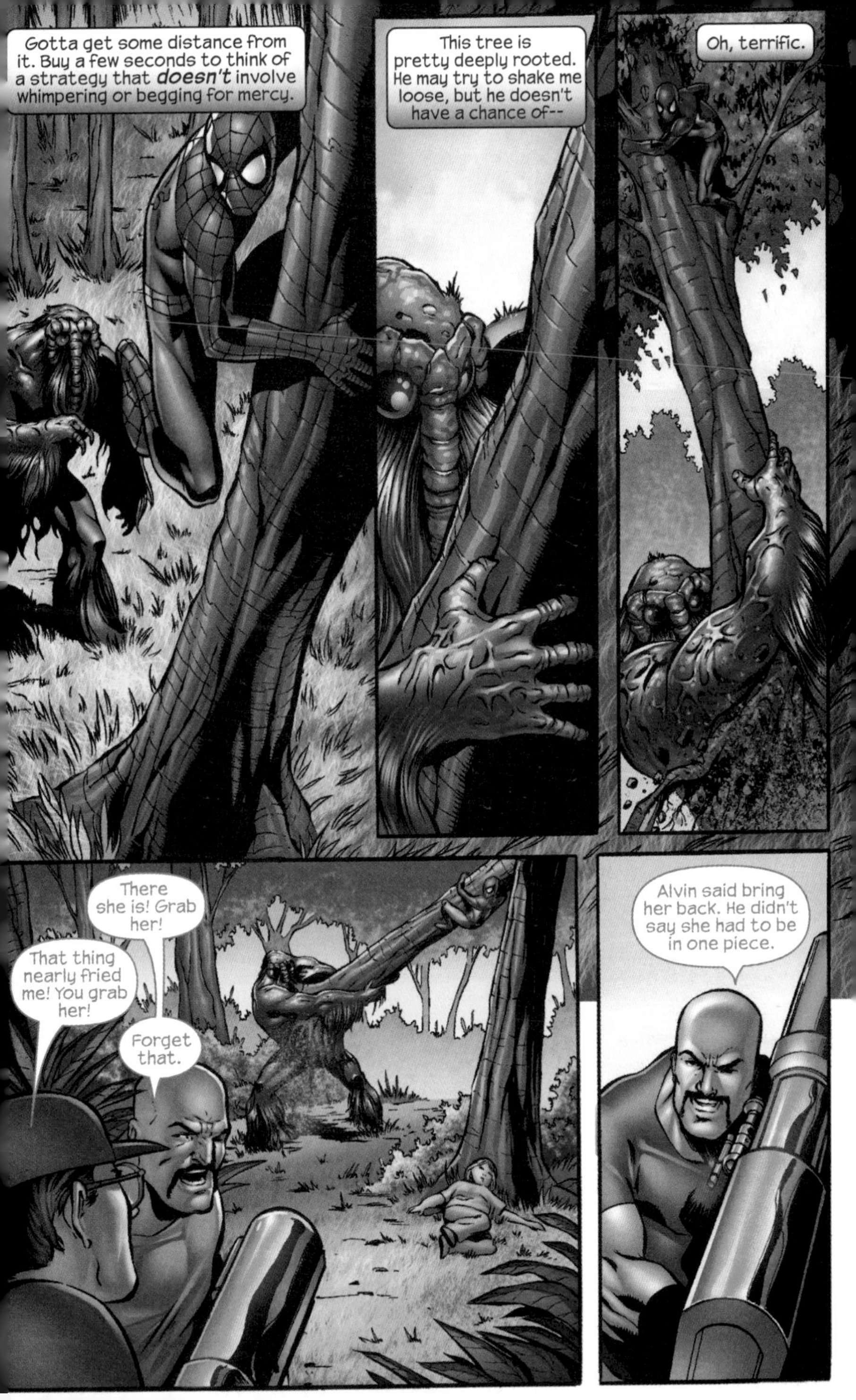
Gotta get some distance from it. Buy a few seconds to think of a strategy that *doesn't* involve whimpering or begging for mercy.
This tree is pretty deeply rooted. He may try to shake me loose, but he doesn't have a chance of--
Oh, terrific.
There she is! Grab her!
That thing nearly fried me! You grab her!
Forget that.
Alvin said bring her back. He didn't say she had to be in one piece.

Spider-sense...going nuts!

A laser-sighter! She's targeted!

Please, please let me be fast enough.

BUTHOOOM

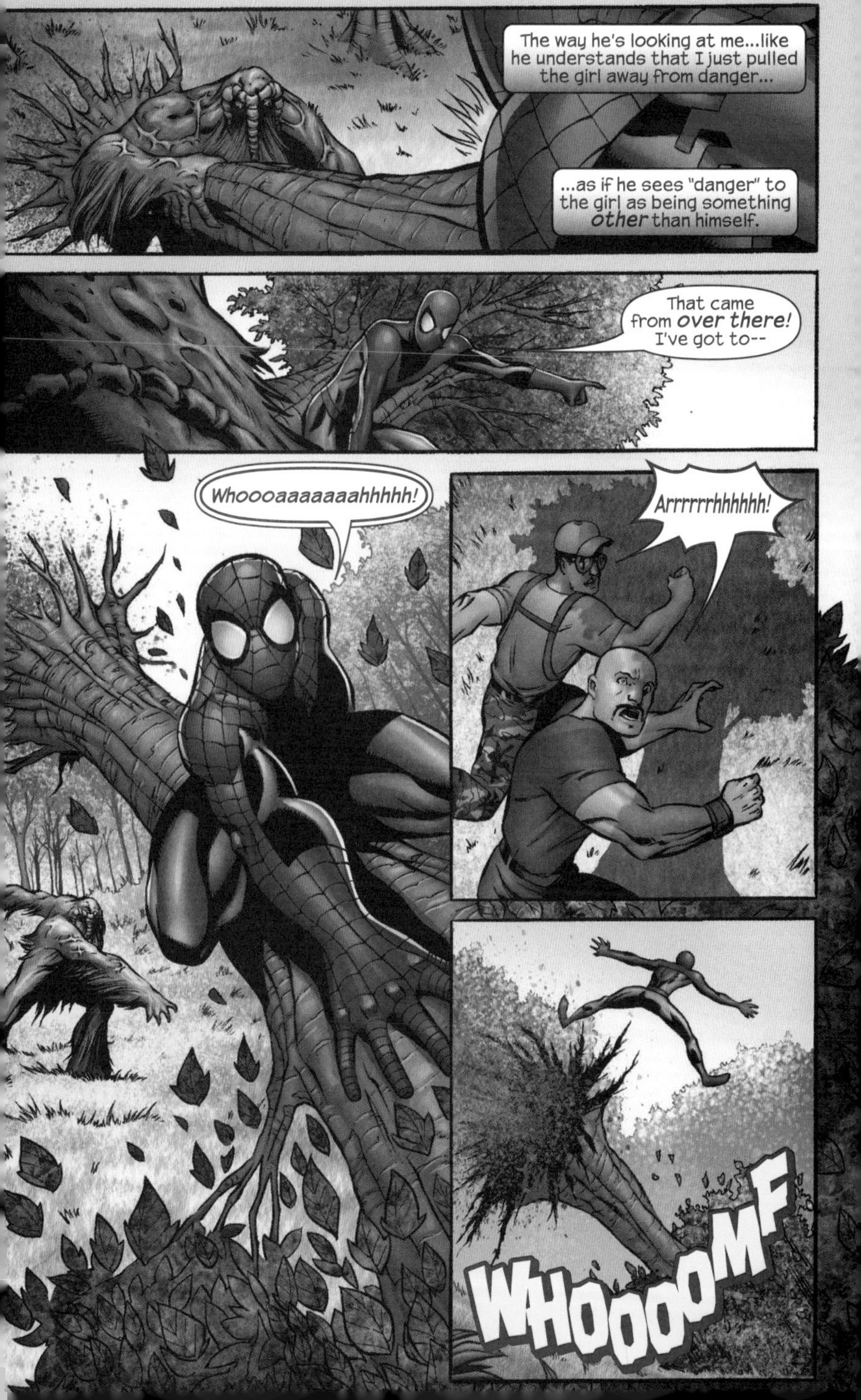
The way he's looking at me...like he understands that I just pulled the girl away from danger...
...as if he sees "danger" to the girl as being something *other* than himself.
That came from **over there!** I've got to--
Whoooaaaaaaahhhhh!
Arrrrrrhhhhhh!
WHOOOOMF

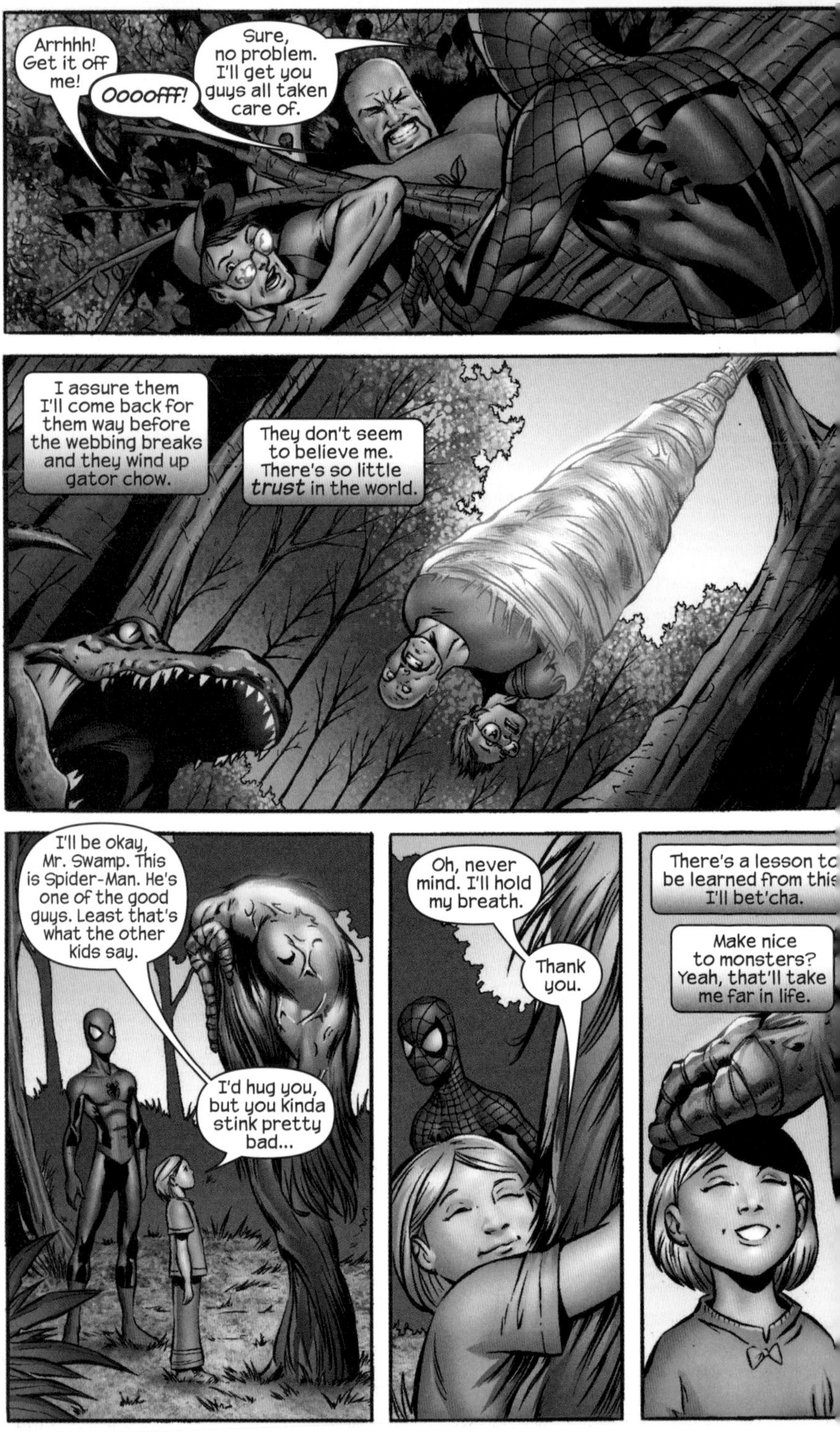
Arrhhh! Get it off me!
Oooofff!
Sure, no problem. I'll get you guys all taken care of.
I assure them I'll come back for them way before the webbing breaks and they wind up gator chow.
They don't seem to believe me. There's so little *trust* in the world.
I'll be okay, Mr. Swamp. This is Spider-Man. He's one of the good guys. Least that's what the other kids say.
I'd hug you, but you kinda stink pretty bad...
Oh, never mind. I'll hold my breath.
Thank you.
There's a lesson to be learned from this I'll bet'cha.
Make nice to monsters? Yeah, that'll take me far in life.

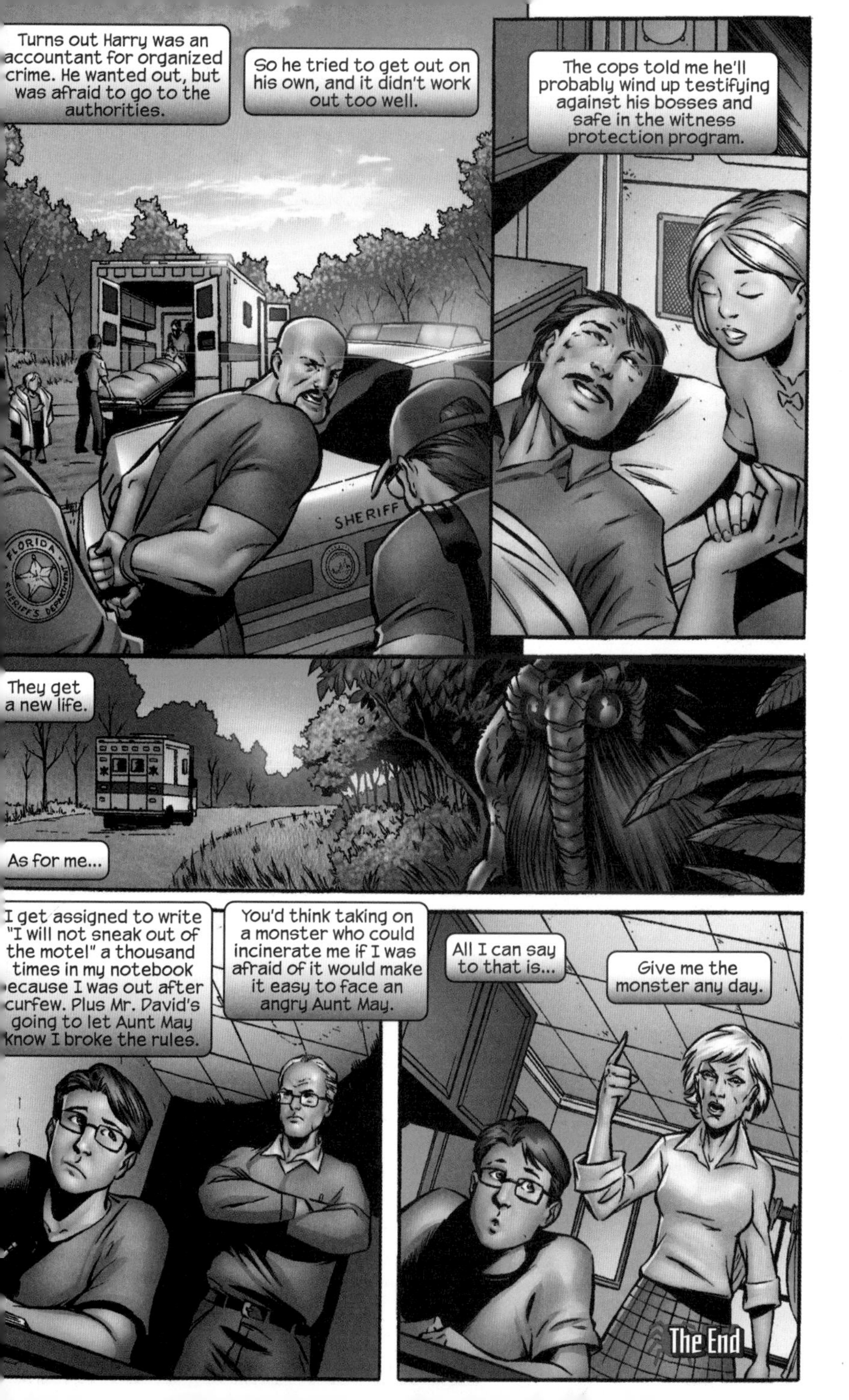
Turns out Harry was an accountant for organized crime. He wanted out, but was afraid to go to the authorities.
So he tried to get out on his own, and it didn't work out too well.
SHERIFF
FLORIDA
SHERIFF'S DEPARTMENT
The cops told me he'll probably wind up testifying against his bosses and safe in the witness protection program.
They get a new life.
As for me...
I get assigned to write "I will not sneak out of the motel" a thousand times in my notebook because I was out after curfew. Plus Mr. David's going to let Aunt May know I broke the rules.
You'd think taking on a monster who could incinerate me if I was afraid of it would make it easy to face an angry Aunt May.
All I can say to that is...
Give me the monster any day.
The End

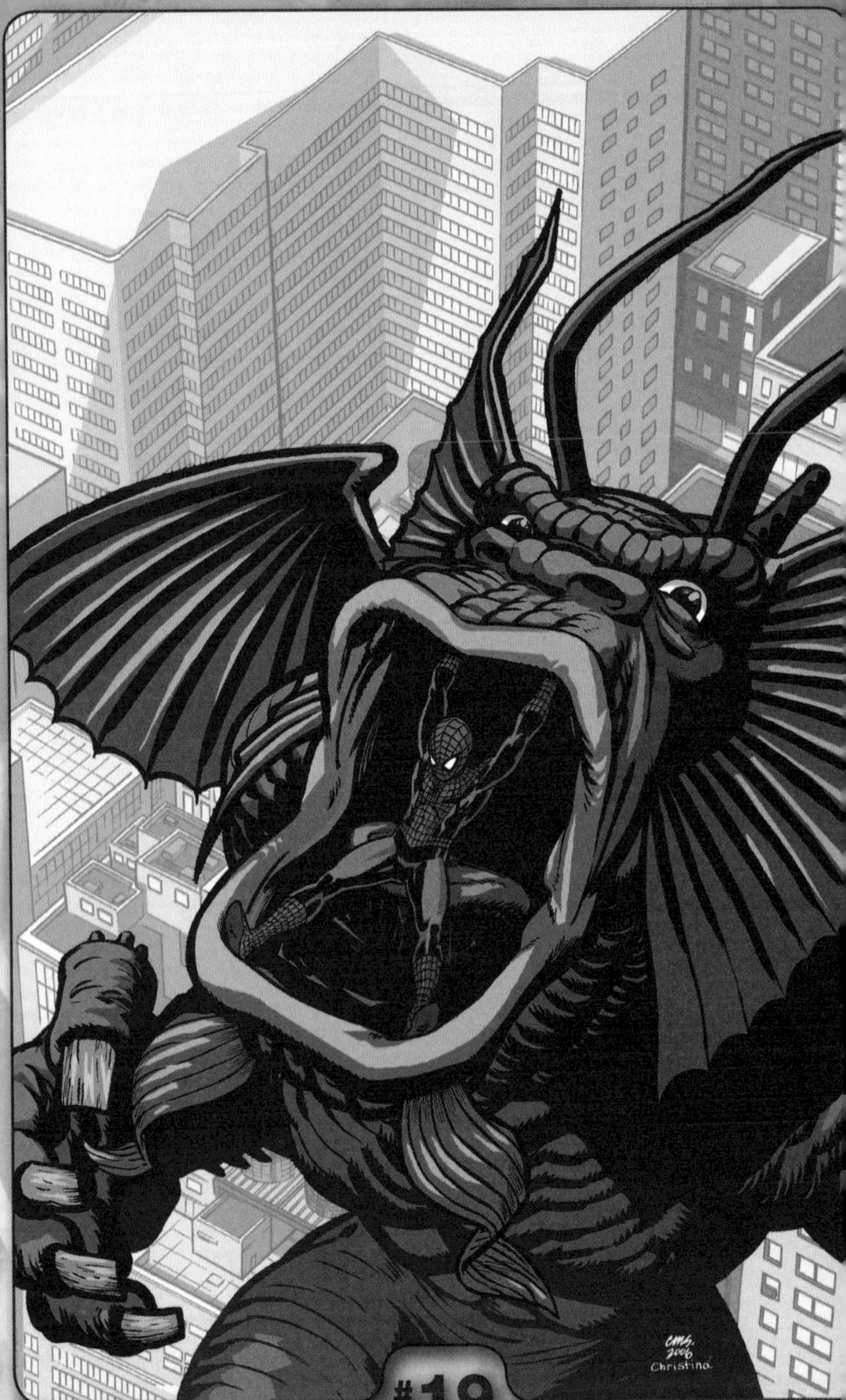
CMS.
2006
Christina

#19

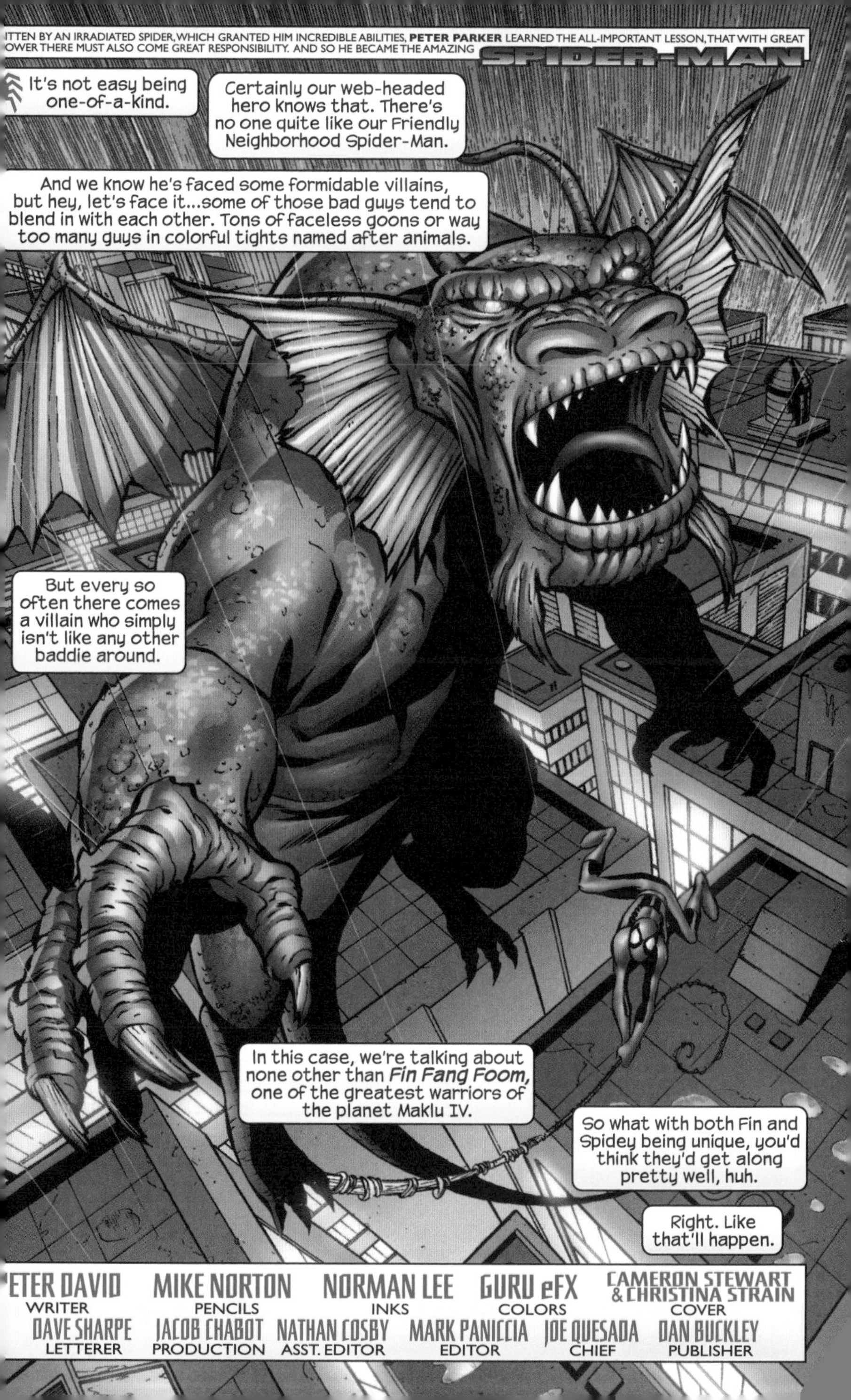
ITTEN BY AN IRRADIATED SPIDER, WHICH GRANTED HIM INCREDIBLE ABILITIES, PETER PARKER LEARNED THE ALL-IMPORTANT LESSON, THAT WITH GREAT
OWER THERE MUST ALSO COME GREAT RESPONSIBILITY. AND SO HE BECAME THE AMAZING
SPIDER-MAN
It's not easy being one-of-a-kind.
Certainly our web-headed hero knows that. There's no one quite like our Friendly Neighborhood Spider-Man.
And we know he's faced some formidable villains, but hey, let's face it...some of those bad guys tend to blend in with each other. Tons of faceless goons or way too many guys in colorful tights named after animals.
But every so often there comes a villain who simply isn't like any other baddie around.
In this case, we're talking about none other than *Fin Fang Foom,* one of the greatest warriors of the planet Maklu IV.
So what with both Fin and Spidey being unique, you'd think they'd get along pretty well, huh.
Right. Like that'll happen.
ETER DAVID WRITER
MIKE NORTON PENCILS
NORMAN LEE INKS
GURU eFX COLORS
CAMERON STEWART & CHRISTINA STRAIN COVER
DAVE SHARPE LETTERER
JACOB CHABOT PRODUCTION
NATHAN COSBY ASST. EDITOR
MARK PANICCIA EDITOR
JOE QUESADA CHIEF
DAN BUCKLEY PUBLISHER

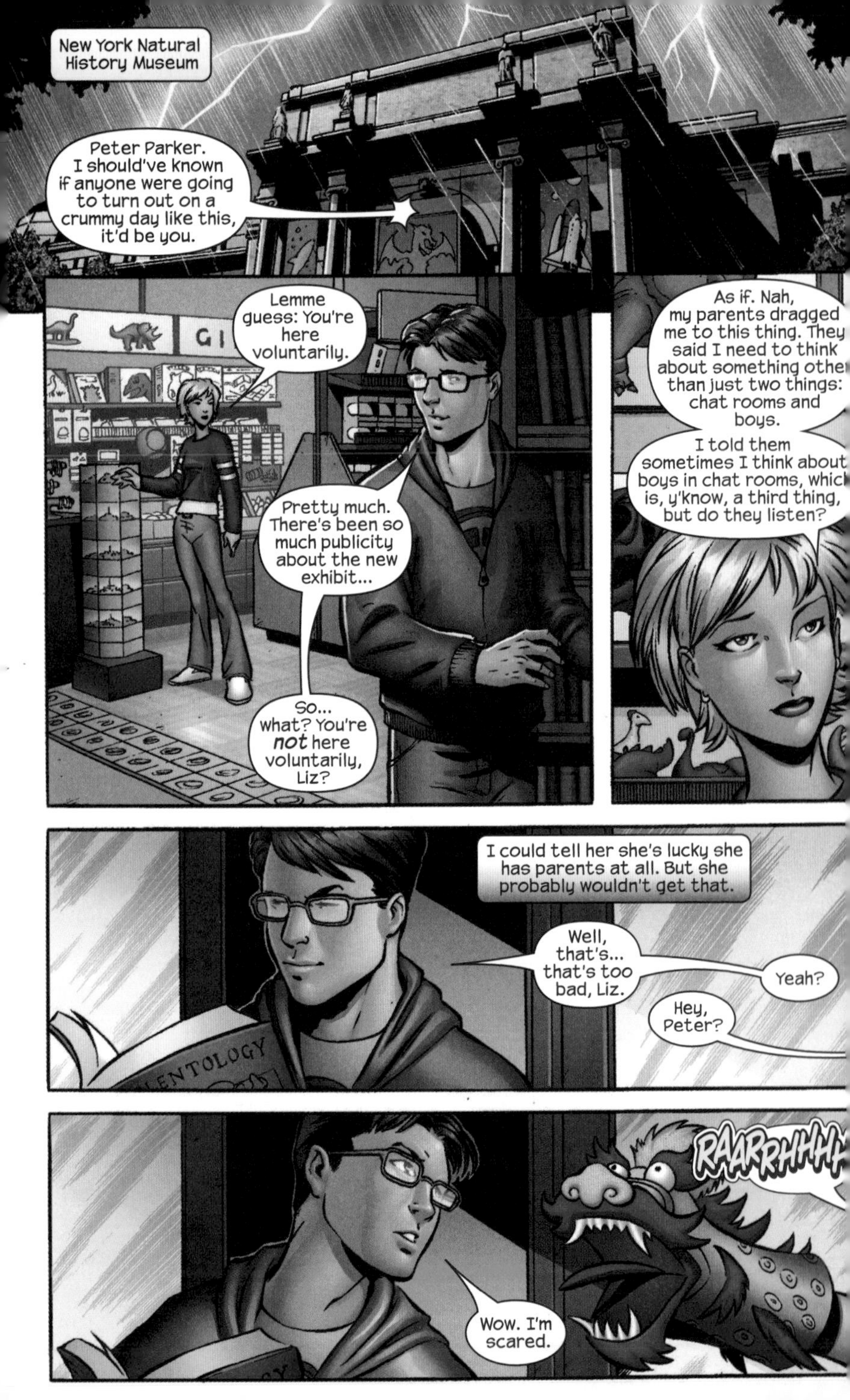
New York Natural History Museum
Peter Parker. I should've known if anyone were going to turn out on a crummy day like this, it'd be you.
Lemme guess: You're here voluntarily.
Pretty much. There's been so much publicity about the new exhibit...
So... what? You're *not* here voluntarily, Liz?
As if. Nah, my parents dragged me to this thing. They said I need to think about something othe than just two things: chat rooms and boys.
I told them sometimes I think about boys in chat rooms, whic is, y'know, a third thing, but do they listen?
I could tell her she's lucky she has parents at all. But she probably wouldn't get that.
Well, that's... that's too bad, Liz.
Yeah?
Hey, Peter?
RAARRHHH
Wow. I'm scared.

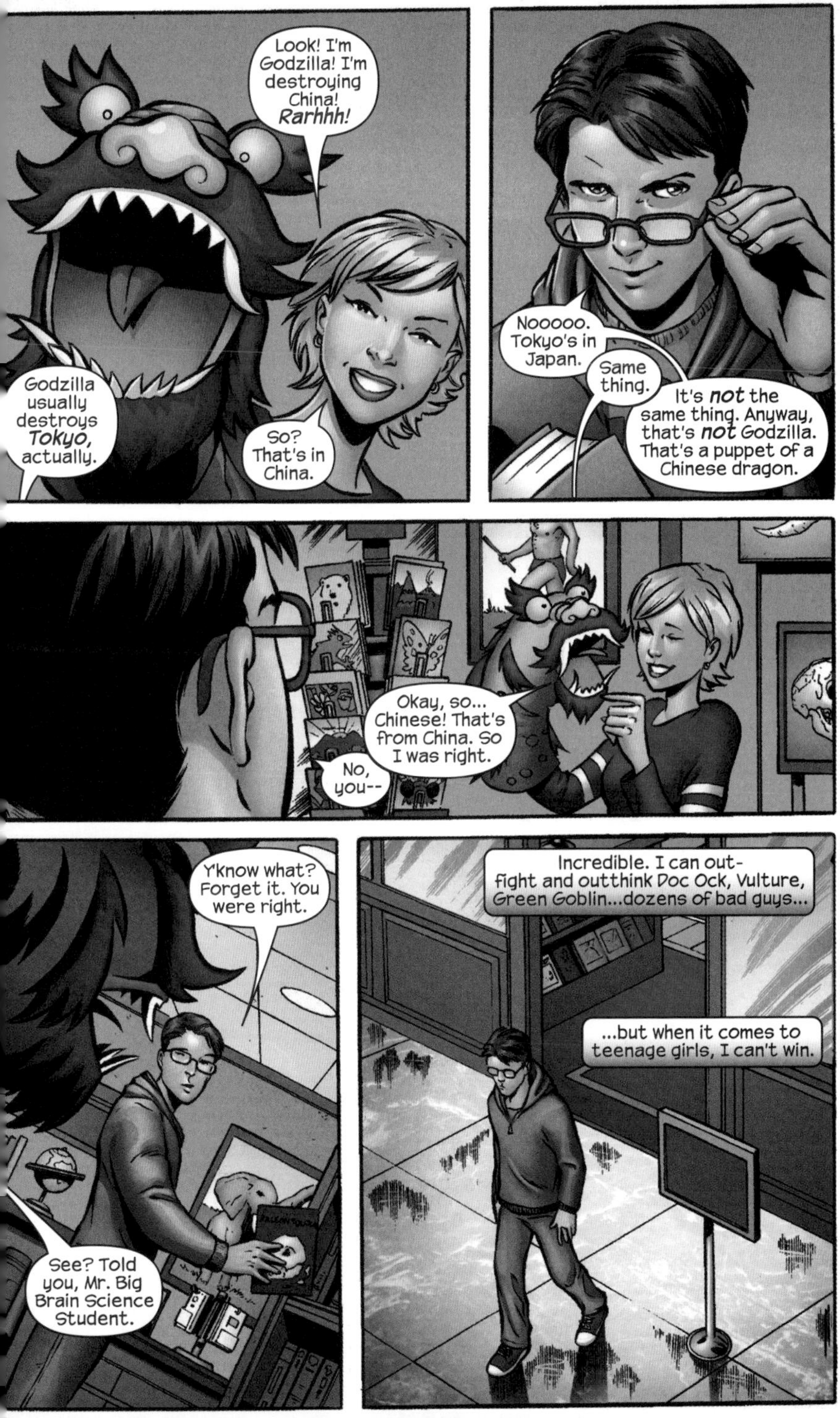
Look! I'm Godzilla! I'm destroying China! Rarhhh!
Godzilla usually destroys Tokyo, actually.
So? That's in China.
Nooooo. Tokyo's in Japan.
Same thing.
It's not the same thing. Anyway, that's not Godzilla. That's a puppet of a Chinese dragon.
Okay, so... Chinese! That's from China. So I was right.
No, you--
Y'know what? Forget it. You were right.
See? Told you, Mr. Big Brain Science Student.
Incredible. I can out-fight and outthink Doc Ock, Vulture, Green Goblin...dozens of bad guys...
...but when it comes to teenage girls, I can't win.

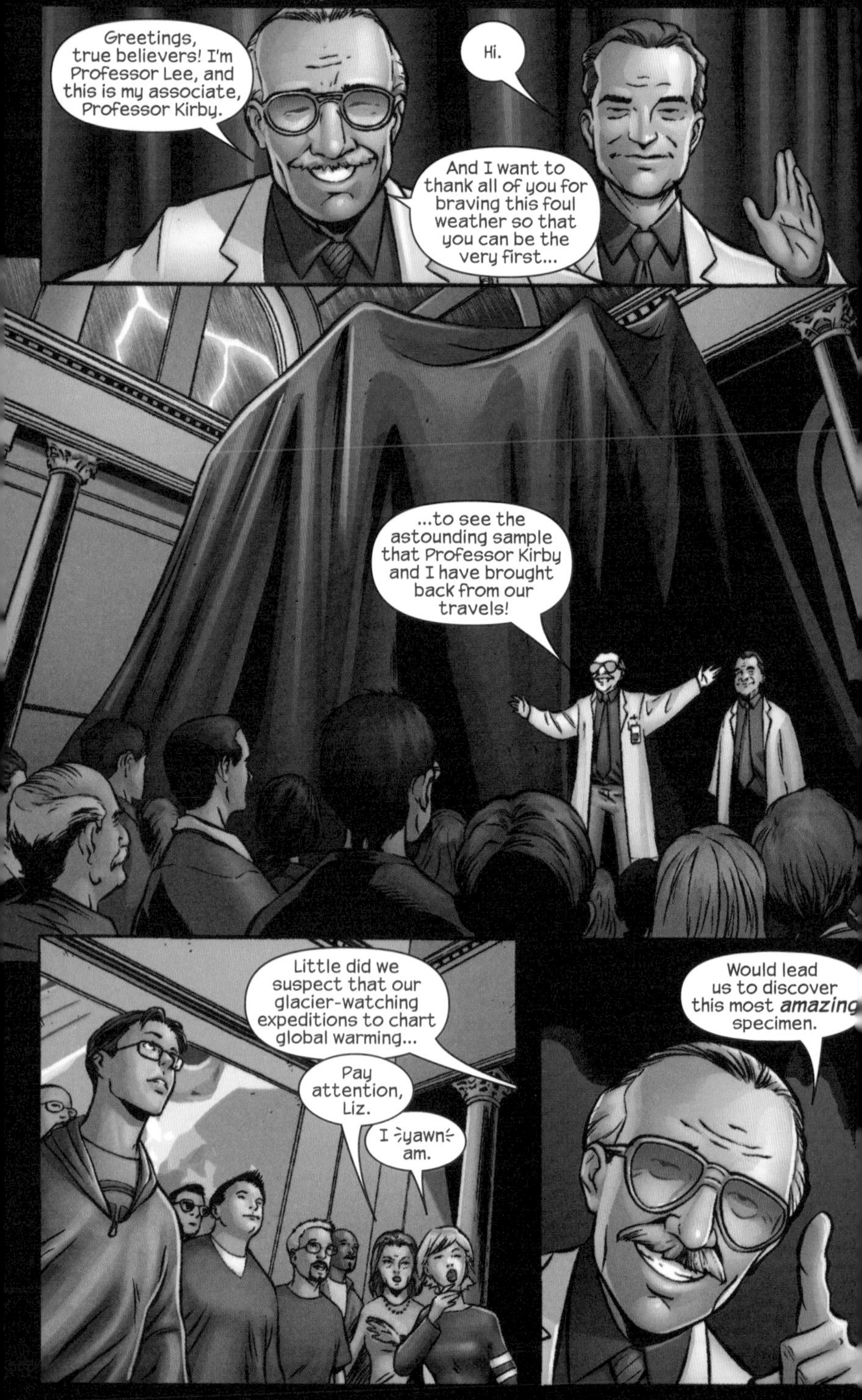
Greetings, true believers! I'm Professor Lee, and this is my associate, Professor Kirby.
Hi.
And I want to thank all of you for braving this foul weather so that you can be the very first...
...to see the astounding sample that Professor Kirby and I have brought back from our travels!
Little did we suspect that our glacier-watching expeditions to chart global warming...
Pay attention, Liz.
I -yawn- am.
Would lead us to discover this most amazing specimen.

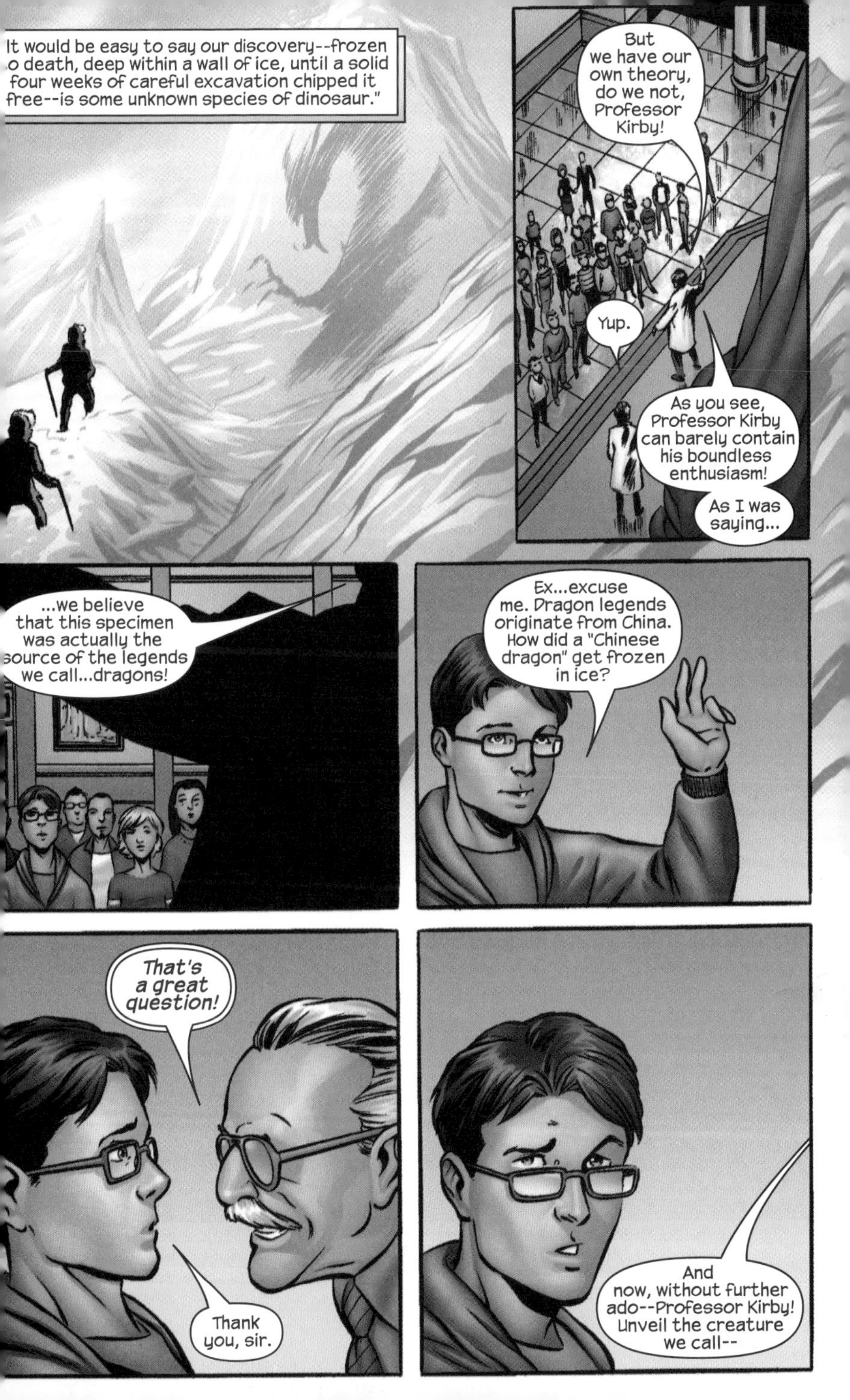

It would be easy to say our discovery--frozen to death, deep within a wall of ice, until a solid four weeks of careful excavation chipped it free--is some unknown species of dinosaur."
But we have our own theory, do we not, Professor Kirby!
Yup.
As you see, Professor Kirby can barely contain his boundless enthusiasm!
As I was saying...
...we believe that this specimen was actually the source of the legends we call...dragons!
Ex...excuse me. Dragon legends originate from China. How did a "Chinese dragon" get frozen in ice?
That's a great question!
Thank you, sir.
And now, without further ado--Professor Kirby! Unveil the creature we call--

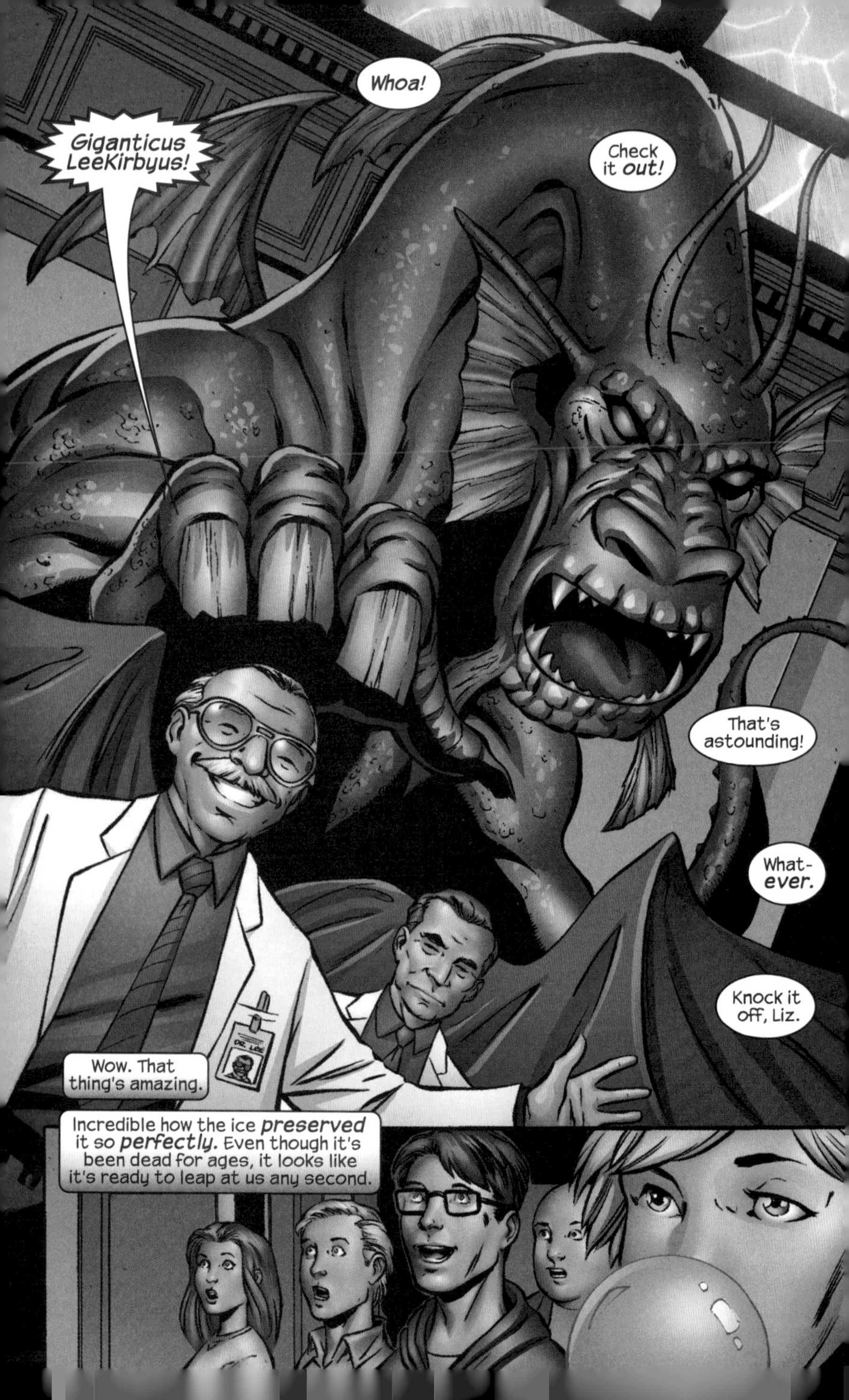
Whoa!
Gigant icus LeeKirbyus!
Check it out!
That's astounding!
What-ever.
Knock it off, Liz.
Wow. That thing's amazing.
Incredible how the ice preserved it so perfectly. Even though it's been dead for ages, it looks like it's ready to leap at us any second.

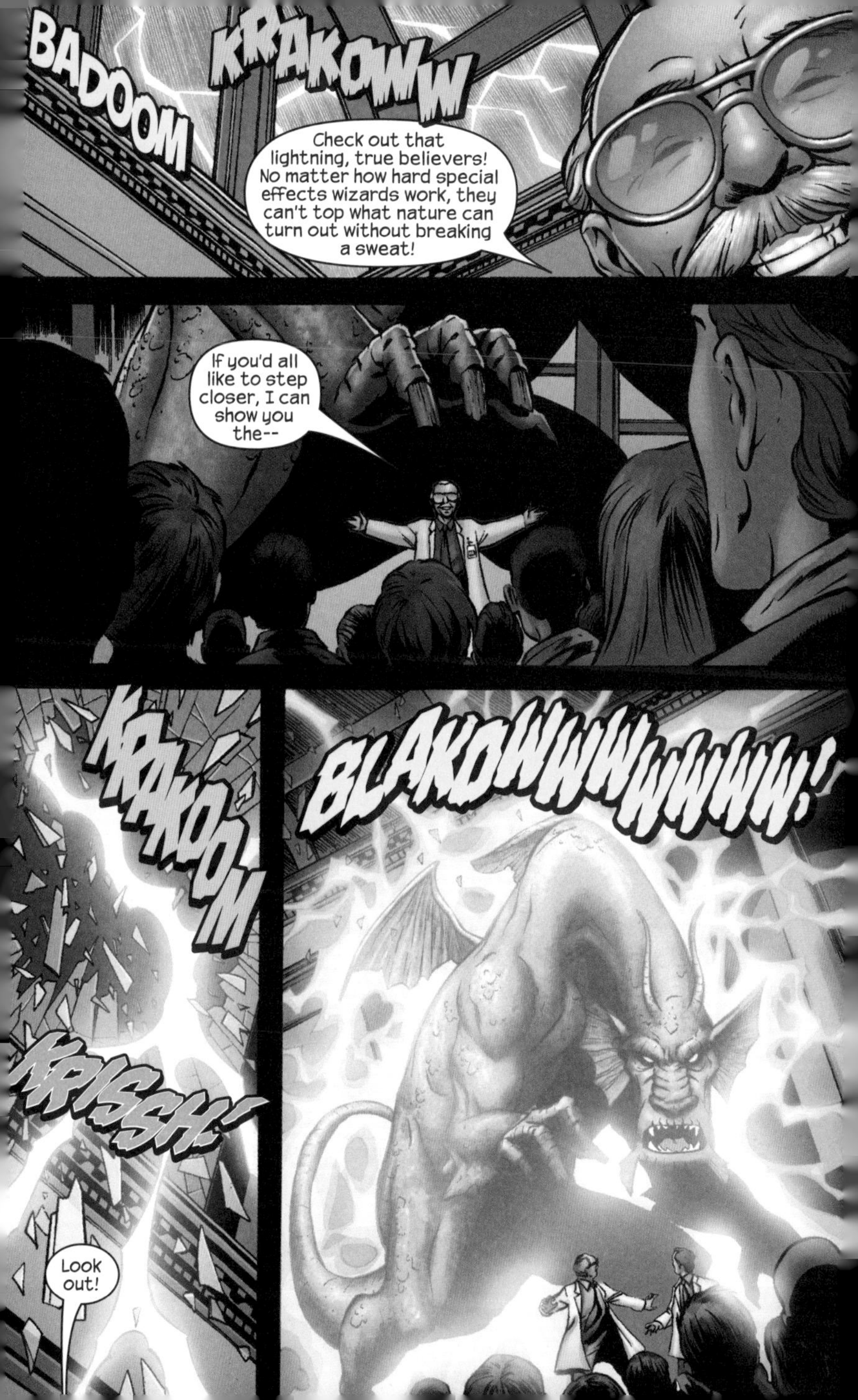
BADOOM
KRAKOWW
Check out that lightning, true believers! No matter how hard special effects wizards work, they can't top what nature can turn out without breaking a sweat!
If you'd all like to step closer, I can show you the--
KRAKOOM
KRISSH!
Look out!
BLAKOWWWWWWWWW!

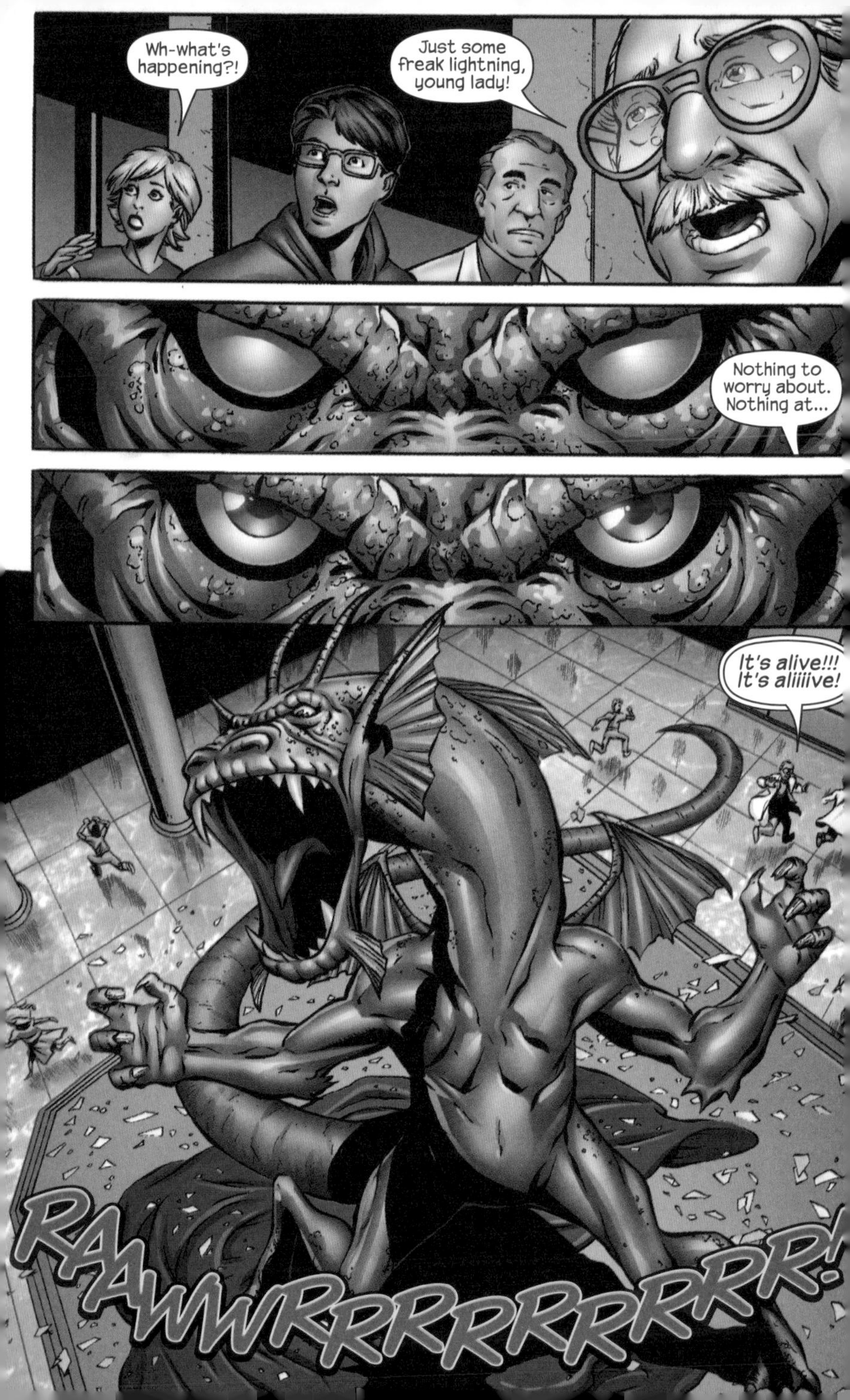

Wh-what's happening?!
Just some freak lightning, young lady!
Nothing to worry about. Nothing at...
It's alive!!! It's aliiiive!
RAAWWRRRRRRRR!

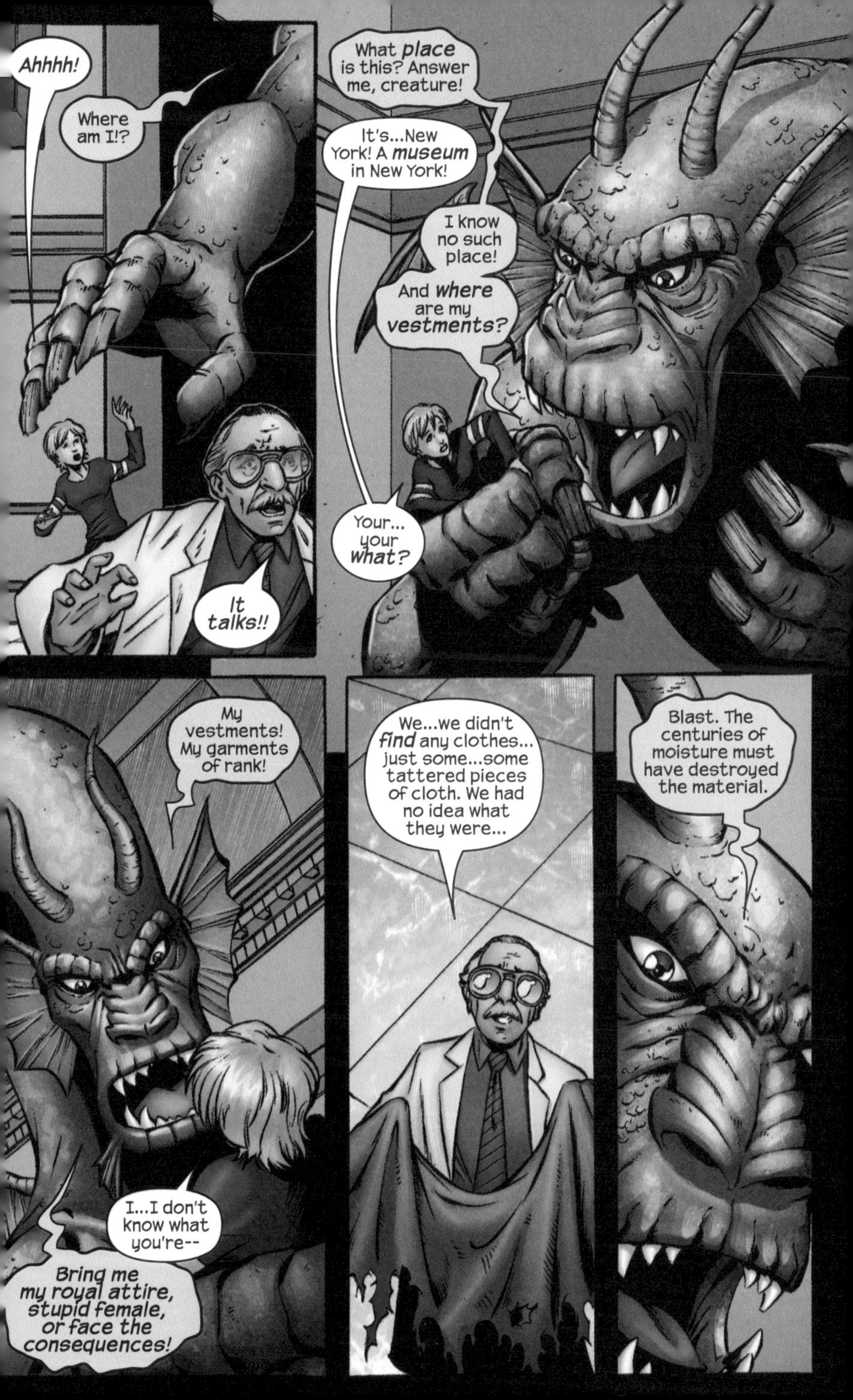
Ahhhh!
Where am I!?
It talks!!
What place is this? Answer me, creature!
It's...New York! A museum in New York!
I know no such place!
And where are my vestments?
Your... your what?
My vestments! My garments of rank!
I...I don't know what you're--
Bring me my royal attire, stupid female, or face the consequences!
We...we didn't find any clothes... just some...some tattered pieces of cloth. We had no idea what they were...
Blast. The centuries of moisture must have destroyed the material.

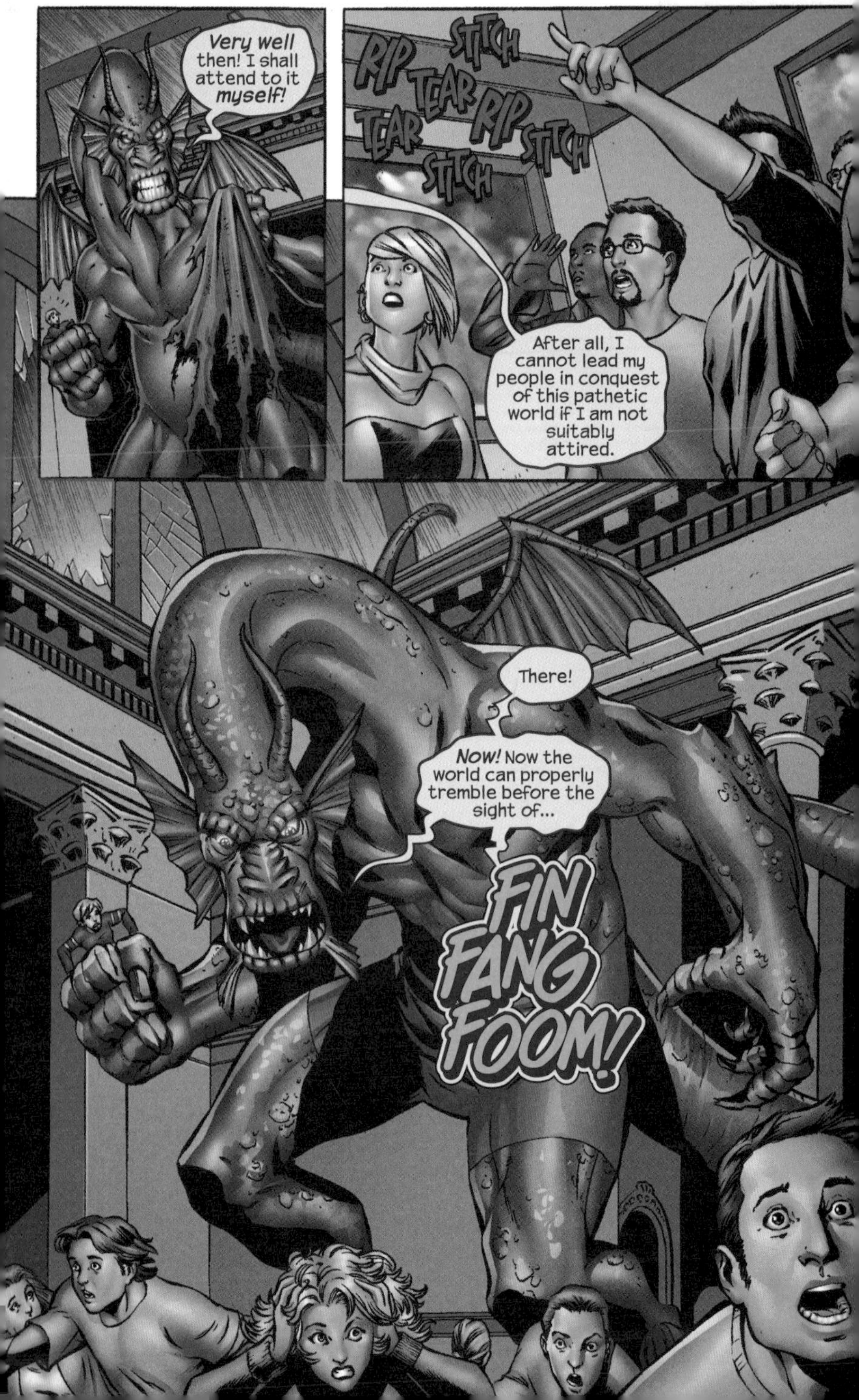
Very well then! I shall attend to it myself!
RIP STITCH TEAR RIP TEAR STITCH STITCH
After all, I cannot lead my people in conquest of this pathetic world if I am not suitably attired.
There!
NOW! Now the world can properly tremble before the sight of...
FIN FANG FOOM!

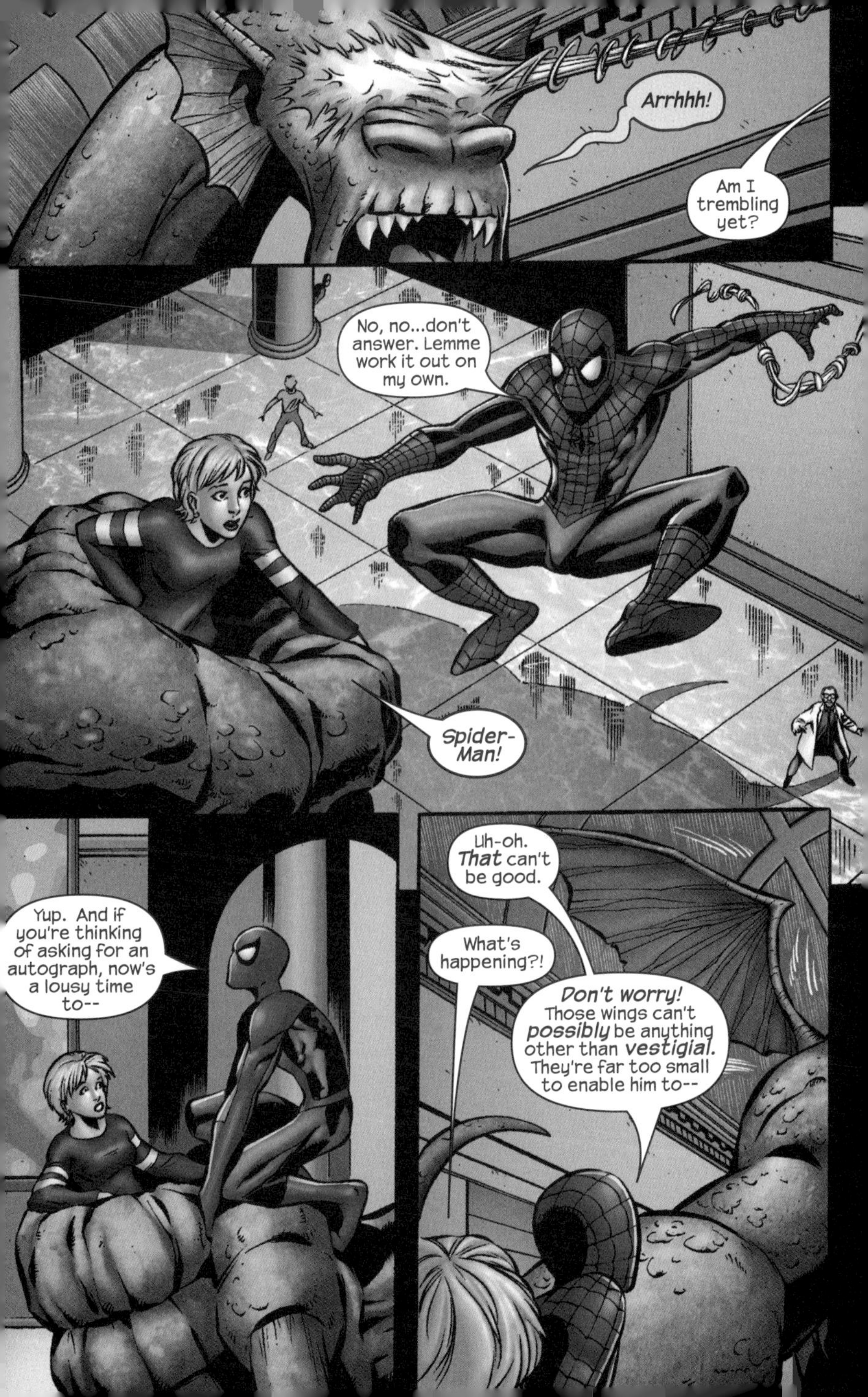
Arrhhh!
Am I trembling yet?
No, no...don't answer. Lemme work it out on my own.
Spider-Man!
Yup. And if you're thinking of asking for an autograph, now's a lousy time to--
Uh-oh. That can't be good.
What's happening?!
Don't worry! Those wings can't possibly be anything other than vestigial. They're far too small to enable him to--

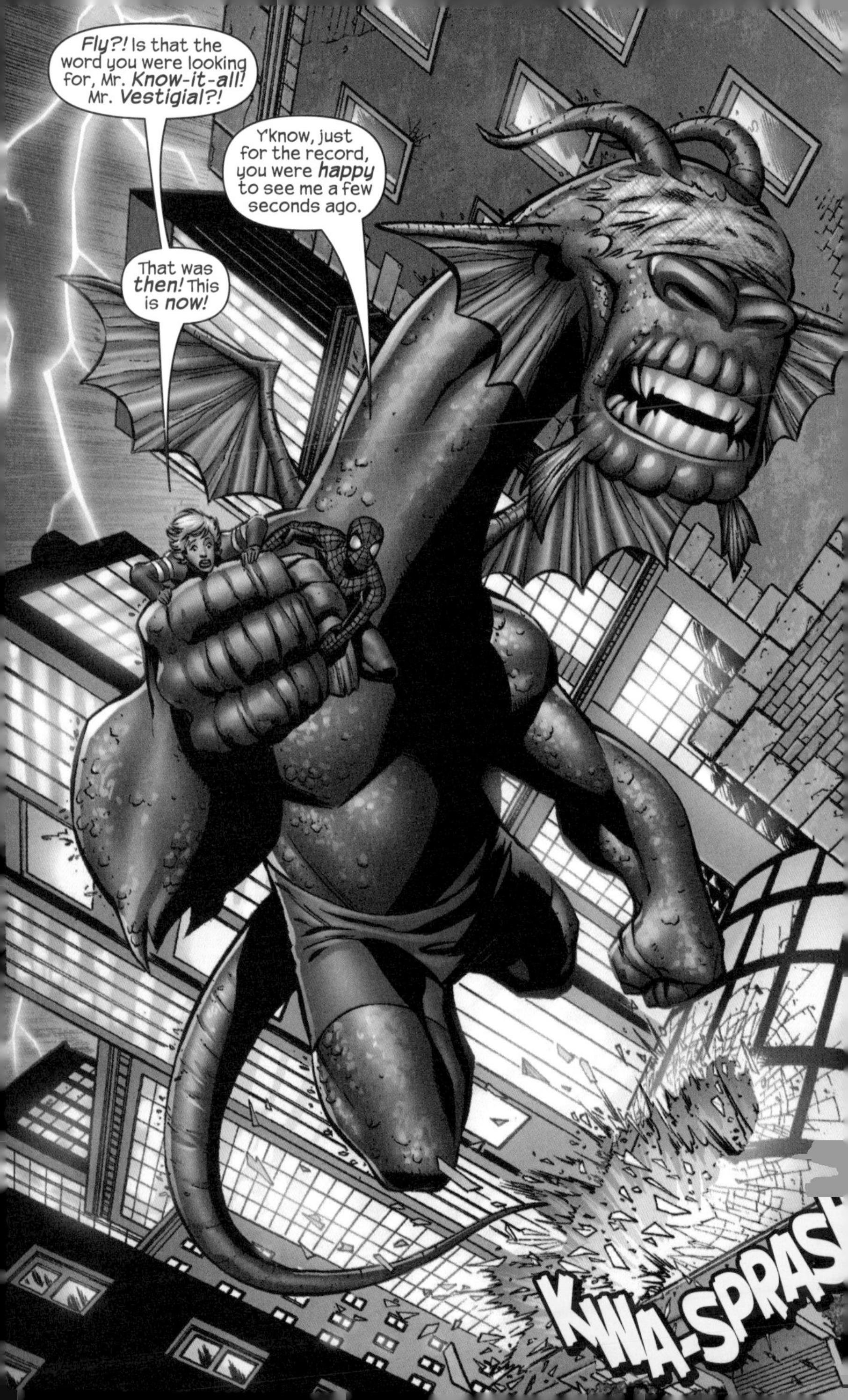

Fly?! Is that the word you were looking for, Mr. Know-it-all! Mr. Vestigial?!
Y'know, just for the record, you were happy to see me a few seconds ago.
That was then! This is now!
KWA-SPRAS

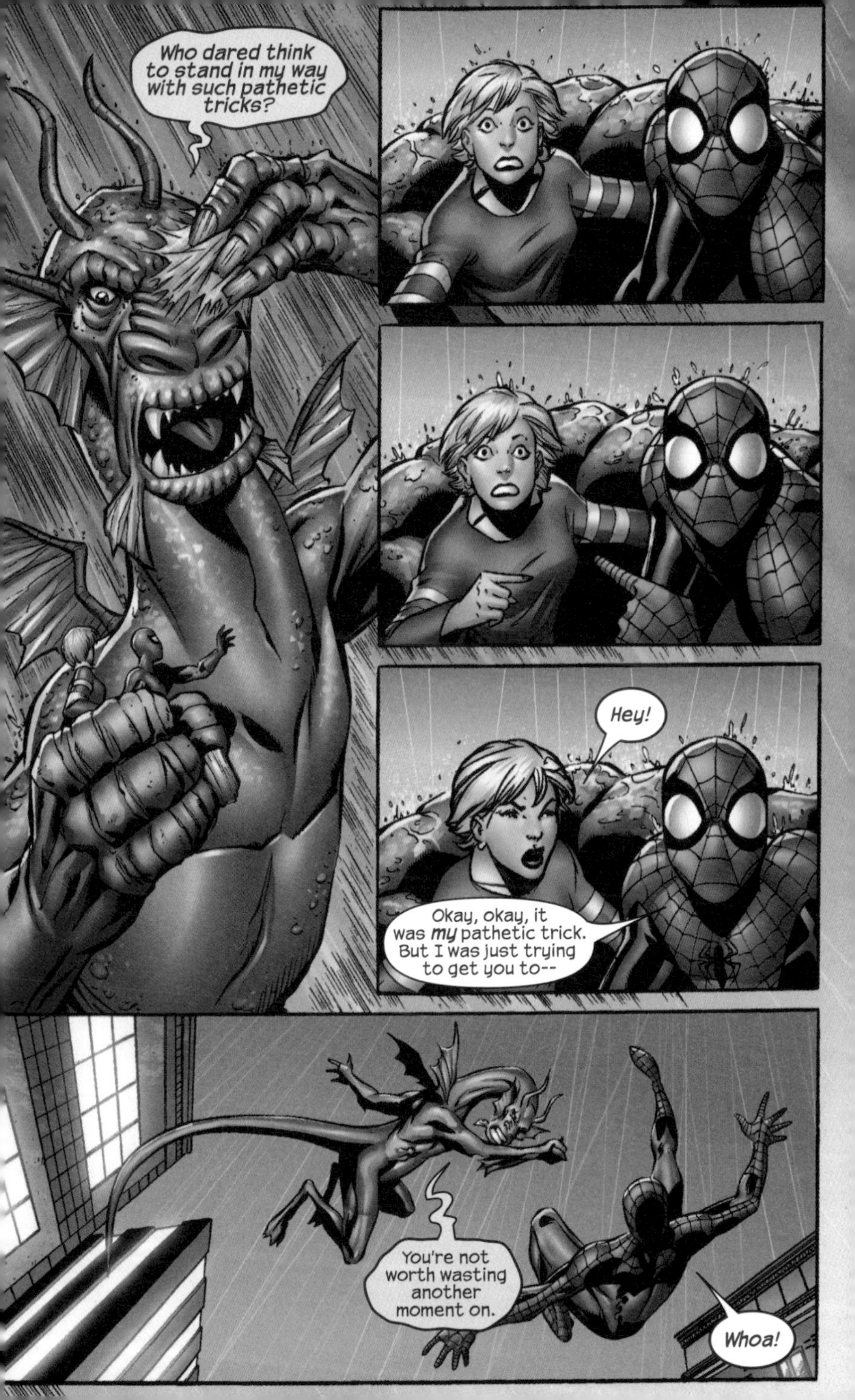
Who dared think to stand in my way with such pathetic tricks?
Hey!
Okay, okay, it was *my* pathetic trick. But I was just trying to get you to--
You're not worth wasting another moment on.
Whoa!

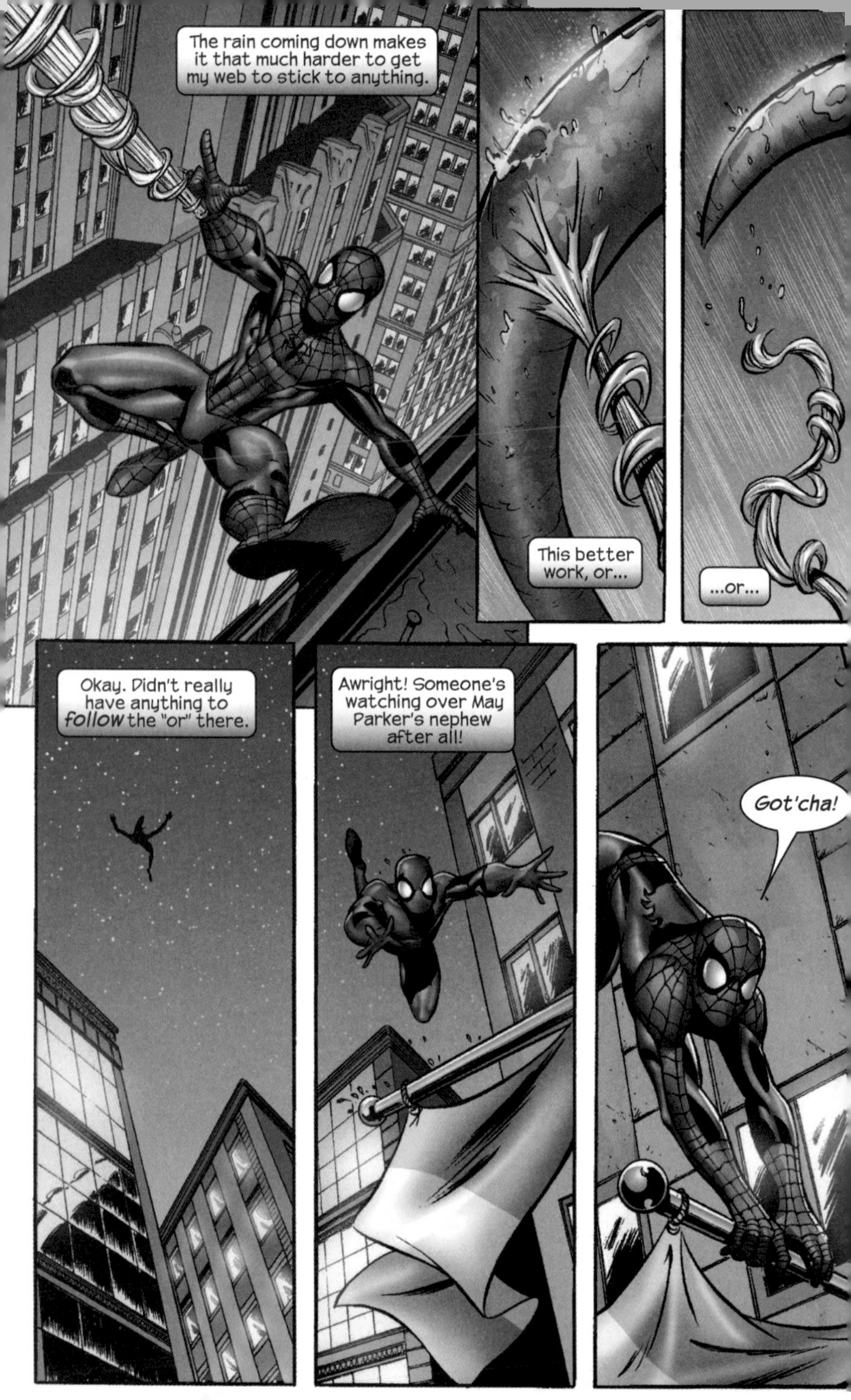
The rain coming down makes it that much harder to get my web to stick to anything.
This better work, or...
...or...
Okay. Didn't really have anything to *follow* the "or" there.
Awright! Someone's watching over May Parker's nephew after all!
Got'cha!

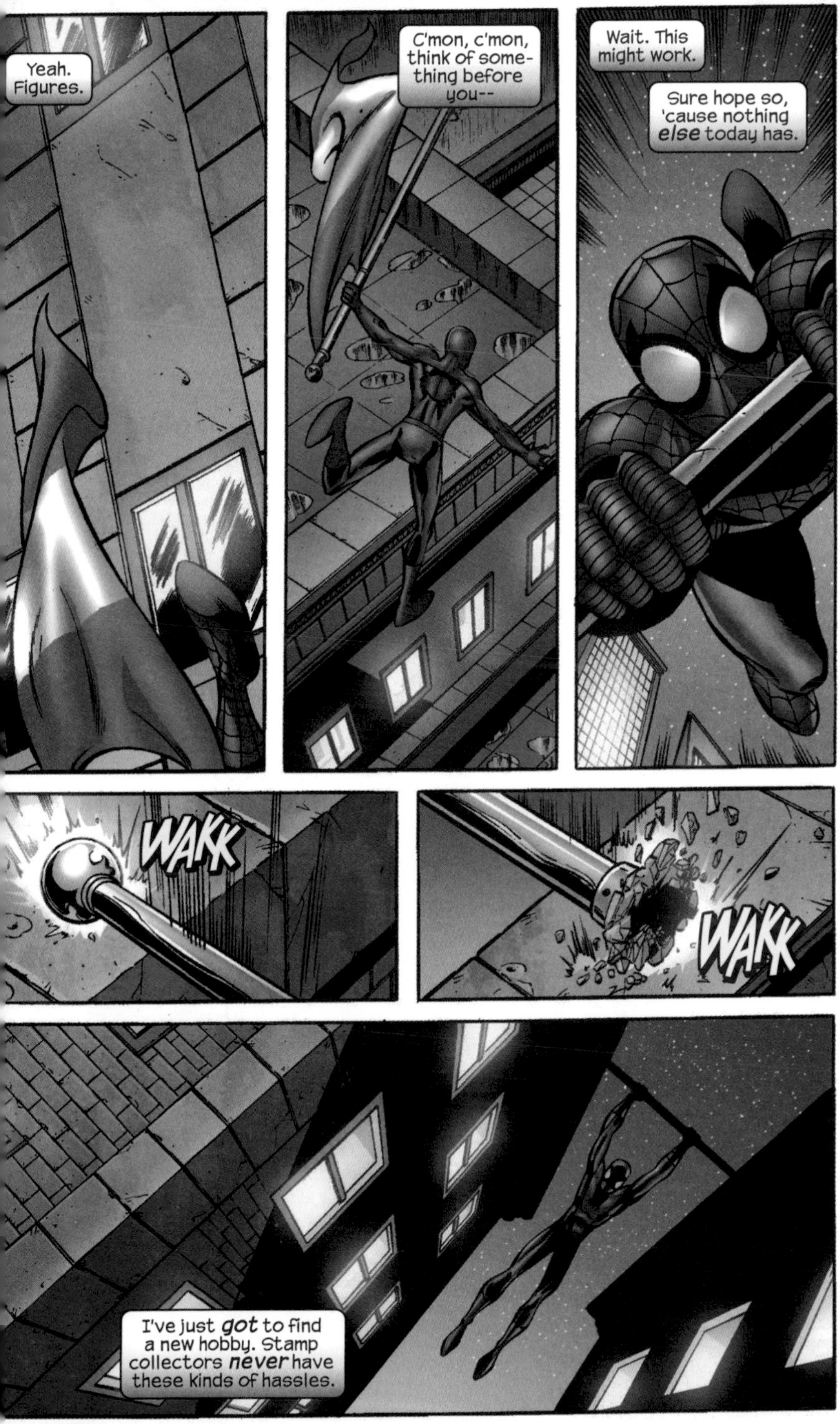
Yeah. Figures.
C'mon, c'mon, think of something before you--
Wait. This might work.
Sure hope so, 'cause nothing *else* today has.
WAKK
WAKK
I've just *got* to find a new hobby. Stamp collectors *never* have these kinds of hassles.

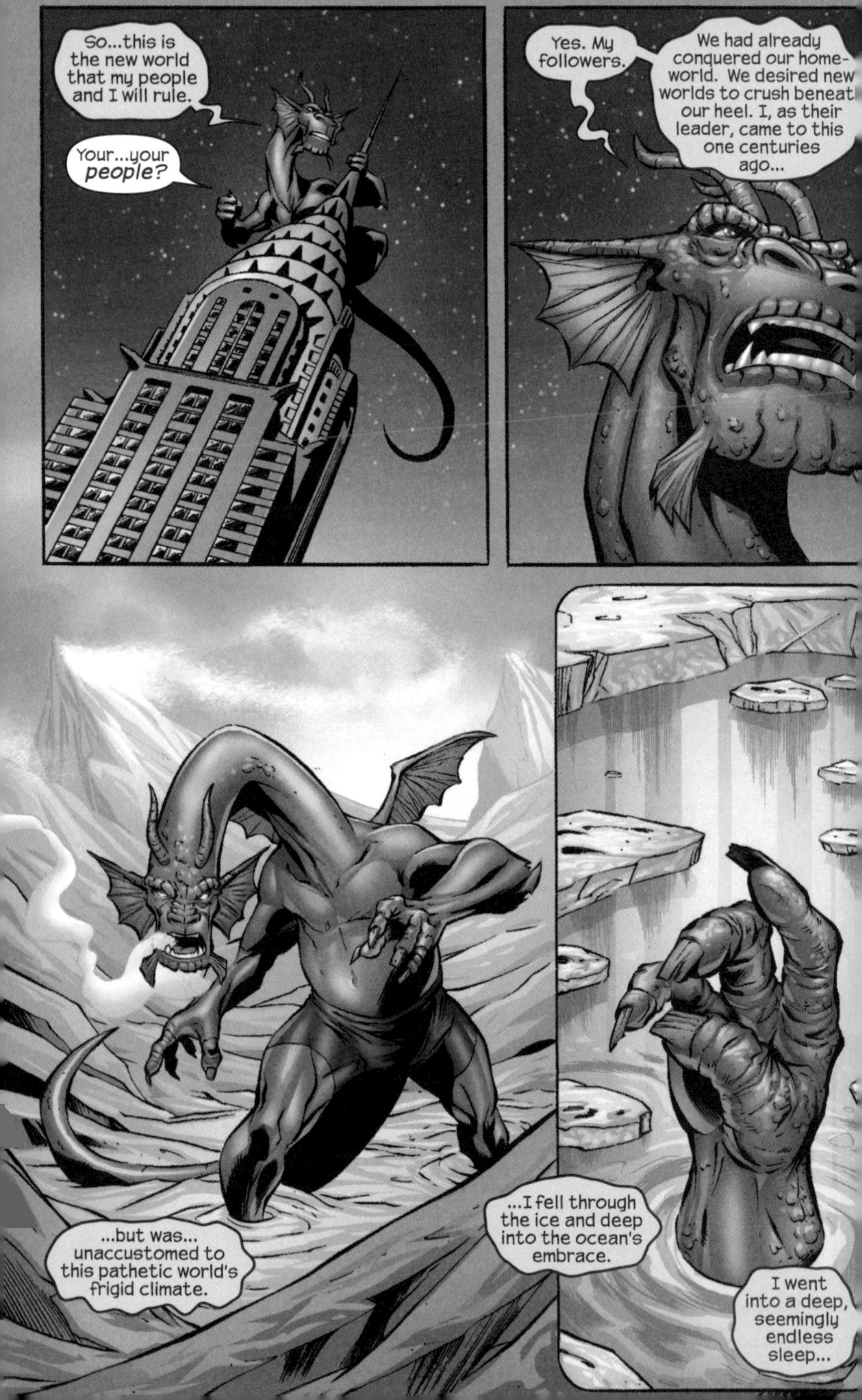
So...this is the new world that my people and I will rule.
Your...your *people?*
Yes. My followers.
We had already conquered our home-world. We desired new worlds to crush beneat our heel. I, as their leader, came to this one centuries ago...
...but was... unaccustomed to this pathetic world's frigid climate.
...I fell through the ice and deep into the ocean's embrace.
I went into a deep, seemingly endless sleep...

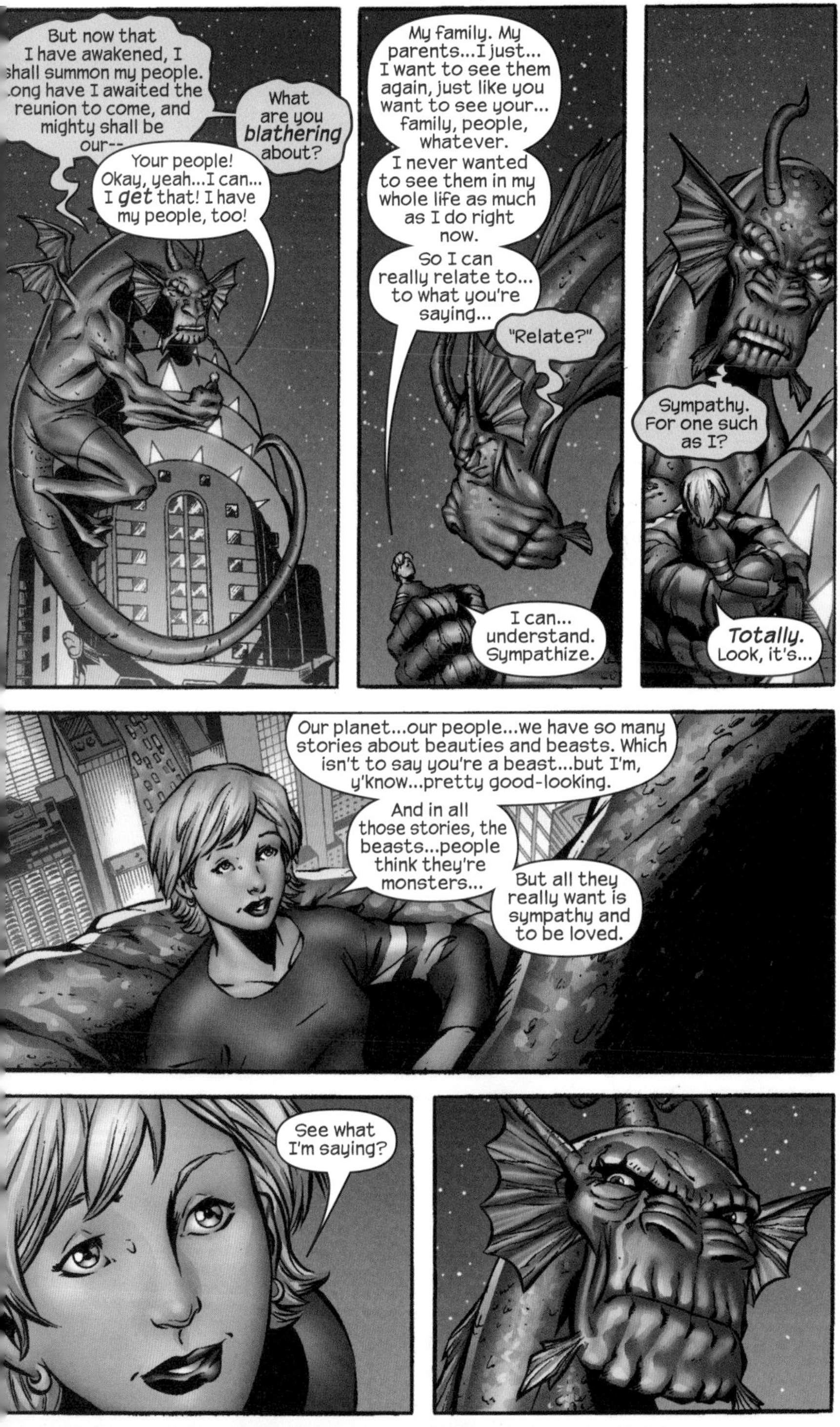
But now that I have awakened, I shall summon my people. Long have I awaited the reunion to come, and mighty shall be our--
What are you *blathering* about?
Your people! Okay, yeah...I can... I *get* that! I have my people, too!
My family. My parents...I just... I want to see them again, just like you want to see your... family, people, whatever.
I never wanted to see them in my whole life as much as I do right now.
So I can really relate to... to what you're saying...
"Relate?"
I can... understand. Sympathize.
Sympathy. For one such as I?
Totally. Look, it's...
Our planet...our people...we have so many stories about beauties and beasts. Which isn't to say you're a beast...but I'm, y'know...pretty good-looking.
And in all those stories, the beasts...people think they're monsters...
But all they really want is sympathy and to be loved.
See what I'm saying?

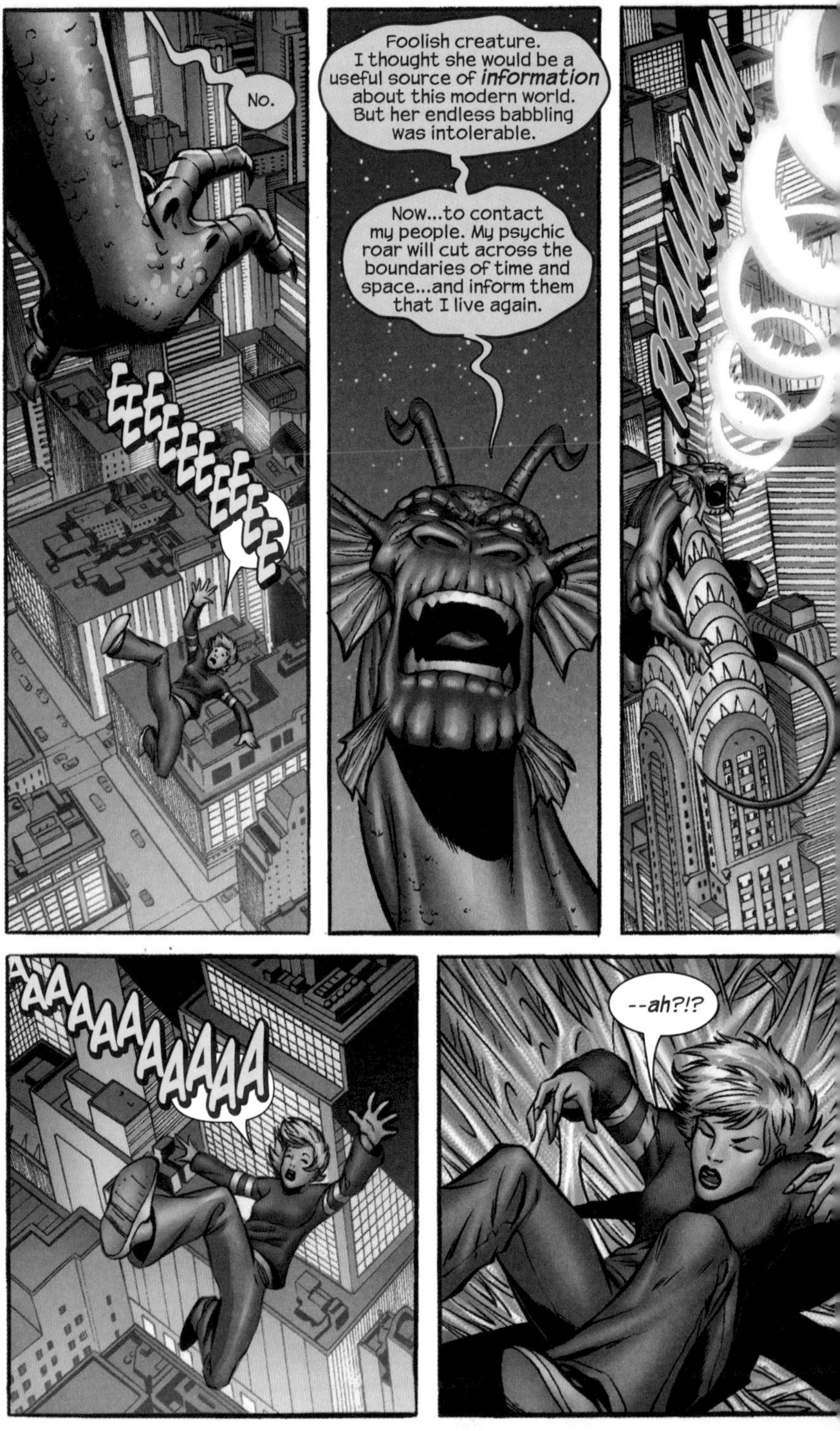
No.
EEEEEEEEEEEEE
Foolish creature. I thought she would be a useful source of *information* about this modern world. But her endless babbling was intolerable.
Now...to contact my people. My psychic roar will cut across the boundaries of time and space...and inform them that I live again.
RRAAAAAAA
AAAAAAAAAAA
--ah?!?

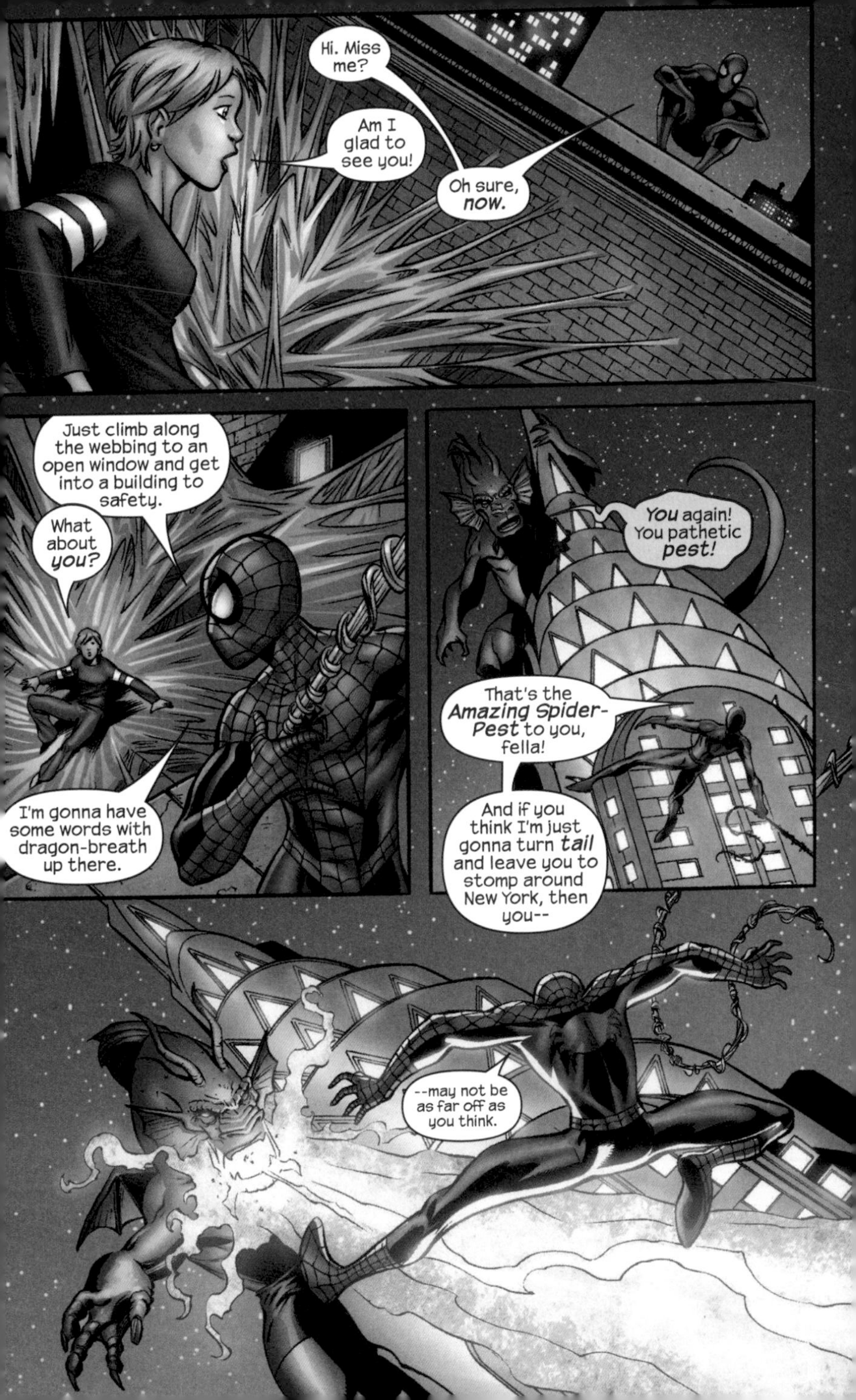
Hi. Miss me?
Am I glad to see you!
Oh sure, *now.*
Just climb along the webbing to an open window and get into a building to safety.
What about *you?*
I'm gonna have some words with dragon-breath up there.
You again! You pathetic *pest!*
That's the *Amazing Spider-Pest* to you, fella!
And if you think I'm just gonna turn *tail* and leave you to stomp around New York, then you--
--may not be as far off as you think.

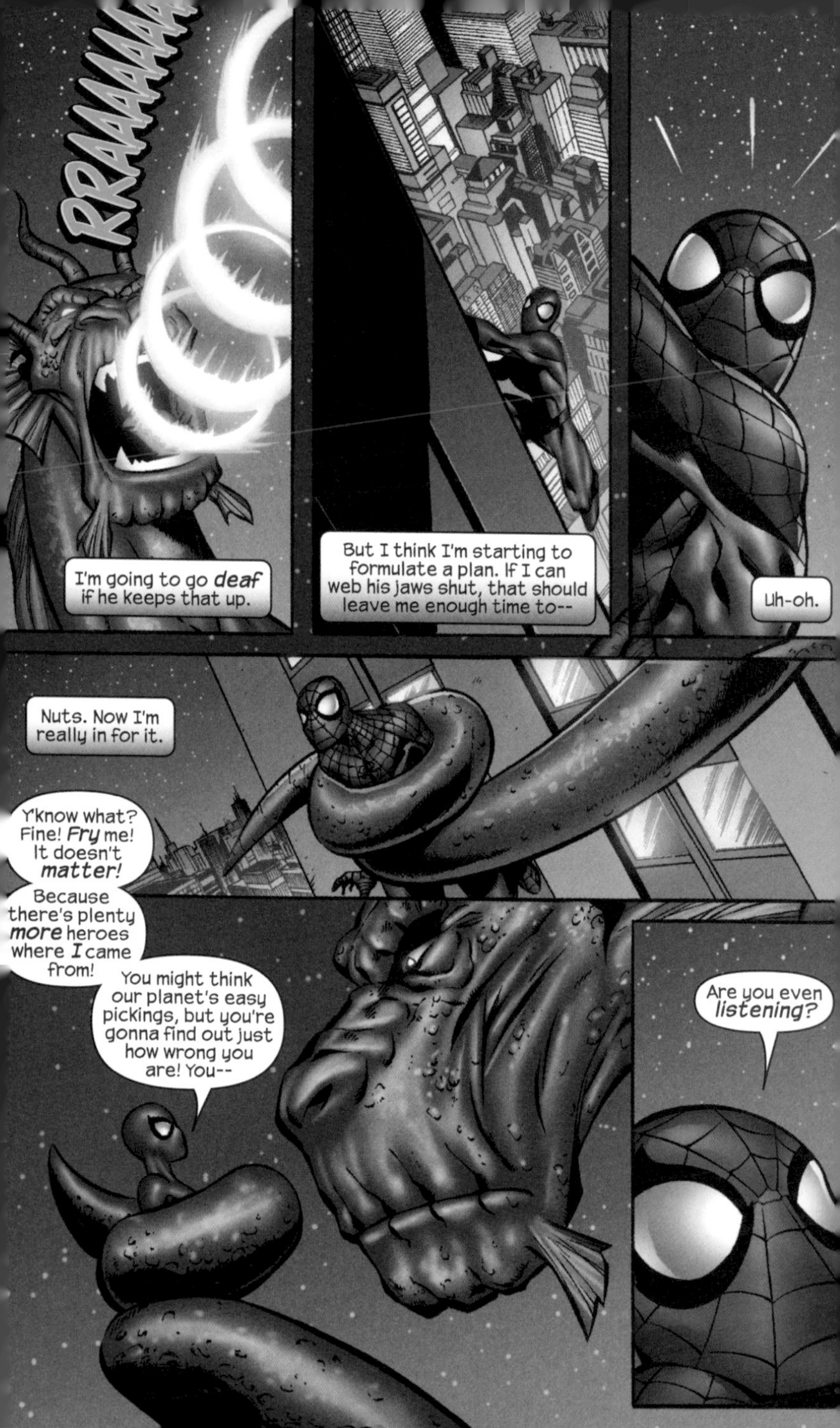
RRAAAAAA
I'm going to go *deaf* if he keeps that up.
But I think I'm starting to formulate a plan. If I can web his jaws shut, that should leave me enough time to--
Uh-oh.
Nuts. Now I'm really in for it.
Y'know what? Fine! *Fry* me! It doesn't *matter!*
Because there's plenty *more* heroes where *I* came from!
You might think our planet's easy pickings, but you're gonna find out just how wrong you are! You--
Are you even *listening?*

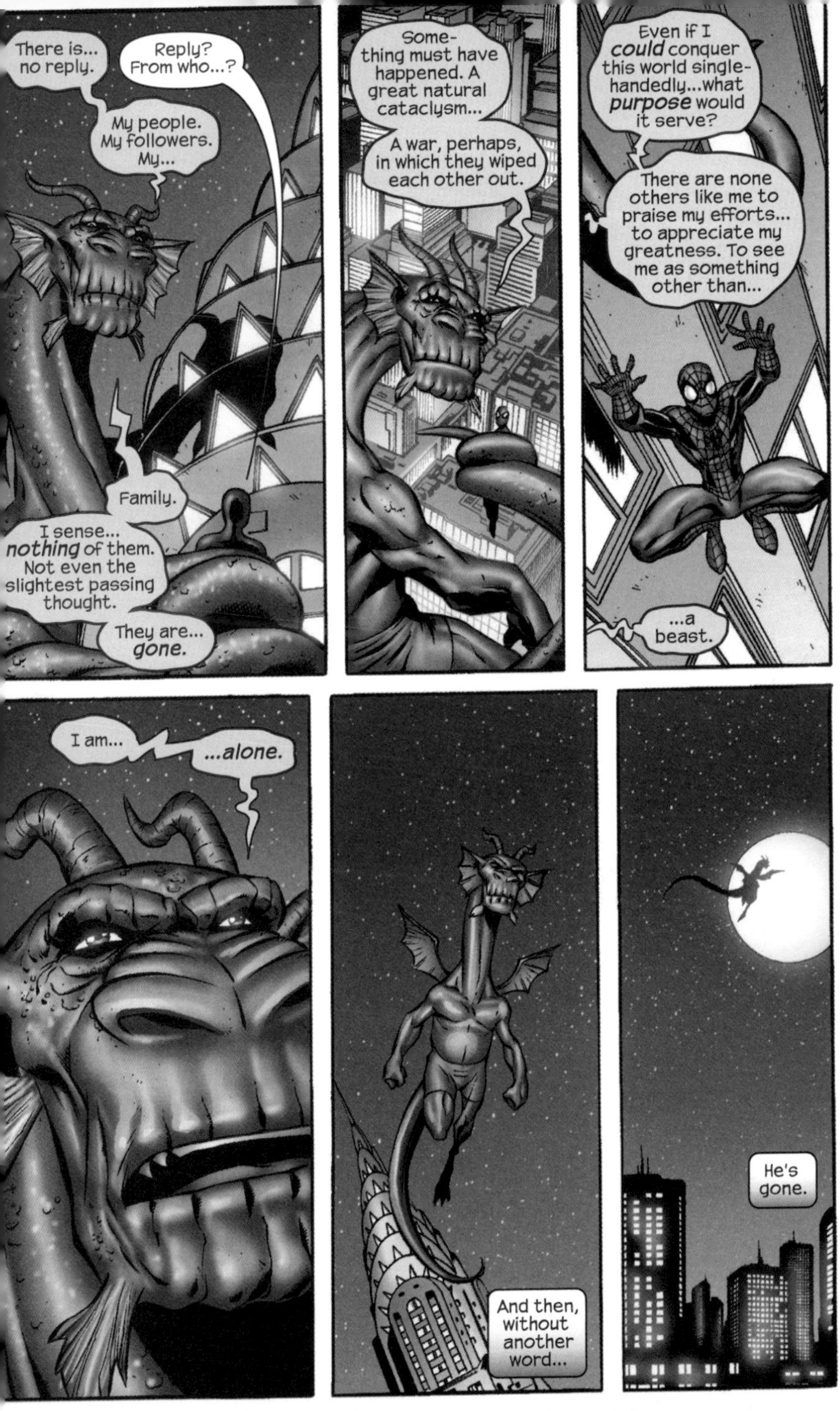
There is... no reply.
Reply? From who...?
My people. My followers. My...
Family.
I sense... *nothing* of them. Not even the slightest passing thought.
They are... *gone.*
Some-thing must have happened. A great natural cataclysm...
A war, perhaps, in which they wiped each other out.
Even if I *could* conquer this world single-handedly...what *purpose* would it serve?
There are none others like me to praise my efforts... to appreciate my greatness. To see me as something other than...
...a beast.
I am...
...alone.
And then, without another word...
He's gone.

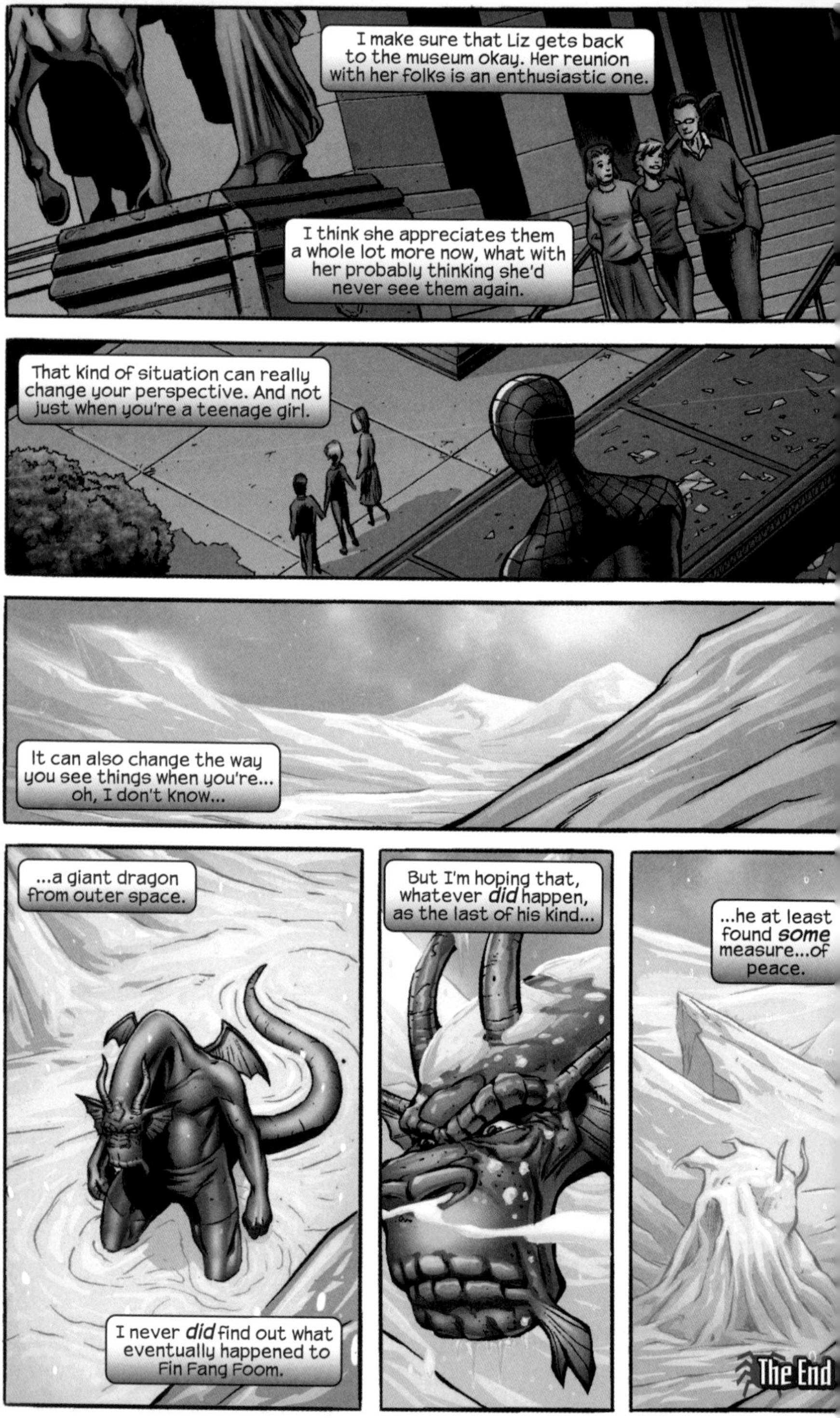
I make sure that Liz gets back to the museum okay. Her reunion with her folks is an enthusiastic one.
I think she appreciates them a whole lot more now, what with her probably thinking she'd never see them again.
That kind of situation can really change your perspective. And not just when you're a teenage girl.
It can also change the way you see things when you're... oh, I don't know...
...a giant dragon from outer space.
I never *did* find out what eventually happened to Fin Fang Foom.
But I'm hoping that, whatever *did* happen, as the last of his kind...
...he at least found *some* measure...of peace.
The End

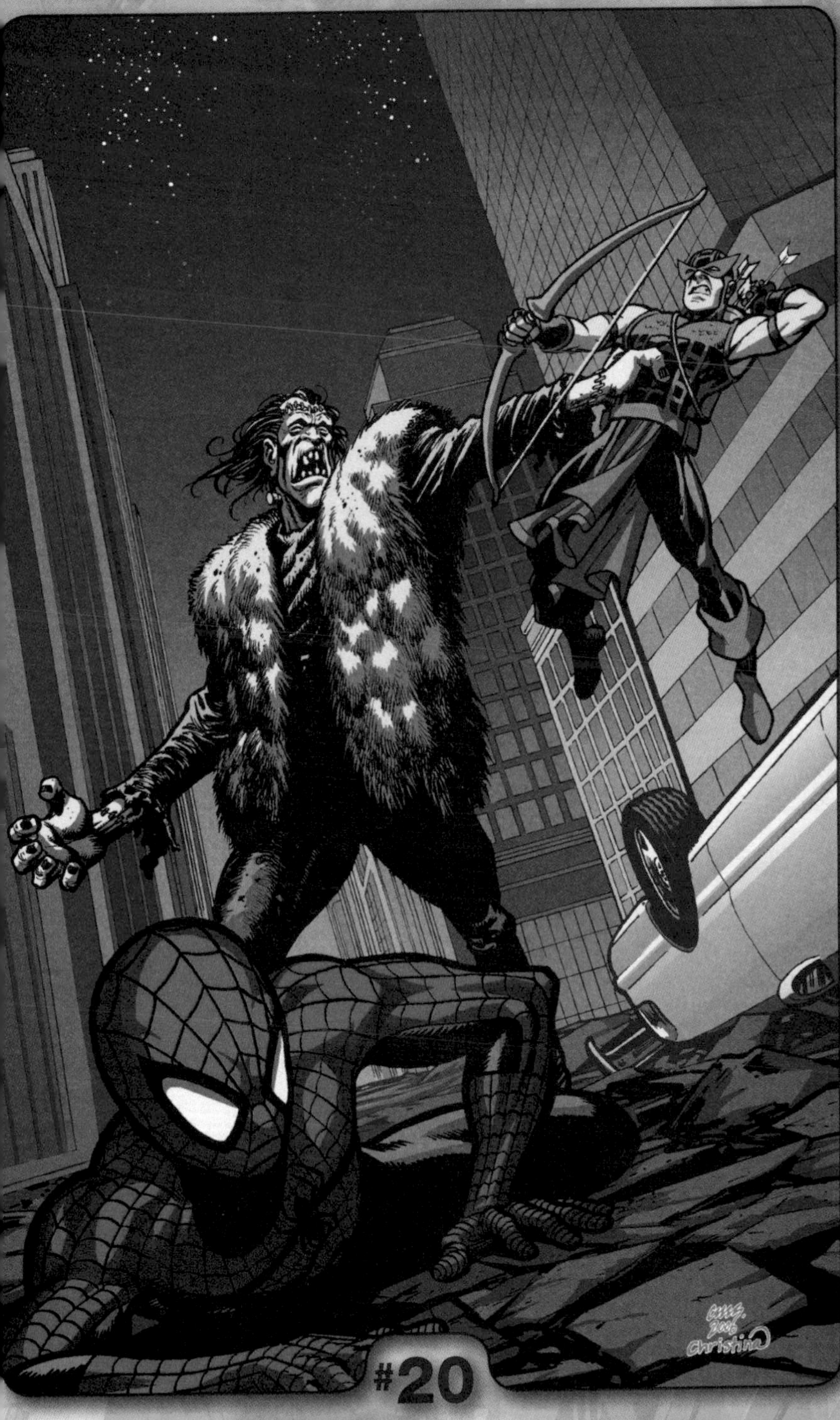

#20

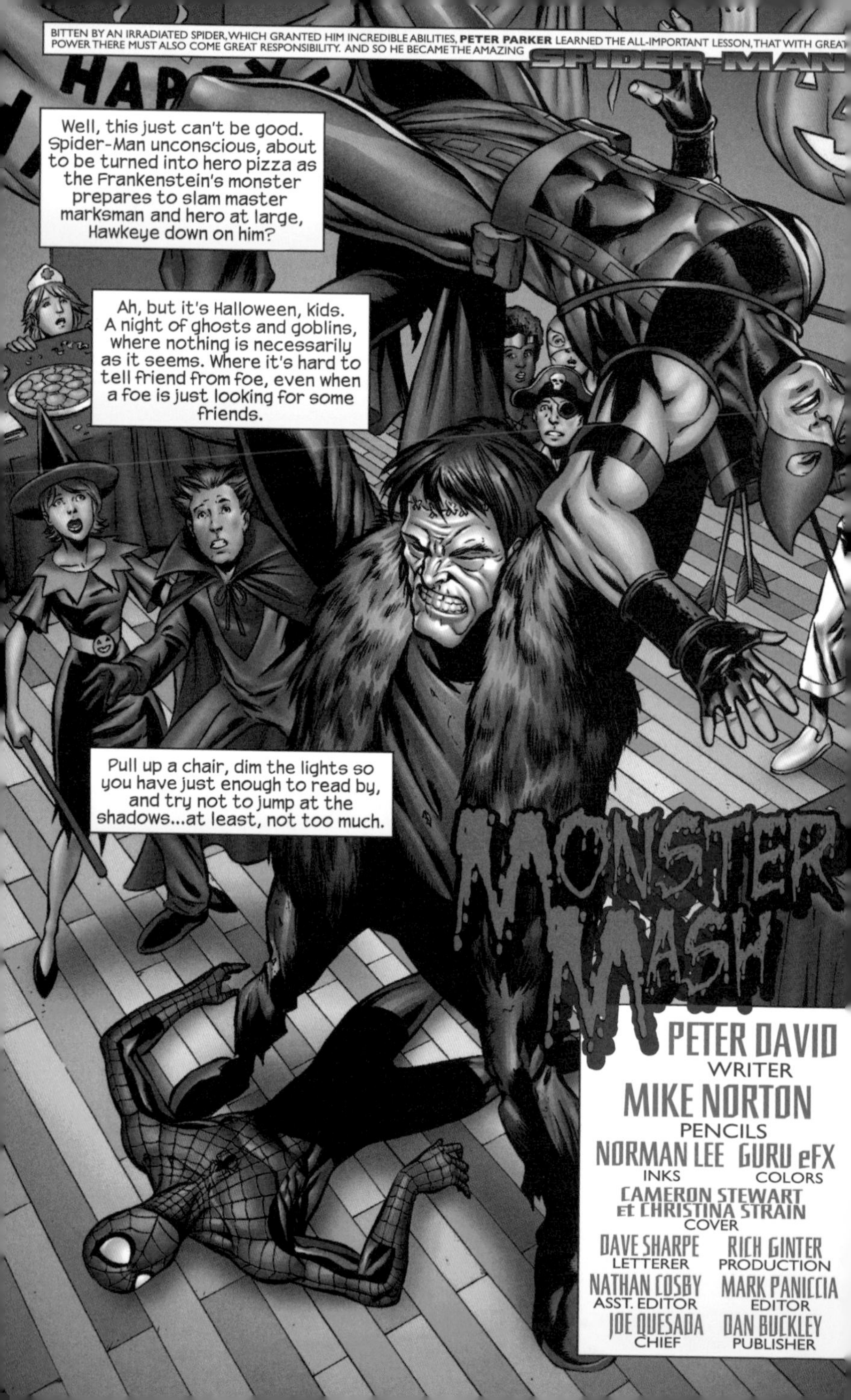
BITTEN BY AN IRRADIATED SPIDER, WHICH GRANTED HIM INCREDIBLE ABILITIES, PETER PARKER LEARNED THE ALL-IMPORTANT LESSON, THAT WITH GREAT POWER THERE MUST ALSO COME GREAT RESPONSIBILITY. AND SO HE BECAME THE AMAZING
SPIDER-MAN
Well, this just can't be good. Spider-Man unconscious, about to be turned into hero pizza as the Frankenstein's monster prepares to slam master marksman and hero at large, Hawkeye down on him?
Ah, but it's Halloween, kids. A night of ghosts and goblins, where nothing is necessarily as it seems. Where it's hard to tell friend from foe, even when a foe is just looking for some friends.
Pull up a chair, dim the lights so you have just enough to read by, and try not to jump at the shadows...at least, not too much.
MONSTER MASH
PETER DAVID
WRITER
MIKE NORTON
PENCILS
NORMAN LEE
INKS
GURU eFX
COLORS
CAMERON STEWART et CHRISTINA STRAIN
COVER
DAVE SHARPE
LETTERER
RICH GINTER
PRODUCTION
NATHAN COSBY
ASST. EDITOR
MARK PANICCIA
EDITOR
JOE QUESADA
CHIEF
DAN BUCKLEY
PUBLISHER

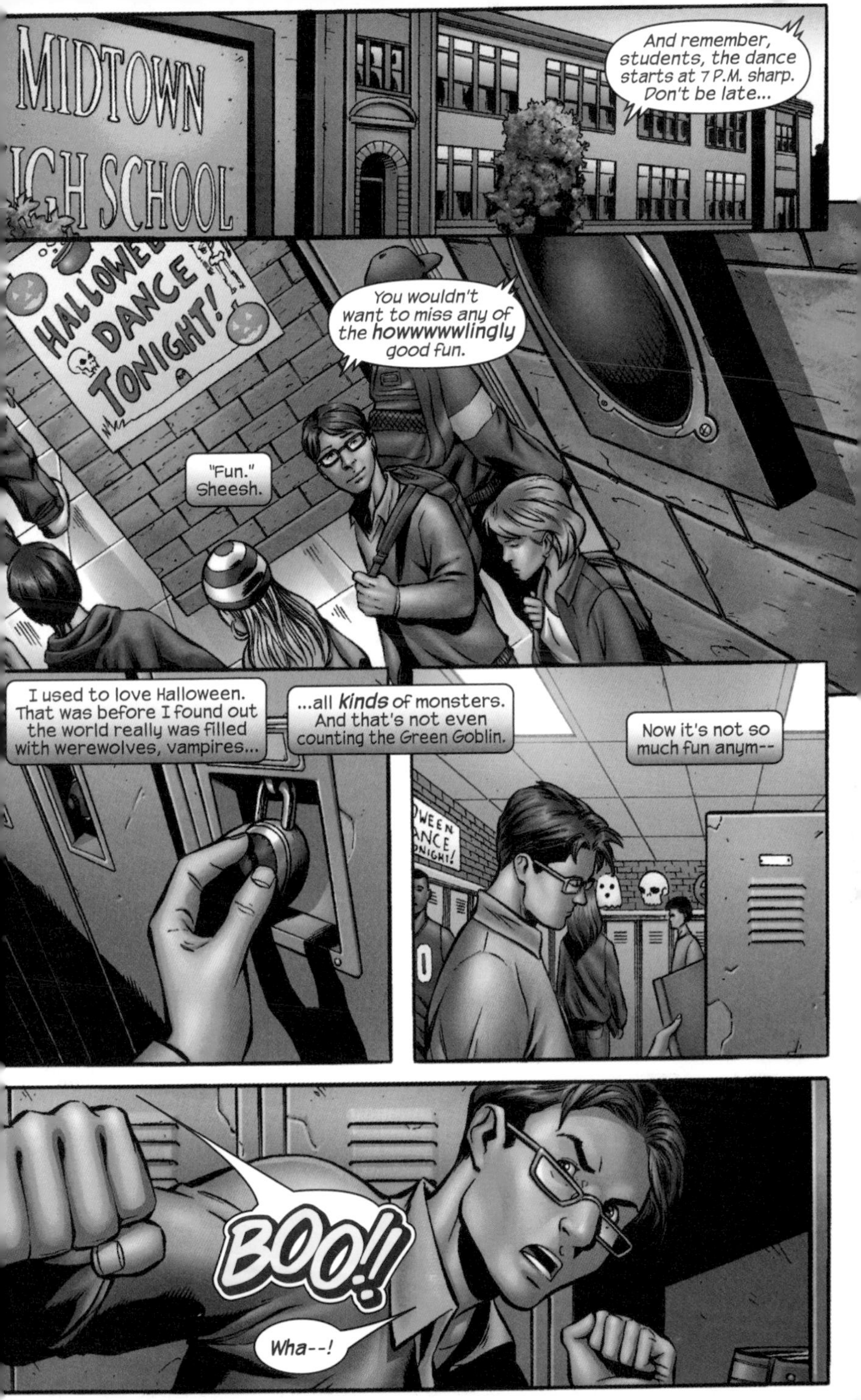
MIDTOWN
IGH SCHOOL
And remember, students, the dance starts at 7 P.M. sharp. Don't be late...
HALLOWE DANCE TONIGHT!
You wouldn't want to miss any of the **howwwwwlingly** good fun.
"Fun." Sheesh.
I used to love Halloween. That was before I found out the world really was filled with werewolves, vampires...
...all *kinds* of monsters. And that's not even counting the Green Goblin.
Now it's not so much fun anym--
BOO!!
Wha--!

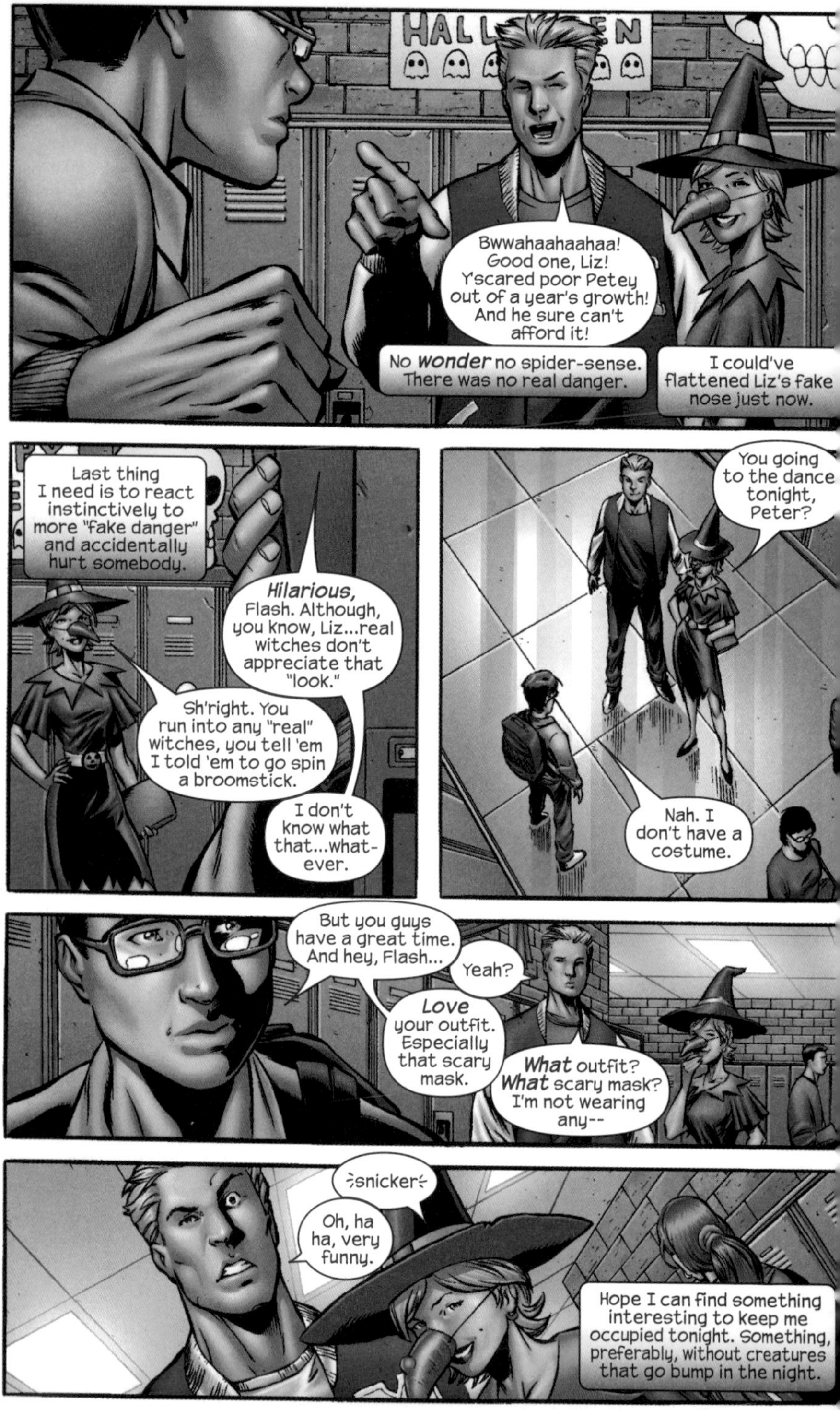

HALL EN
Bwwahaaahaahaa! Good one, Liz! Y'scared poor Petey out of a year's growth! And he sure can't afford it!
No *wonder* no spider-sense. There was no real danger.
I could've flattened Liz's fake nose just now.
Last thing I need is to react instinctively to more "fake danger" and accidentally hurt somebody.
Hilarious, Flash. Although, you know, Liz...real witches don't appreciate that "look."
Sh'right. You run into any "real" witches, you tell 'em I told 'em to go spin a broomstick.
I don't know what that...whatever.
You going to the dance tonight, Peter?
Nah. I don't have a costume.
But you guys have a great time. And hey, Flash...
Yeah?
Love your outfit. Especially that scary mask.
What outfit? *What* scary mask? I'm not wearing any--
snicker
Oh, ha ha, very funny.
Hope I can find something interesting to keep me occupied tonight. Something, preferably, without creatures that go bump in the night.

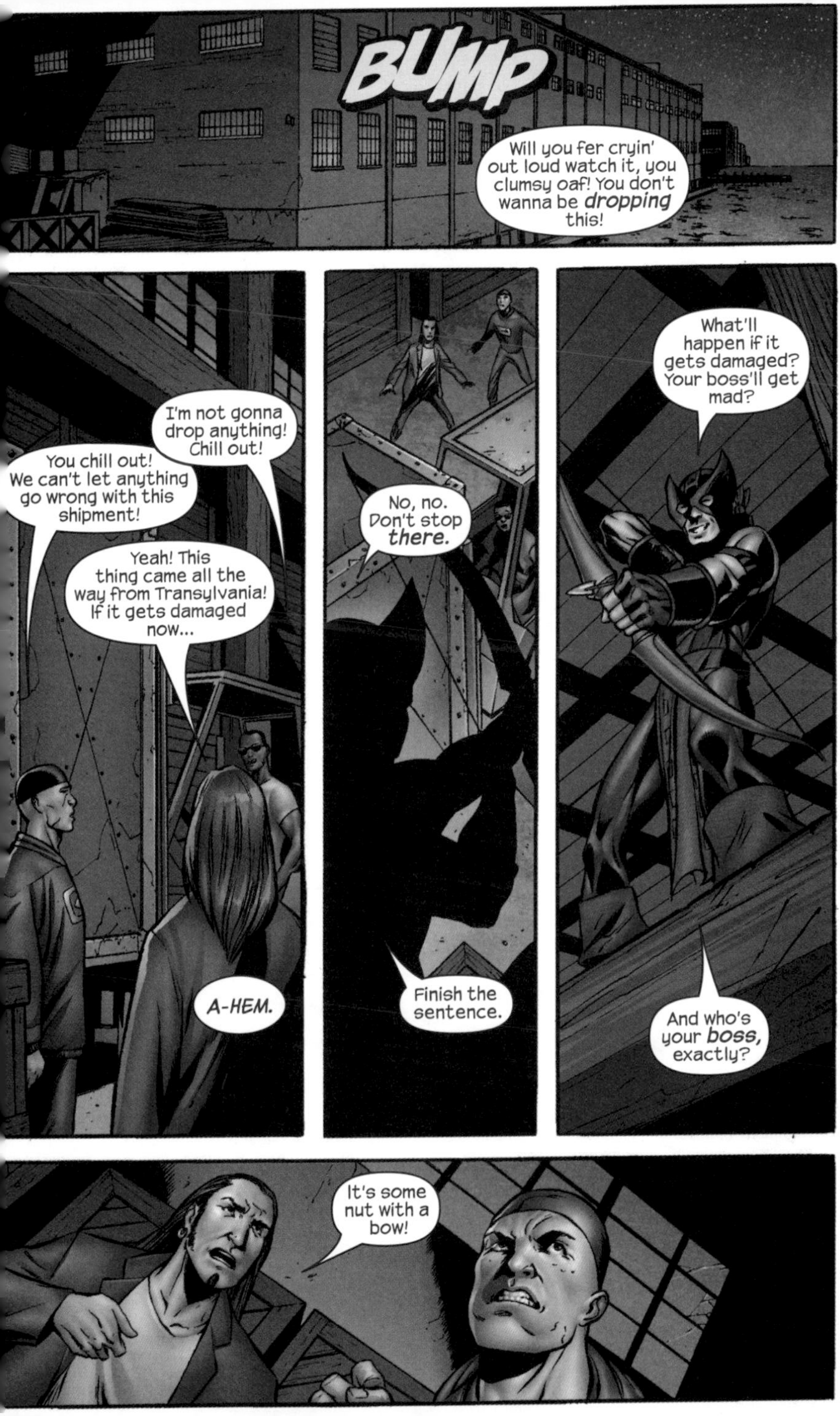
BUMP
Will you fer cryin' out loud watch it, you clumsy oaf! You don't wanna be *dropping* this!
I'm not gonna drop anything! Chill out!
You chill out! We can't let anything go wrong with this shipment!
Yeah! This thing came all the way from Transylvania! If it gets damaged now...
A-HEM.
No, no. Don't stop *there.*
Finish the sentence.
What'll happen if it gets damaged? Your boss'll get mad?
And who's your *boss,* exactly?
It's some nut with a bow!

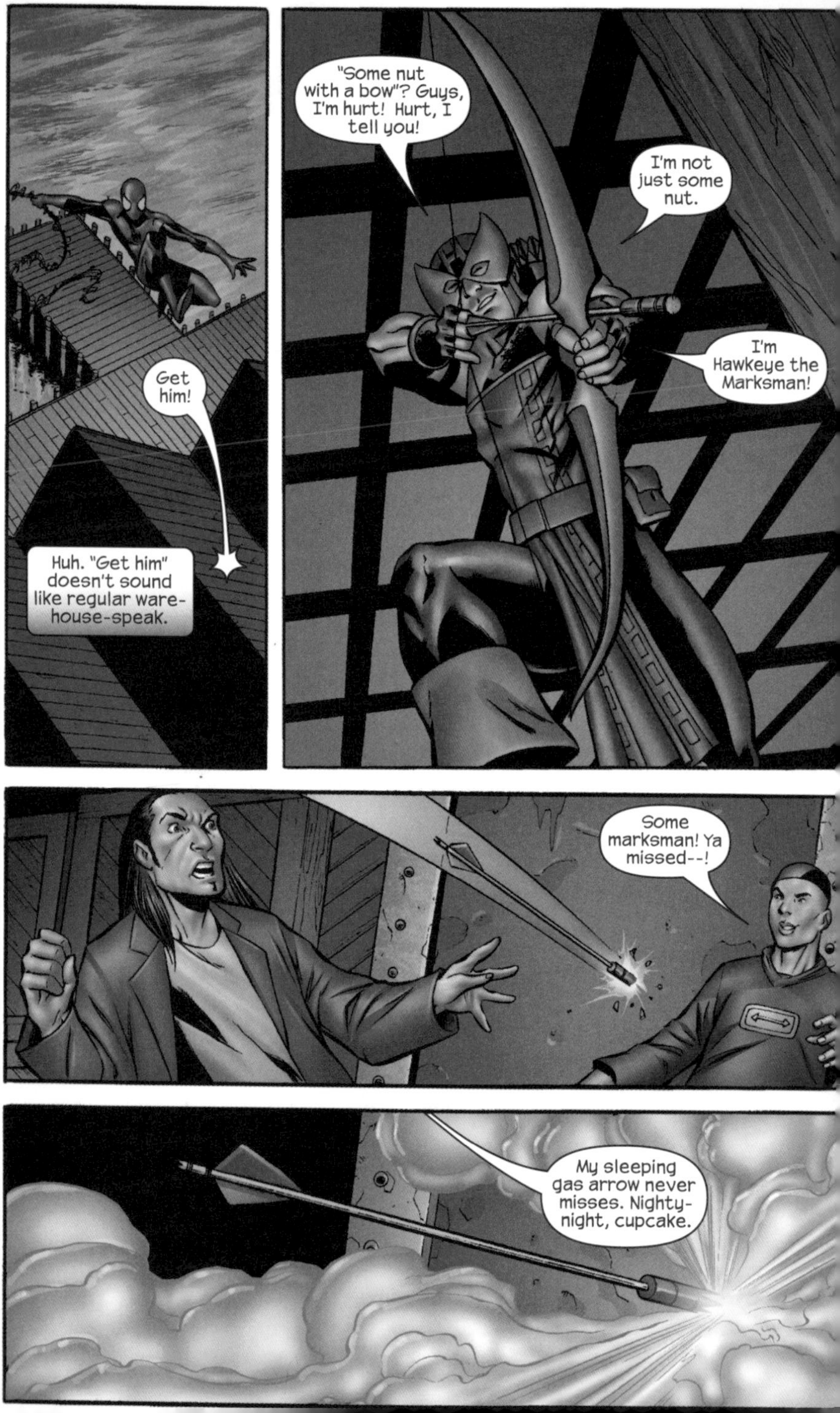
"Some nut with a bow"? Guys, I'm hurt! Hurt, I tell you!
I'm not just some nut.
I'm Hawkeye the Marksman!
Get him!
Huh. "Get him" doesn't sound like regular ware-house-speak.
Some marksman! Ya missed--!
My sleeping gas arrow never misses. Nighty-night, cupcake.

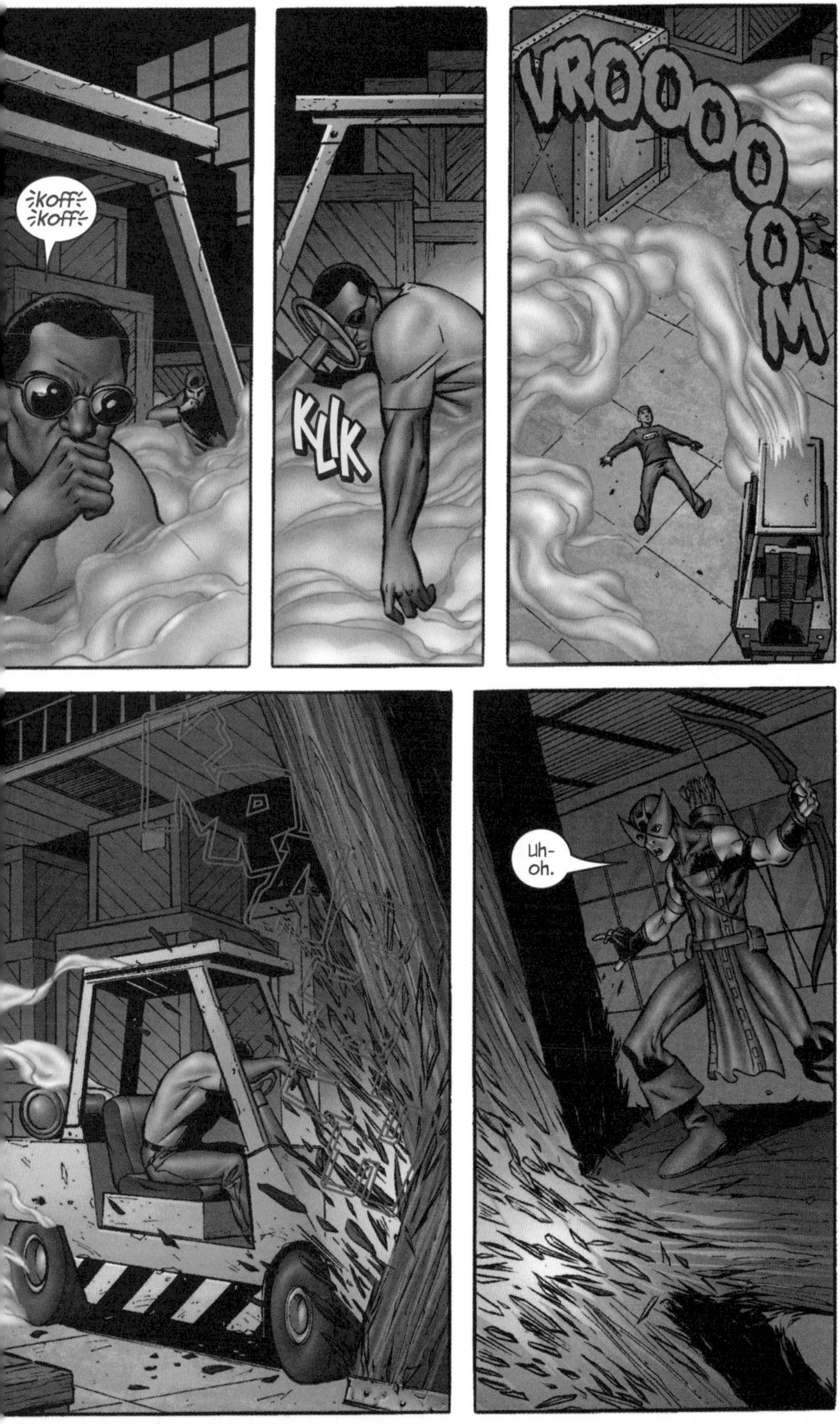

KOFF KOFF
KLIK
VROOOOOM
Uh-oh.

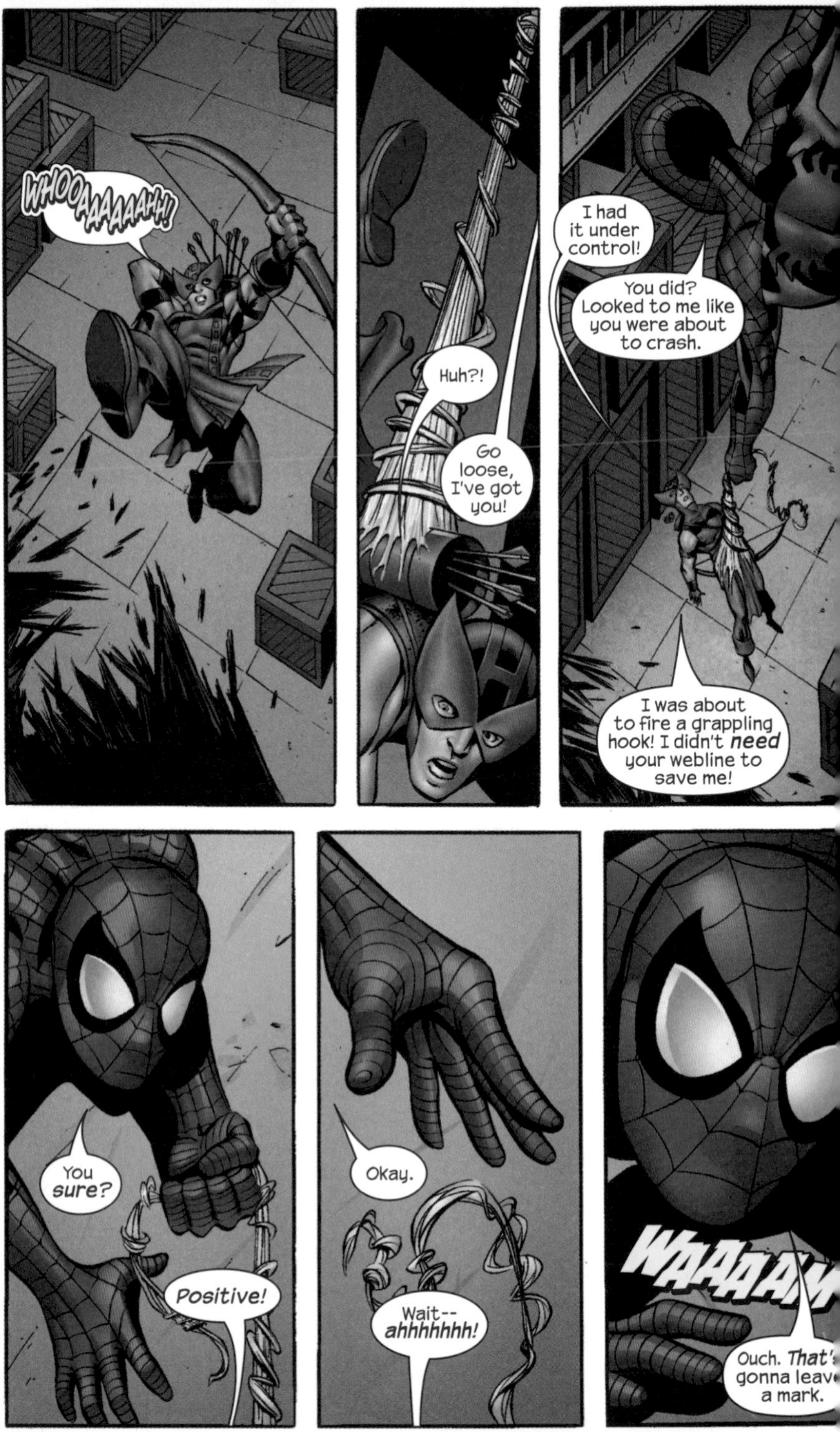
WHOOAAAAAAHH!
Huh?!
Go loose, I've got you!
I had it under control!
You did? Looked to me like you were about to crash.
I was about to fire a grappling hook! I didn't *need* your webline to save me!
You *sure?*
Positive!
Okay.
Wait-- *ahhhhhhh!*
WAAAAM
Ouch. *That's* gonna leave a mark.

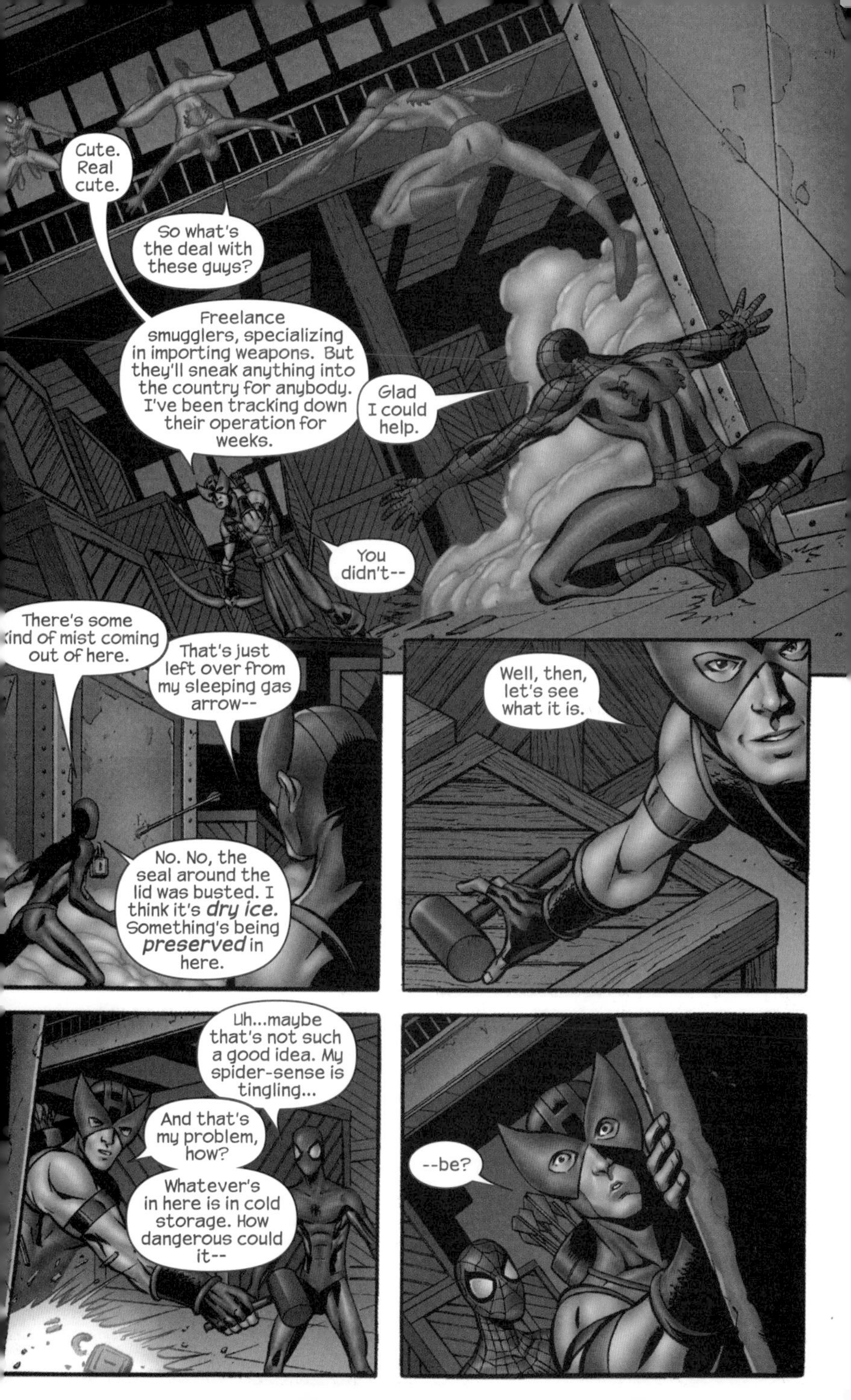
Cute. Real cute.
So what's the deal with these guys?
Freelance smugglers, specializing in importing weapons. But they'll sneak anything into the country for anybody. I've been tracking down their operation for weeks.
Glad I could help.
You didn't--
There's some kind of mist coming out of here.
That's just left over from my sleeping gas arrow--
No. No, the seal around the lid was busted. I think it's *dry ice.* Something's being *preserved* in here.
Well, then, let's see what it is.
Uh...maybe that's not such a good idea. My spider-sense is tingling...
And that's my problem, how?
Whatever's in here is in cold storage. How dangerous could it--
--be?

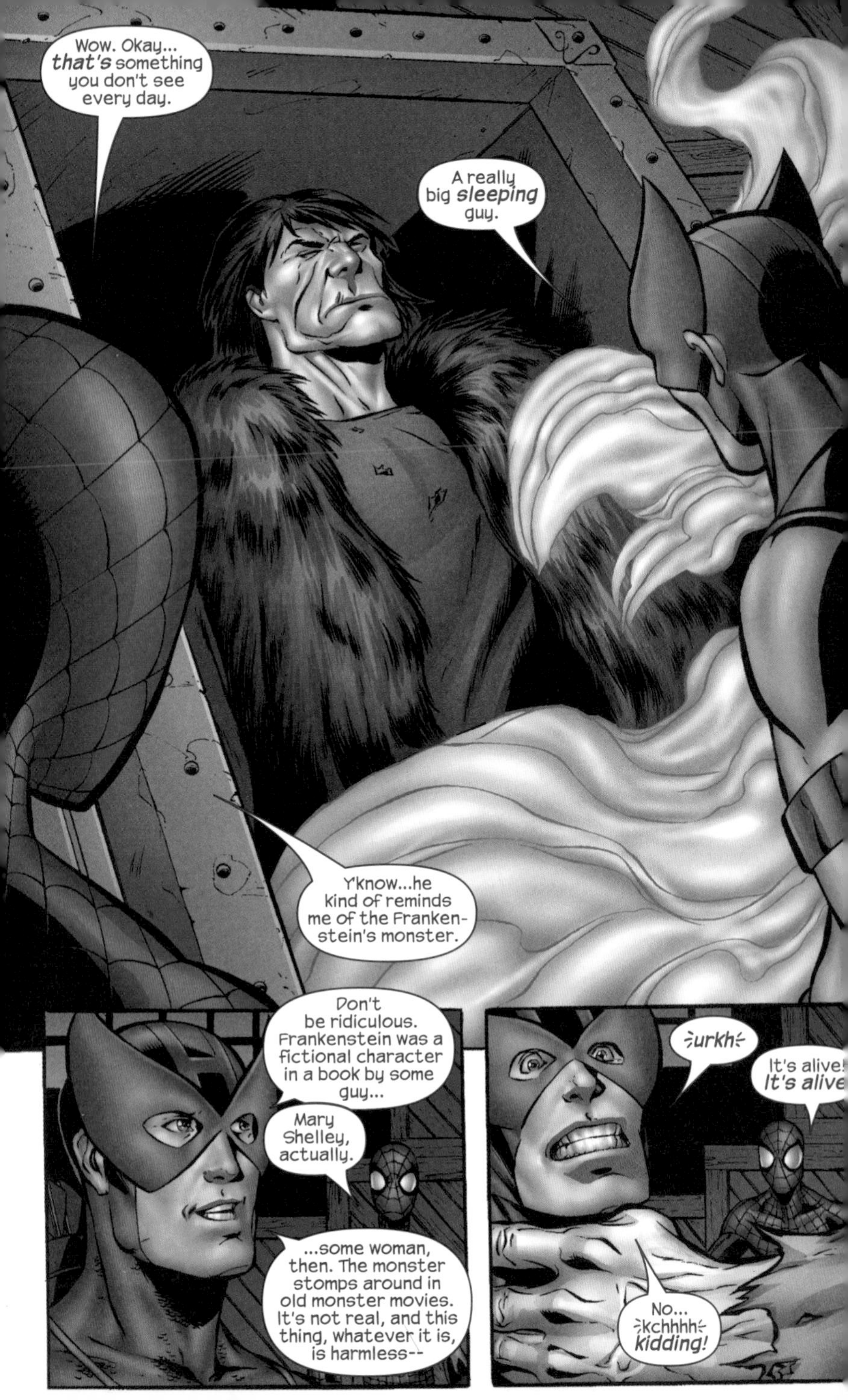
Wow. Okay... *that's* something you don't see every day.
A really big *sleeping* guy.
Y'know...he kind of reminds me of the Franken-stein's monster.
Don't be ridiculous. Frankenstein was a fictional character in a book by some guy...
Mary Shelley, actually.
...some woman, then. The monster stomps around in old monster movies. It's not real, and this thing, whatever it is, is harmless--
urkh
It's alive! *It's alive*
No... kchhhh *kidding!*

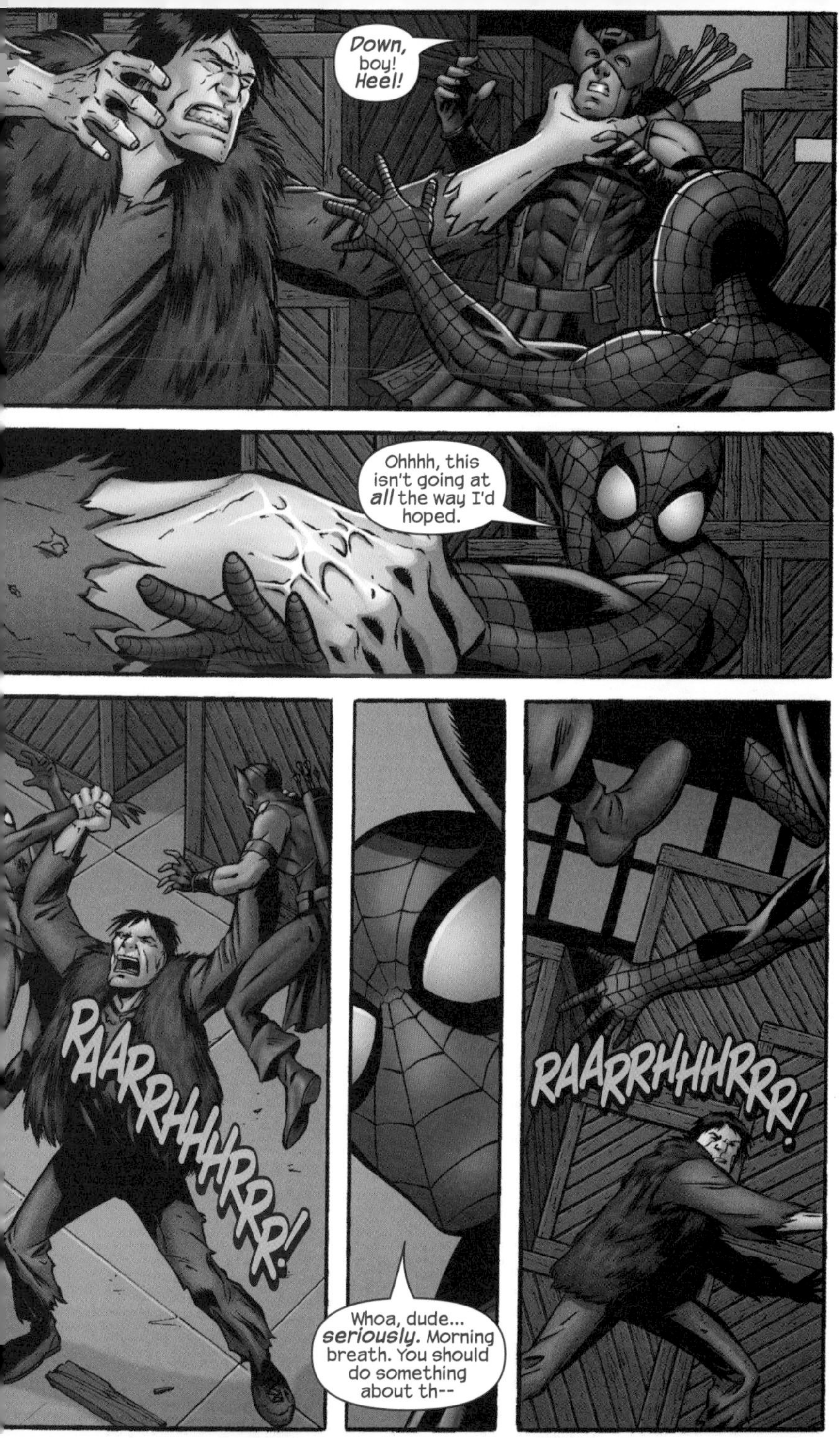
Down, boy! Heel!
Ohhhh, this isn't going at all the way I'd hoped.
RAARRHHHRRR!
Whoa, dude... seriously. Morning breath. You should do something about th--
RAARRHHHRRR!

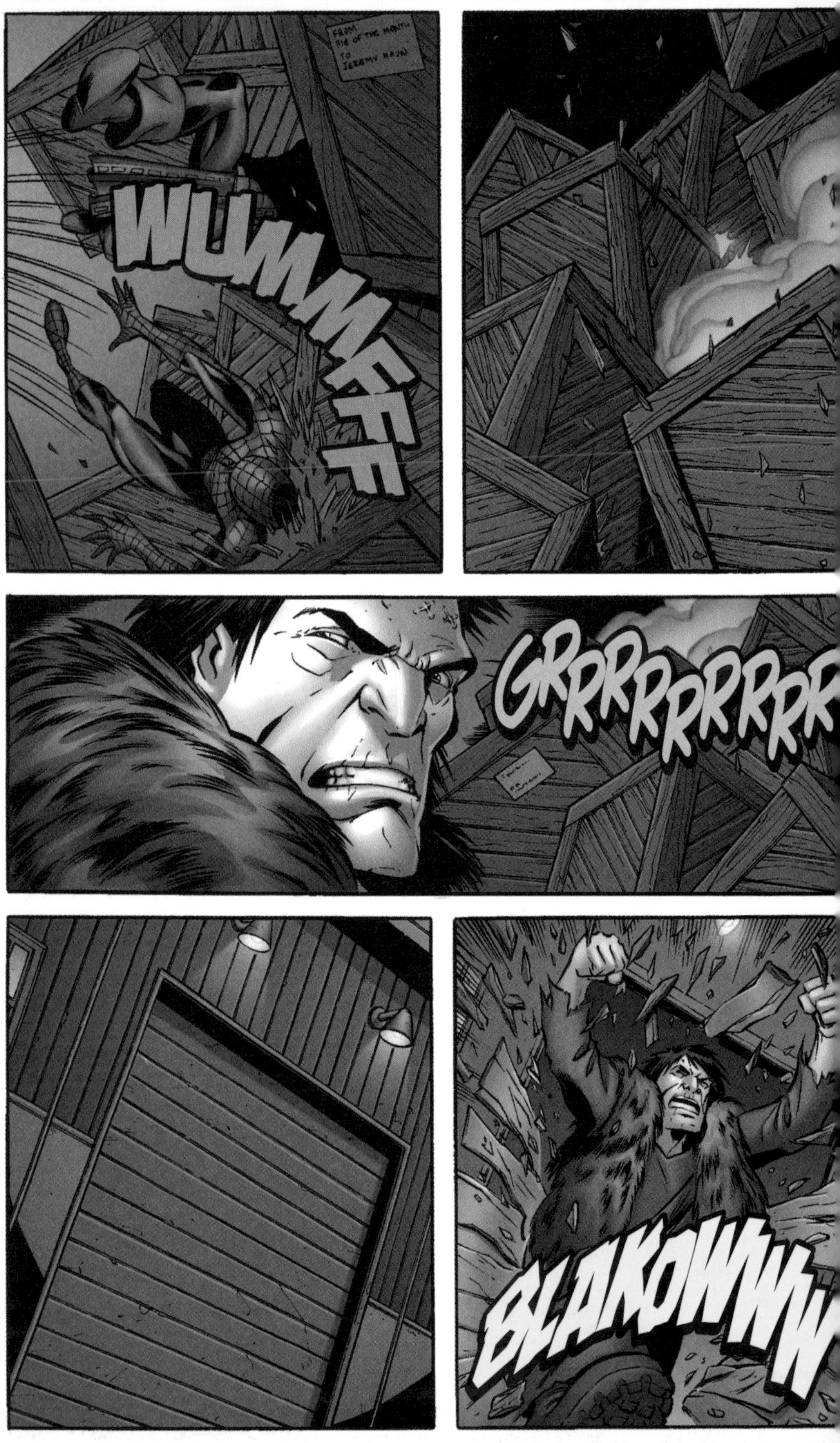
FROM:
PIE OF THE MONTH
TO
JEREMY RAUN
WUMMMFFF
GRRRRRRRRR
BLAKOWWW

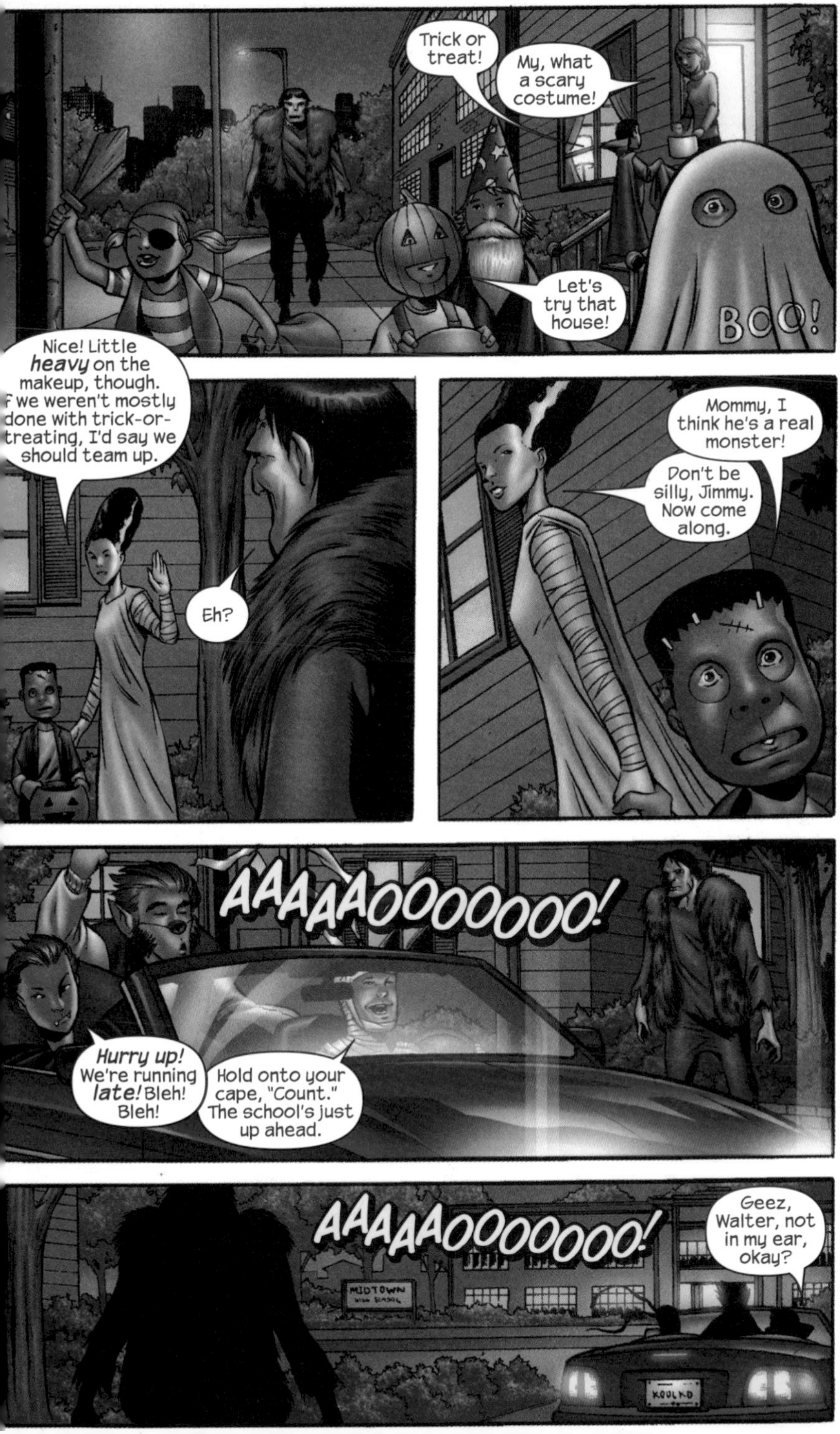

Trick or treat!
My, what a scary costume!
Let's try that house!
BOO!
Nice! Little *heavy* on the makeup, though. If we weren't mostly done with trick-or-treating, I'd say we should team up.
Eh?
Mommy, I think he's a real monster!
Don't be silly, Jimmy. Now come along.
AAAAAOOOOOOOO!
Hurry up! We're running *late!* Bleh! Bleh!
Hold onto your cape, "Count." The school's just up ahead.
AAAAAOOOOOOOO!
Geez, Walter, not in my ear, okay?
MIDTOWN

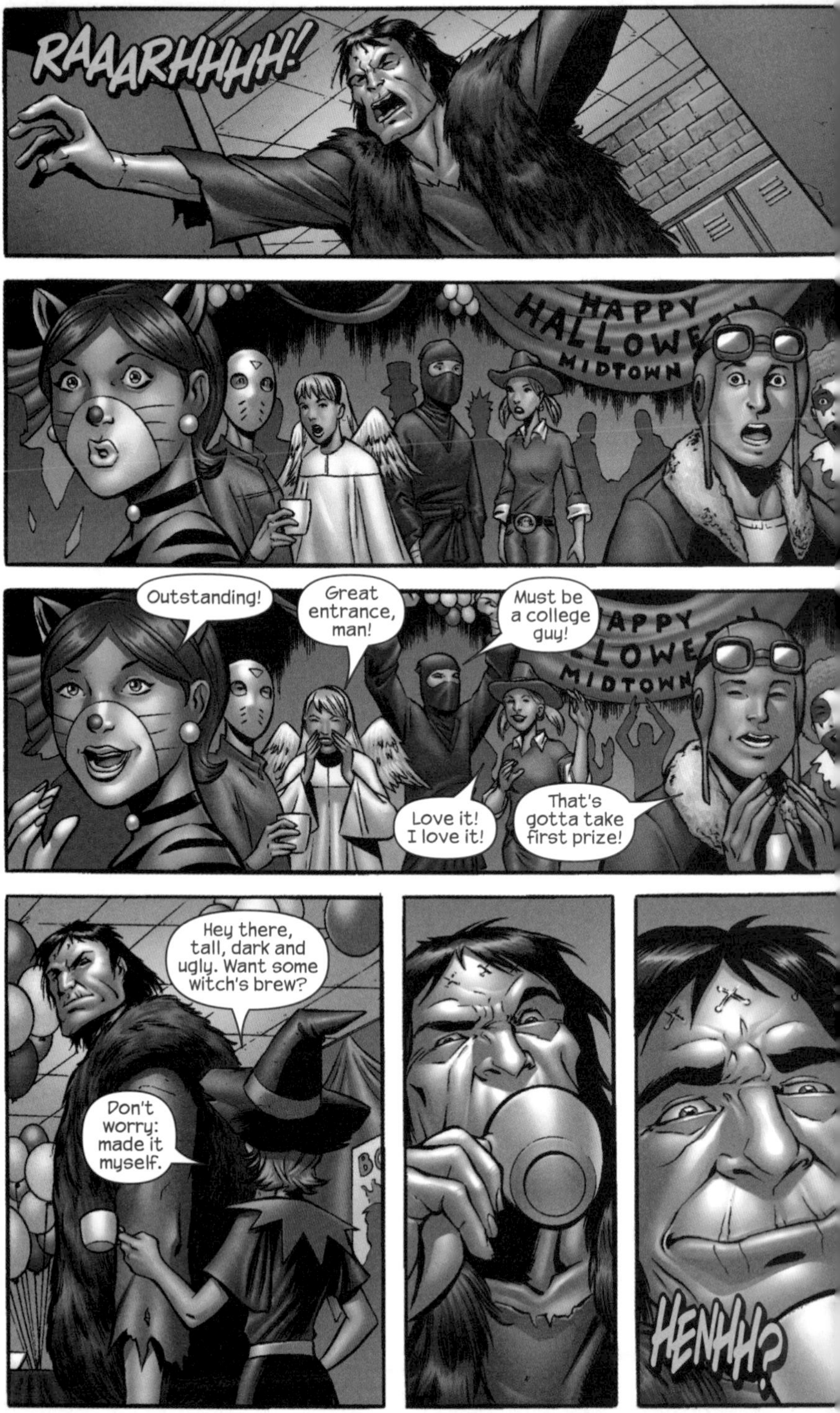
RAAARHHHH!
HAPPY HALLOWE
MIDTOWN
Outstanding!
Great entrance, man!
Must be a college guy!
Love it! I love it!
That's gotta take first prize!
Hey there, tall, dark and ugly. Want some witch's brew?
Don't worry: made it myself.
HENHH?

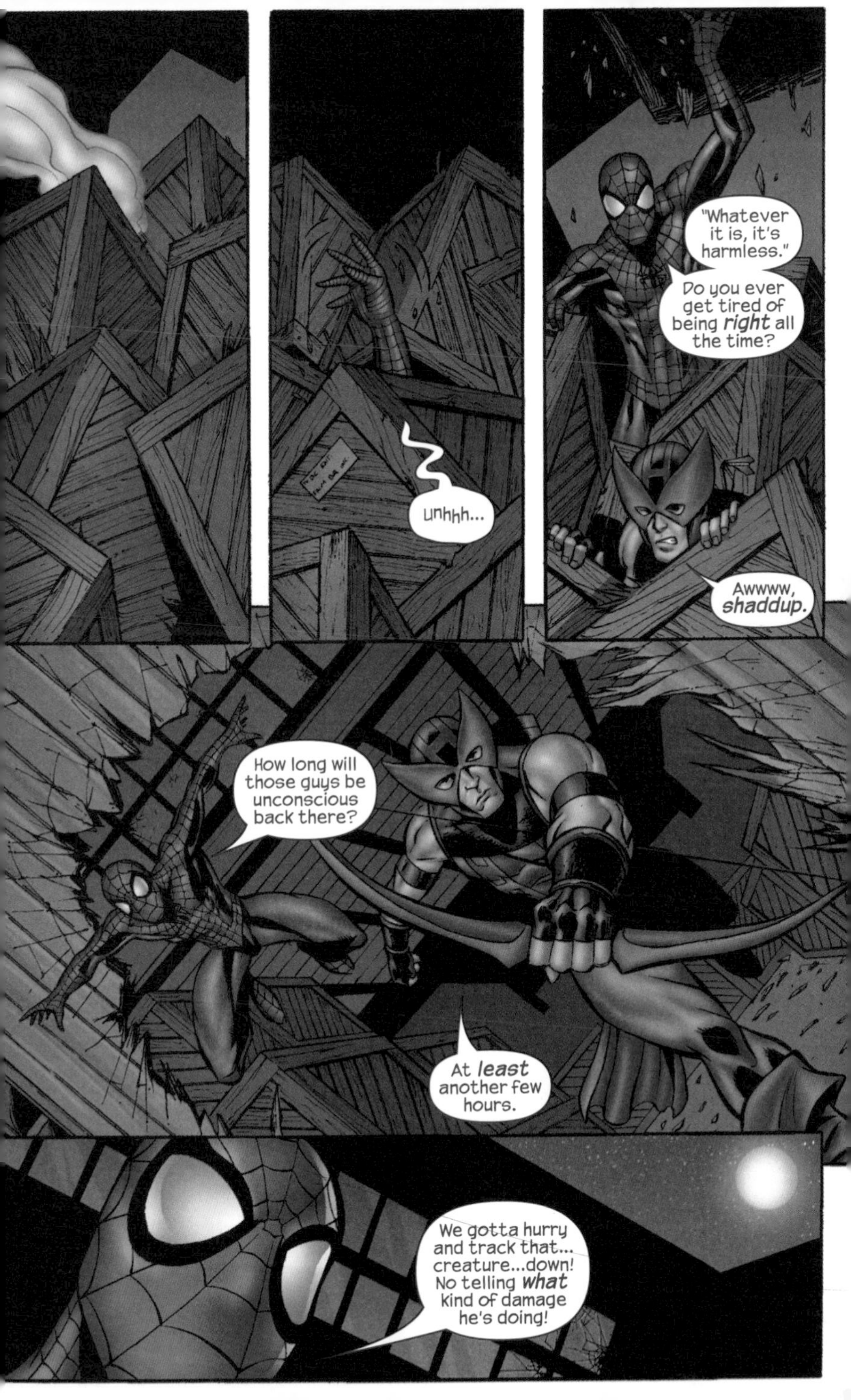
Unhhh...
"Whatever it is, it's harmless."
Do you ever get tired of being *right* all the time?
Awwww, *shaddup.*
How long will those guys be unconscious back there?
At *least* another few hours.
We gotta hurry and track that... creature...down! No telling *what* kind of damage he's doing!

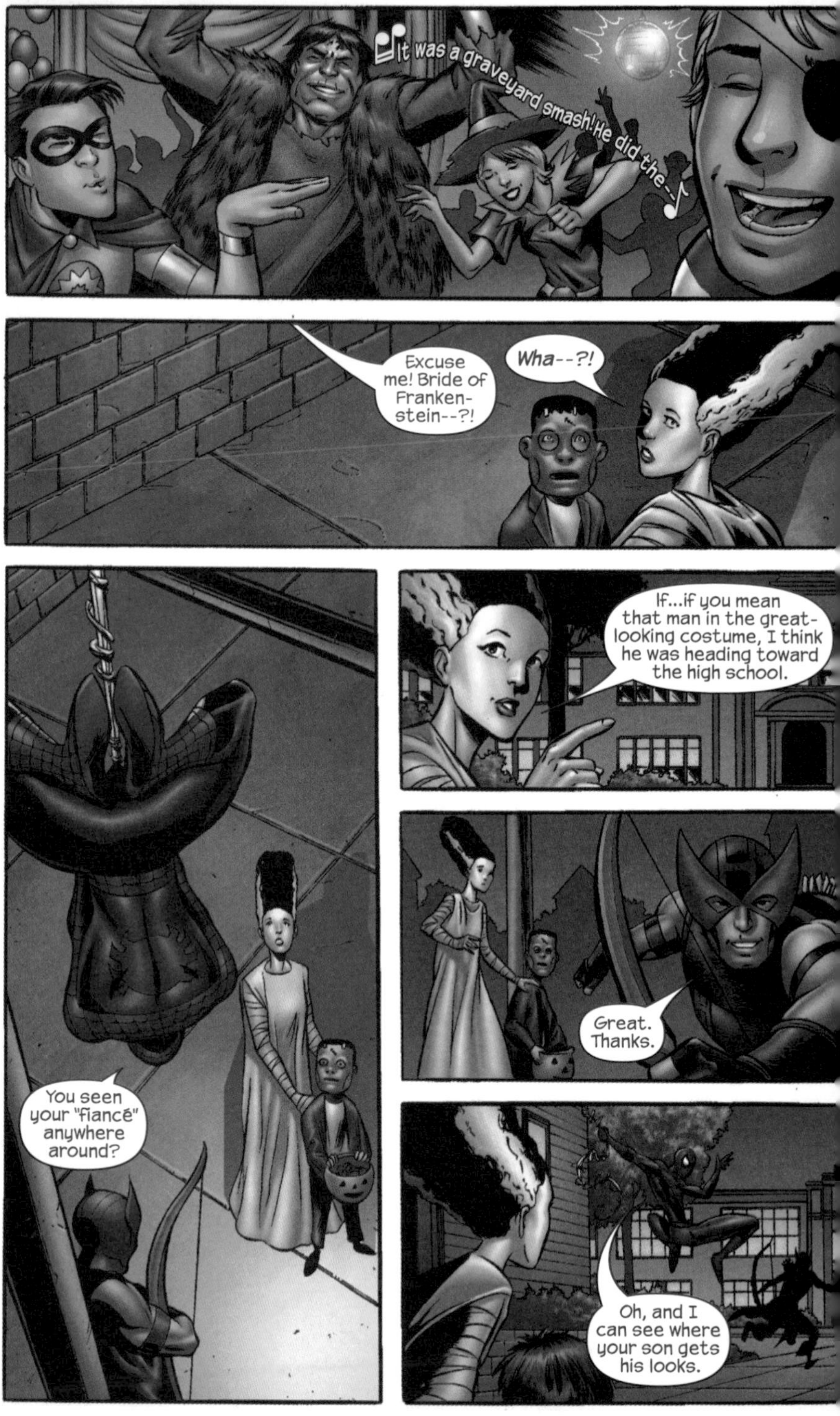
It was a graveyard smash! He did the--
Excuse me! Bride of Franken-stein--?!
Wha--?!
You seen your "fiancé" anywhere around?
If...if you mean that man in the great-looking costume, I think he was heading toward the high school.
Great. Thanks.
Oh, and I can see where your son gets his looks.

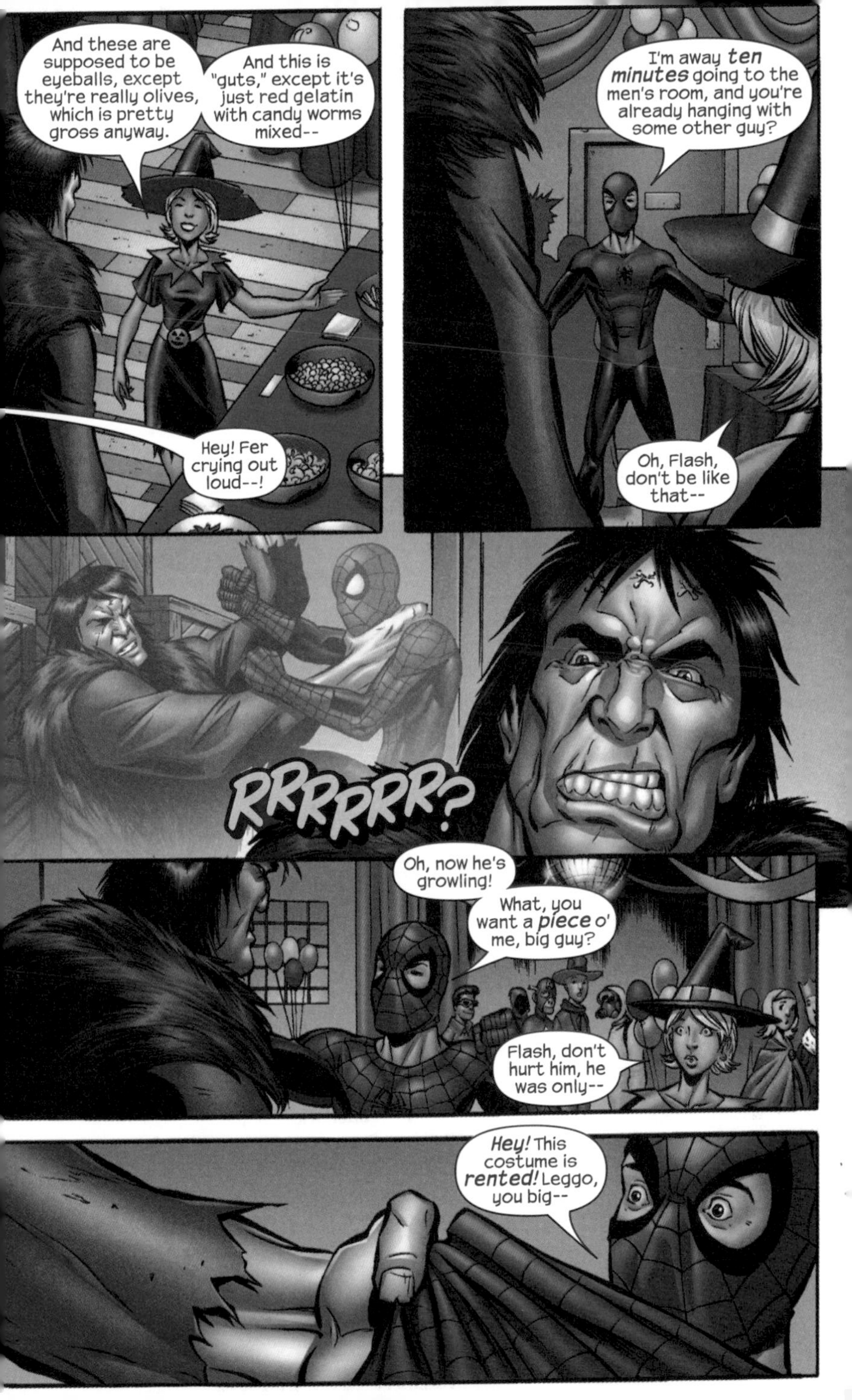
And these are supposed to be eyeballs, except they're really olives, which is pretty gross anyway.
And this is "guts," except it's just red gelatin with candy worms mixed--
Hey! Fer crying out loud--!
I'm away ten minutes going to the men's room, and you're already hanging with some other guy?
Oh, Flash, don't be like that--
RRRRRR?
Oh, now he's growling!
What, you want a piece o' me, big guy?
Flash, don't hurt him, he was only--
Hey! This costume is rented! Leggo, you big--

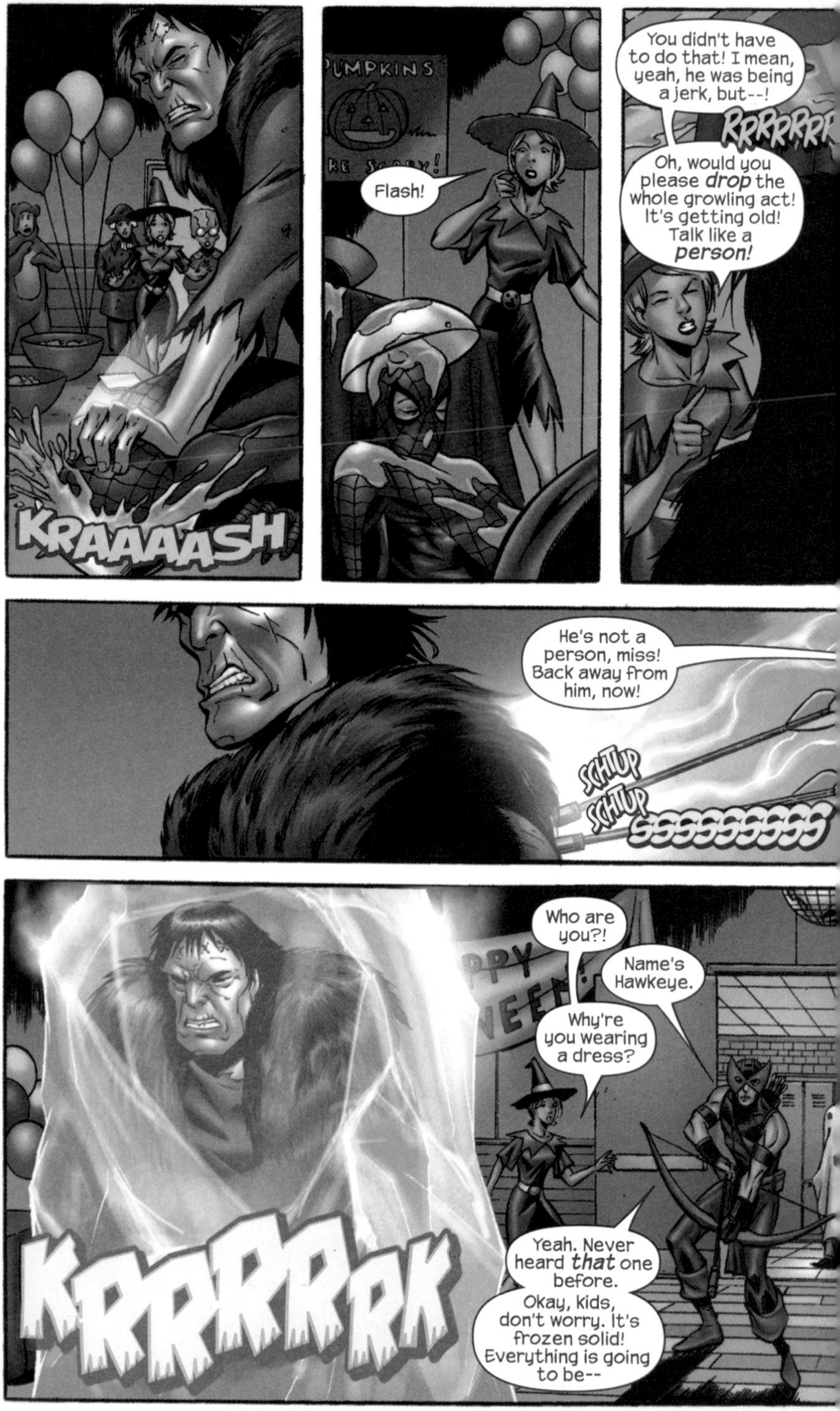
KRAAAASH
Flash!
You didn't have to do that! I mean, yeah, he was being a jerk, but--!
RRRRRRR
Oh, would you please *drop* the whole growling act! It's getting old! Talk like a *person!*
He's not a person, miss! Back away from him, now!
SCHTUP
SCHTUP
SSSSSSSSS
Who are you?!
Name's Hawkeye.
Why're you wearing a dress?
Yeah. Never heard *that* one before.
Okay, kids, don't worry. It's frozen solid! Everything is going to be--
KRRRRRK

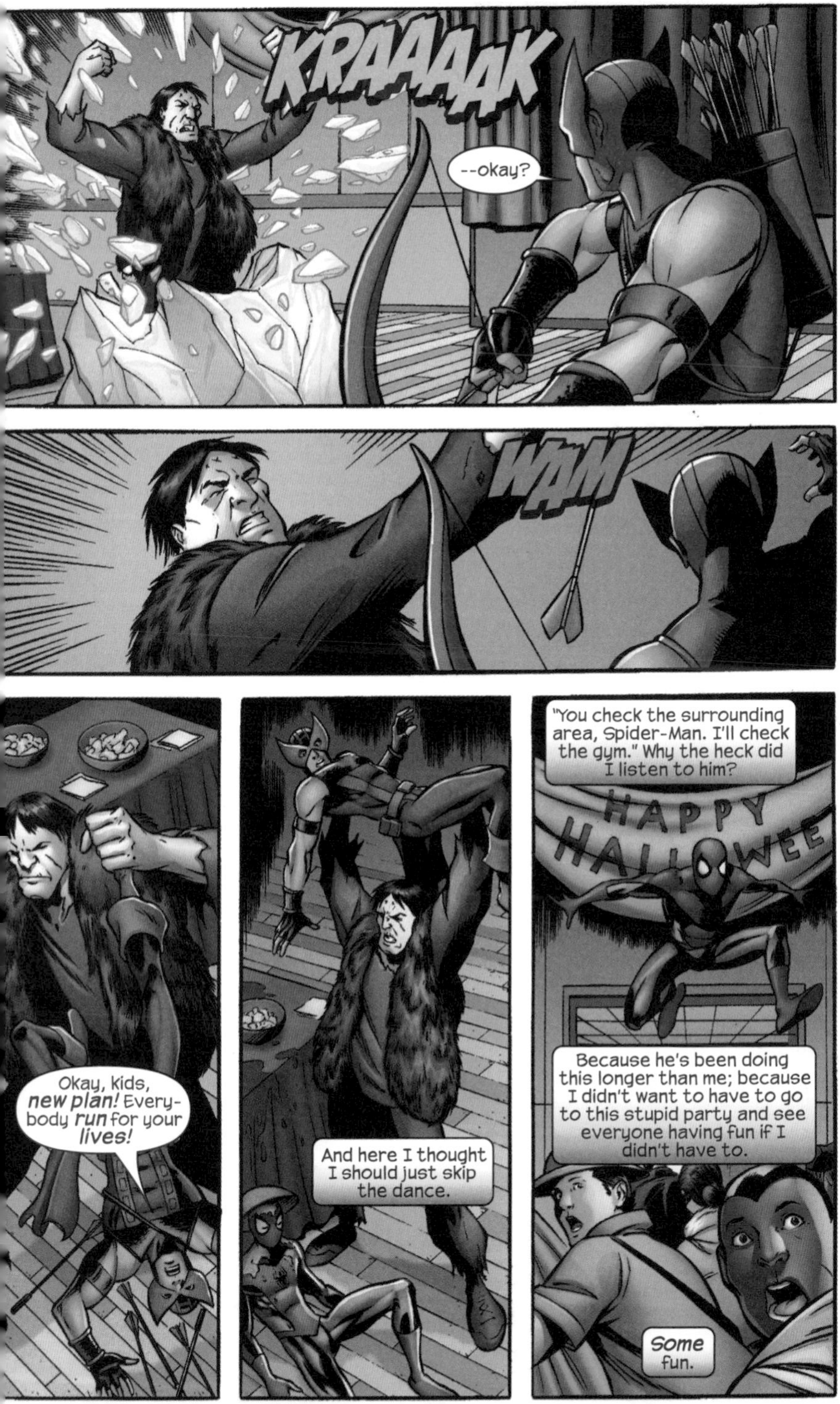
KRAAAAK
--okay?
WAM
Okay, kids, new plan! Everybody run for your lives!
And here I thought I should just skip the dance.
"You check the surrounding area, Spider-Man. I'll check the gym." Why the heck did I listen to him?
HAPPY HALLOWEE
Because he's been doing this longer than me; because I didn't want to have to go to this stupid party and see everyone having fun if I didn't have to.
Some fun.

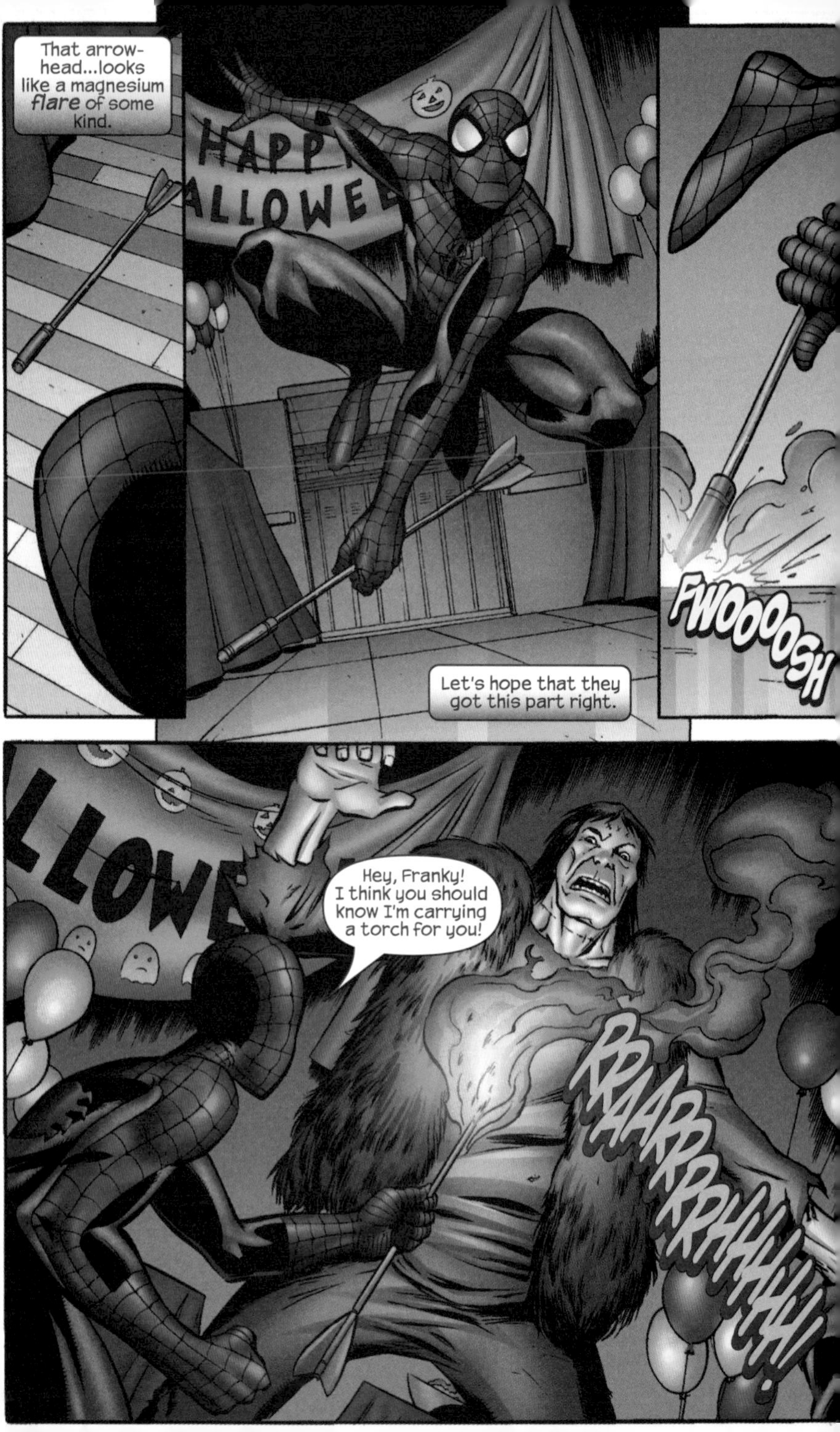
That arrow-head...looks like a magnesium *flare* of some kind.
HAPP
ALLOWEE
Let's hope that they got this part right.
FWOOOOSH
LLOWE
Hey, Franky! I think you should know I'm carrying a torch for you!
RRAARRRHHHHH!

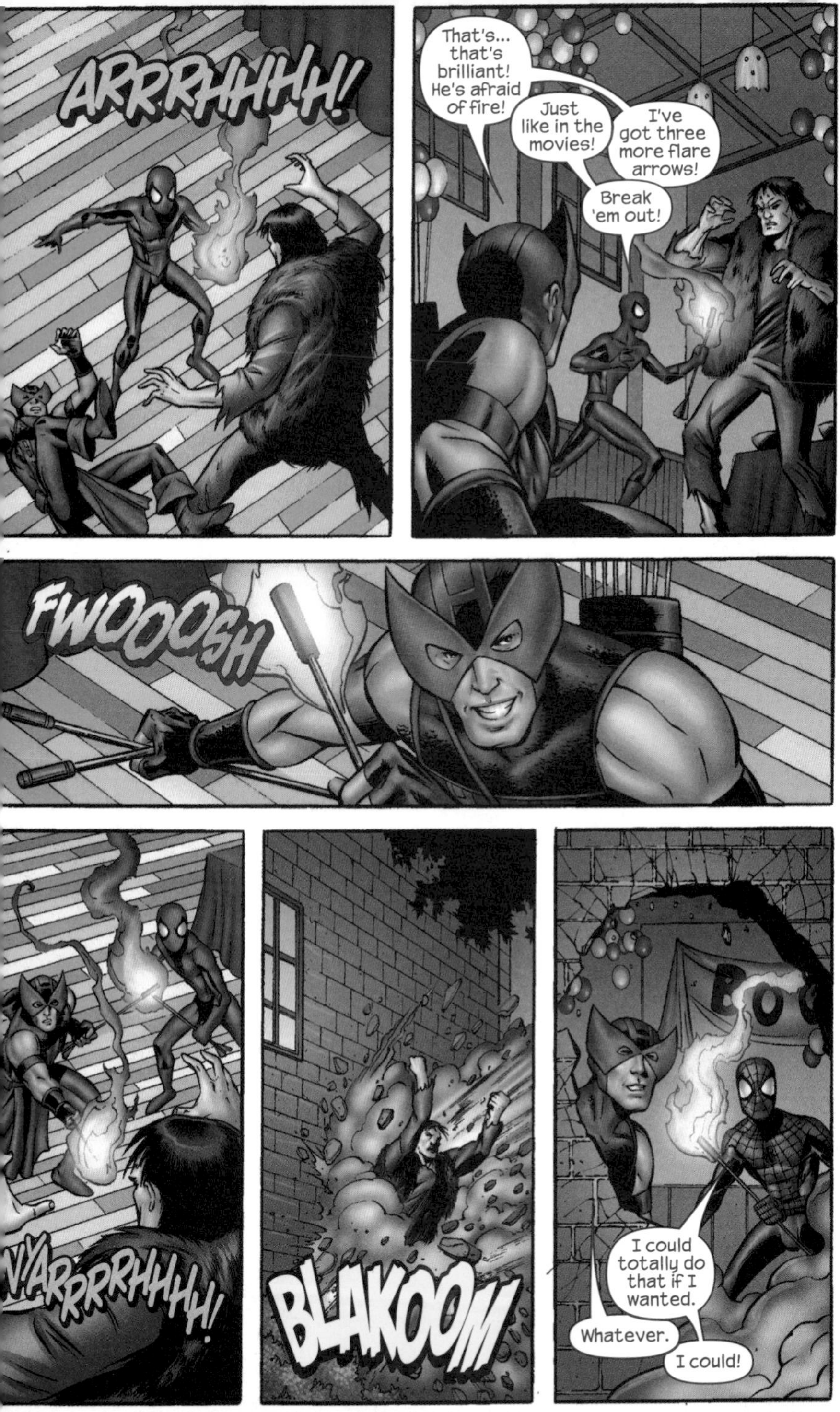
ARRRHHHH!
That's... that's brilliant! He's afraid of fire!
Just like in the movies!
I've got three more flare arrows!
Break 'em out!
FWOOOSH
NYARRRRHHHH!
BLAKOOM
I could totally do that if I wanted.
Whatever.
I could!

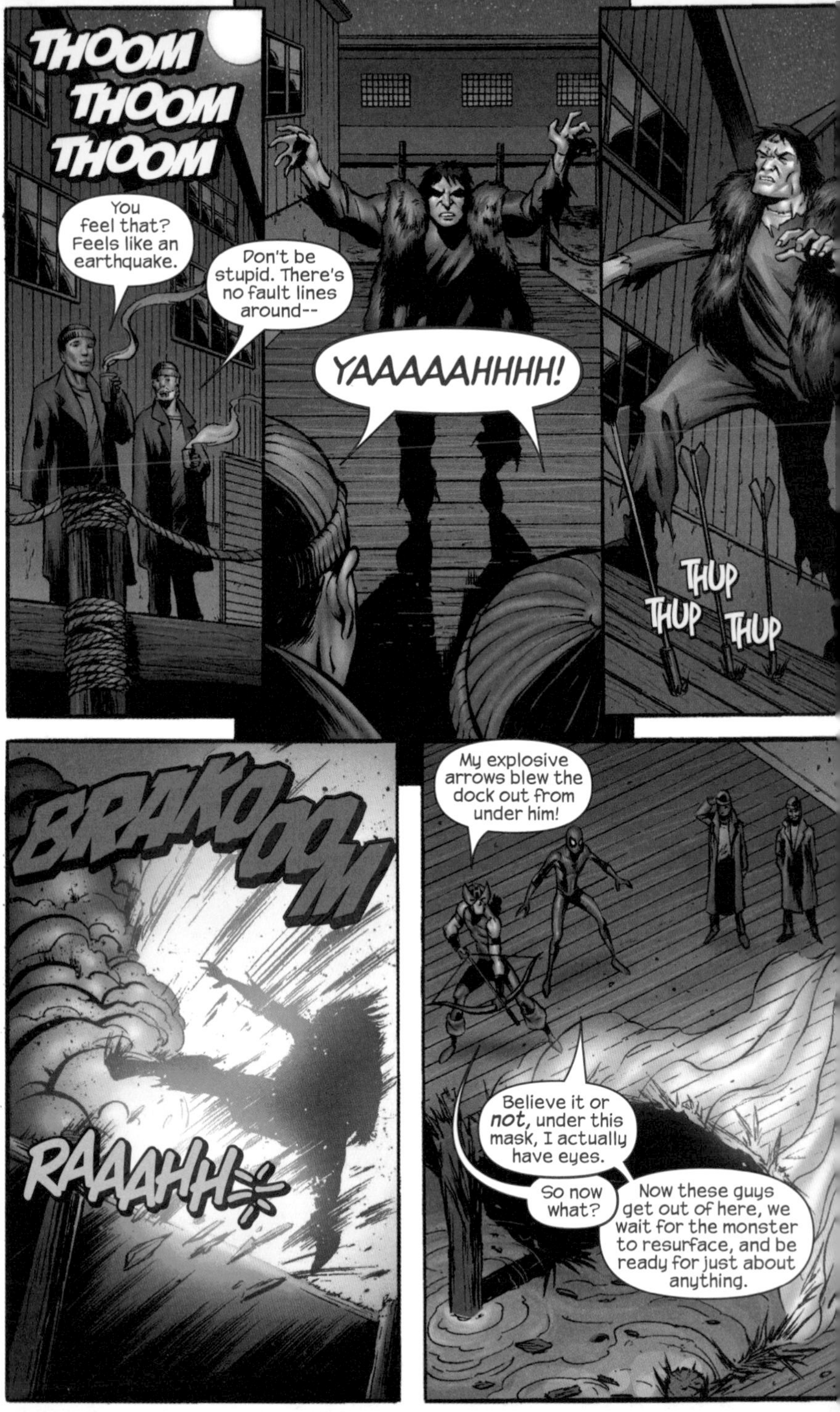
THOOM
THOOM
THOOM
You feel that? Feels like an earthquake.
Don't be stupid. There's no fault lines around--
YAAAAAHHHH!
THUP
THUP
THUP
BRAKOOOM
RAAAHH!
My explosive arrows blew the dock out from under him!
Believe it or not, under this mask, I actually have eyes.
So now what?
Now these guys get out of here, we wait for the monster to resurface, and be ready for just about anything.

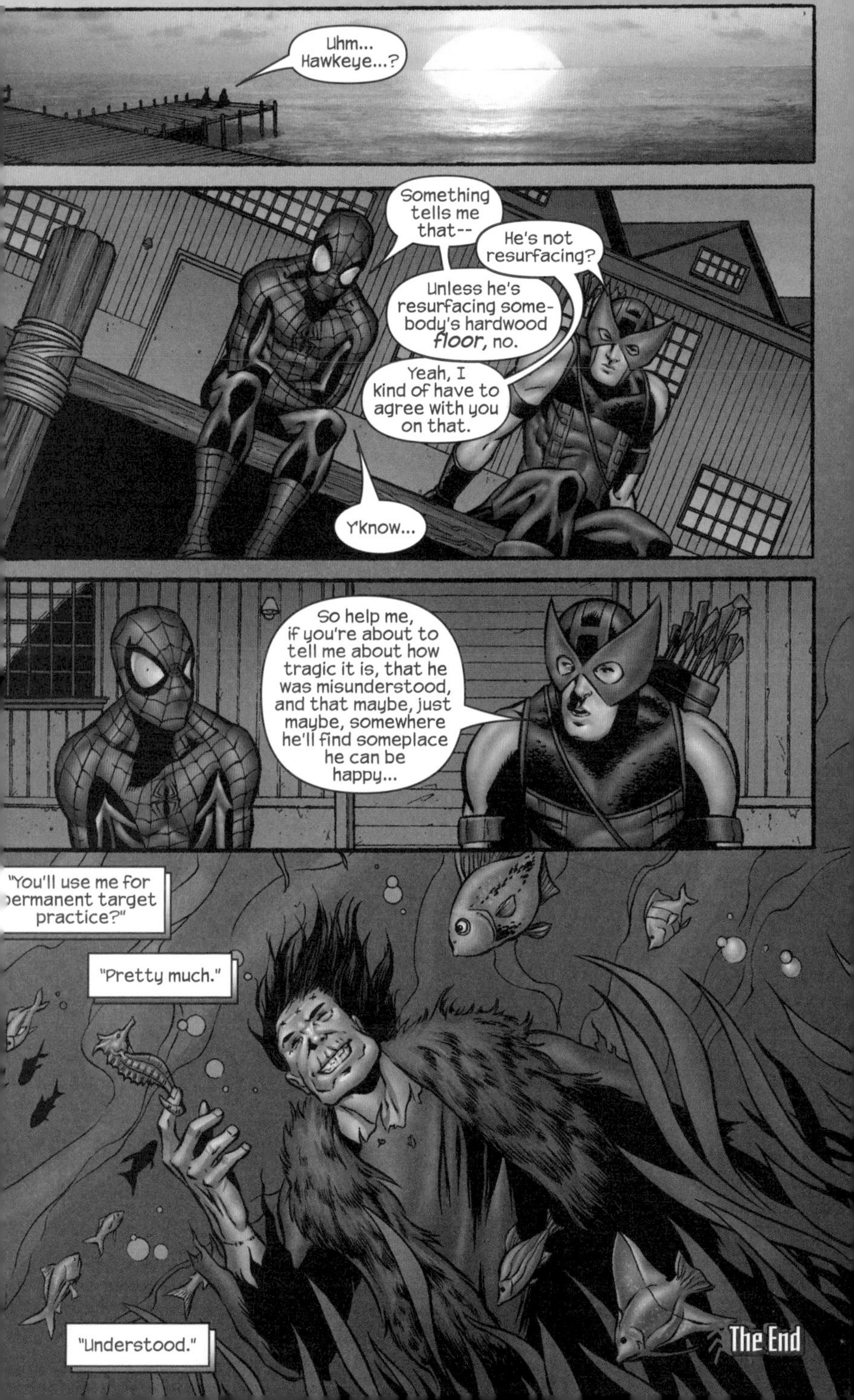

Uhm... Hawkeye...?
Something tells me that--
He's not resurfacing?
Unless he's resurfacing some-body's hardwood *floor*, no.
Yeah, I kind of have to agree with you on that.
Y'know...
So help me, if you're about to tell me about how tragic it is, that he was misunderstood, and that maybe, just maybe, somewhere he'll find someplace he can be happy...
"You'll use me for permanent target practice?"
"Pretty much."
"Understood."
The End

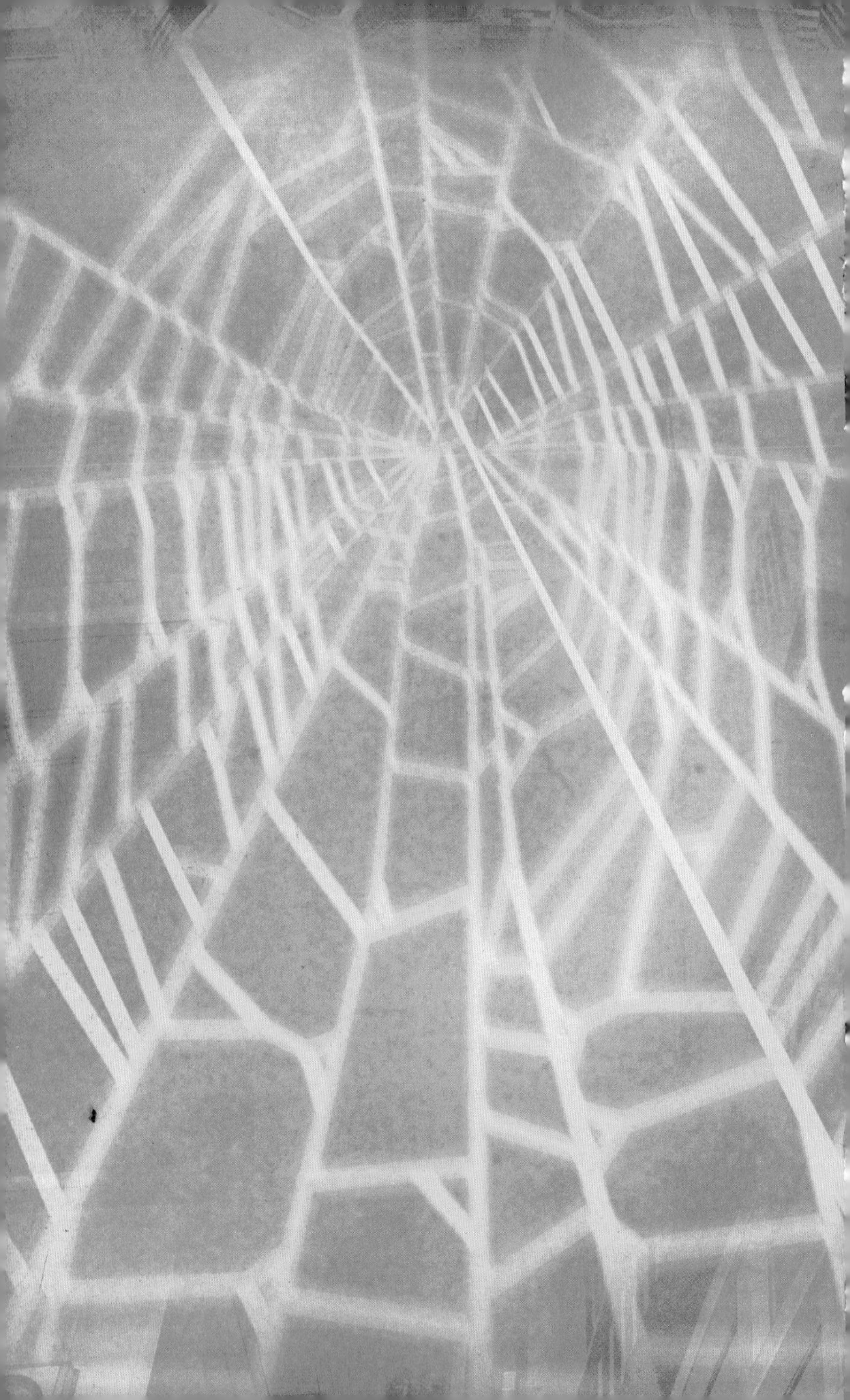